POINT REYES
SHERIFF'S CALLS

For Alissa and Chris

Point Reyes sheriff's calls / Susanna Solomon. — Henderson, Nev. : HD Media Press Inc., c2013

p. ; cm.

ISBN: 978-0-9854930-8-0 (cloth); 978-0-9854930-9-7 (paper)

Summary: A short story collection based on places in and around the rural northern California town of Point Reyes. Although the characters are fictitious, the author conceived of their adventures by pondering on actual 'Sheriff's Calls' published in the "Point Reyes Light", her local newspaper.— Publisher.

Point Reyes (Calif.)—Fiction. 2. Crime—California—Point Reyes—Fiction. 3. Criminals—California—Point Reyes—Fiction. 4. Sheriffs—California—Point Reyes—Fiction. 5. California—Fiction. 6. Short stories, American. 7. Short stories.

PS3619.O4372 P65 2013
813.6—dc23
2013917646
1311

Cover and page design by Tanya Quinlan

POINT REYES

SHERIFF'S CALLS

A Collection of Short Stories

Susanna Solomon

H
D

HD Media Press Inc.

POINT REYES STATION: There were no local calls. Good job, West Marin.

Sheriff's Calls

Beatrice Darcy, 92, stepped into her tub at 12053 Drakes View Drive and did not slip.

Mace McKinley, practicing horse jumping for the first time at her cousin Freda's house in Inverness, did not fall off the horse when the filly saw a blue tent in the woods, bucked, and charged off the trail.

Miles Foreman, a software developer from Sunnyvale, in a hurry to attend his best friend's wedding, did not drive his BMW into a ditch on the Petaluma-Point Reyes Road.

In Bolinas, six teenagers from East San Rafael, who had been drinking all day and playing volleyball, did not pass out on the beach under a tarp. Actually, no one was camping at all on the beach, first time that had happened in more than 150 days.

Giacomini's cows, out on Route One, nudged and pushed over a barbed-wire fence near Marshall, hunting for the bright green grass at the edge of the road. A black MG Speedster, convertible, going 60 miles an hour in a 35 zone, sped by, radio blaring. The cows, content with mouthfuls of green grass, nosed their way back inside their pasture.

Frank Turner, 24, despondent over the loss of his girlfriend, his job, and his house in a matter of months, took a last sip of his father's Jim Beam that Dad had left on the counter by mistake, and reached for the Seconal to down them all as he had thought about all day; instead he staggered to the bathroom and fell asleep wedged under the porcelain throne. In the morning he had a hell of a headache and the pills had vanished from his hands.

No one was out in front of Smiley's Saloon, in Bolinas, yelling obscenities, wearing bright orange and blue clothes and talking to dogs.

Out in San Geronimo, five youths, wearing white T-shirts and basketball shorts and holding bags of half-rotten apples, eyed the Stagecoach bus heading for a stop. They hid behind some trees. Thomas, the youngest, heard his mother calling him in for dinner. He dropped his apples and the other boys followed. They were hungry too.

In Lagunitas, a white middle-aged man wearing a white shirt and blue jeans was talking to himself and picking up trash. Deputy Linda Kettleman, sitting nearby in her overheated car, took a bite out of her muffin and turned off her radio.

In Muir Beach, Sandra Littlejohn, 42, was upset because someone had parked on the street in front of her home. Instead of calling 911, she headed to the Pelican Inn for a drink.

William Havens, faced his tenant, a distraught Penny Hennessy, who was not having one of her best days. Unable to fork over rent and two months in arrears, she pleaded with William to give her a little more time. Instead of filing a three-day eviction notice, as he was about to do, his cell phone buzzed in his rear pocket. It was his mother, asking for a ride to church. William gave Penny another month and straightened his tie.

All over West Marin a miracle occurred, no one who got drunk drove, the usual reality-challenged residents did not call the Sheriff for an imaginary trespasser; no one stole a wallet, a bicycle, a camera, or a cell phone. No one sped into a ditch, no bicyclists crashed, no one was evicted, and people holding firecrackers behaved sensibly.

"What is the world coming to?" asked Mildred Rhinehart, of Point Reyes Station, flipping through the pages of the *Light*. She checked to see if her husband was looking and took a long drink from her flask. "I'm disappointed, Fred. How 'bout you?"

Fred, a deeply devoted Giants fan, rose out of his chair while watching Lincecum pitch. "What exactly are you looking for, Mildred?"

"Trouble," she said, loading her gun.

From the Sheriff's Calls Section in the *Point Reyes Light*, January 30, 2011

LAGUNITAS: At 5:48 p.m. a woman discovered a man asleep in a sleeping bag in her back shed. The man told the woman he was cold.

It's Your Lucky Day

Cold? Beth wondered. What do I care about him being cold?

She hurried inside to get a lantern and a gun. Anyone sleeping in her shed, cold or not, had to go. Taking her blue point hound and her .22, she marched back outside.

She jammed the shed door opened with her foot.

"This ain't no hotel, Mister." Beth raised her rifle, racked the slide, and rested her finger on the trigger guard.

The guy eyed the rifle.

"Sorry to bother you, ma'am." His rheumy eyes were bloodshot. "I was riding, horse saw something, and bucked me. I know it's not public property, ma'am."

Again that pleading through bloodshot eyes.

Beth frowned. "This is my house. My land."

"Sure enough." He licked his lips. "Can I stay the night? Ain't no bother. If you like, I can sleep with the horses? The lambs? The pigs?"

"Fat chance of that."

The hound sniffed the man, stood back, a low rumble in his throat.

The man bent down, pegged the hound as a friend. "I used to hunt in Alabama, ma'am."

Again that rhythm of talk she'd heard all her life. The lilt that made her hate her father, angry during the day with that voice, those intonations, silent at night when he came into her room.

The hound buried his muzzle in between the man's knees, tail low and moving fast.

"Not from around here. Don't recognize you at all," she said.

"Fit as a fiddle except for this leg. But I'll leave if you like." The man lifted his foot, ankle not holding right. He rubbed the hound's ears. "See? Me and Bessie's already best friends."

"Tristan, get your ass over here." The hound left the man, came to Beth, rolled up in the crouch position, tail down.

An owl called in the night.

Beth's hand shook as she held the lantern. Five miles down a dirt road outside Point Reyes Station. Closest house ten miles away. A hound who was useless to her. A gun loaded and cocked. A man who sounded like her father. She had no choice. She raised her grandfather's Remington 34.

The man dropped to his knees. "Please."

A crow cawed.

"Ma'am?"

"Hush," she said. "God's talking."

She paused. "Well, okay then." She dropped the rifle to her side and turned toward the house. "God's in a good mood. It's your lucky day. Come on in and have some coffee. It's cold outside."

INVERNESS PARK: At 11:52 a.m. someone thought they heard gunshots. Deputies found that it was just a domestic argument.

Just a Domestic Argument

"Just a domestic argument?" Mildred Rhinehart drew a bead on the little door of the cuckoo clock over her mantel. "Watch this, Fred."

Precisely at 12 p.m. the door on the clock burst open and a little yellow bird let out a song. Mildred's blast blew the bird to smithereens along with the cuckoo clock and some photos nearby.

"You didn't have to shoot Dad!" Fred sprang to the mantel and tried to find all the pieces of his father's photo. "Take it outside, Mildred. This house isn't big enough for the two of us."

"That's what the deputy said and what does he know." She took sight of the red and white gingham curtains in the kitchen window, the ones her sister put there, the ones she'd always hated.

"Mildred, no! You'll break the window."

"You think?" Mildred's shot shattered the glass.

"Second time this week. I'm taking you to your sister's." Fred slipped closer to his wife of fifty years and tried to get behind her. She spun, aimed her weapon at him, and he fled out the door into his burgundy Buick. He would've been at the fire station in Point Reyes Station in five minutes if he'd kept his foot on it. Instead he slowed, stopped and turned around on Levee Road. Mildred needed him and he'd missed her terribly the last time she'd been gone. As far as going to her sister's, that would take $1,000 and a flight to Kansas. He wasn't ready for either.

By the time he got home, the house was quiet. That didn't mean Mildred wasn't still around. He cased the joint like those guys from NCIS, checking each room. He found her on the flowered sofa, the rifle by her side, an afghan pulled half way up to her shoulders, her droopy knee-high nylons slipped to her ankles, her Oxford shoes tied tight. Her snores filled the air. Fred carefully removed the rifle and disarmed it. In the pantry he found some more shells hidden in a Special K box from Costco. He stashed those in the freezer.

He'd already discontinued her credit card when she'd bought ammo from QVC in the middle of the night. He threw the rifle in the well, hearing it clink along with the others. Coming back into the living room, he watched her sleep, her deep breaths making the afghan slowly rise and fall, her cheeks looking a little bit more sunken these days. He'd known her since she was fourteen and couldn't bear to lose her.

He went to kiss her and hesitated. Anything could set her off, even something as soft as a kiss. Outside, the bright sun was overcome by a thin fog, a mist coming over the ridge, and the light dimmed. Fred turned on a few table lamps and watched his wife sleep.

He'd have to wake her soon, otherwise she'd have another sleepless night and do God knows what while watching TV. He would cancel his cable, but he loved watching "Deadliest Catch." He was trying to remember the names of the ships when he felt something on his arm. It was Mildred. Her bony fingers tightened around his wrist.

"Oh Fred." Her eyes flew open. Light blue eyes, eyes he could swim in. "I had the most horrible dream."

"Yes, dear," he replied, uneasy still. Maybe it was time to increase her daily dosage of Prozac? But how much was too much? He didn't want her to sleep all the time. He murmured hello back at her, swept her hair off her forehead.

"I've got something in my pocket that's digging into my hip," she said and pulled out a tiny pistol and aimed it at his head.

"Ah sheesh, Mildred." He started to sweat, knowing he couldn't run this time.

"I can't hold it, I'm so nervous." The gun twisted in her hand, the weight heavy against her slender wrist. "They're coming to get me." She struggled to sit upright.

"Who?" Fred tried to pull away. Her fingernails dug in.

"Deputies. It's only a matter of time, Fred, until they get the both of us. Now get out of the way. I hear them at the door."

From the Sheriff's Calls Section in the *Point Reyes Light*, August 25, 2011

NICASIO: At 9:12 a.m. a man reported finding 30 to 40 marijuana plants on his property.

Predictable as an Old Goat

"Fred – come on, it can't be possible, no one would be so slow that they wouldn't notice all those plants on their property." Mildred put down her paper and let her reading glasses slide off her nose. "Honestly, what were they thinking – waiting for the plants to be six feet high, then call the cops?"

Fred was accustomed to his wife reading things in the *Point Reyes Light* and getting agitated. It seemed to be part of her Thursday routine. Go to the post office, get the paper, get all worked up, get her hair done. All in the space of an hour or two. Predictable as an old goat.

He readjusted his weight in the sky-blue recliner – a new chair for him since he'd broken the couch. This one had no duct tape. He felt a thrill. He eased his hands along the ridges of his wide-wale corduroy pants. Things could be better. Mildred's cooking for one thing, his eyesight, his hearing, and, he didn't want to think it aloud, but the most important thing, his, well, you know. He hobbled into the kitchen for a drink.

Except for the occasional beer. He didn't drink much, but since things hadn't been working well in *that* area, he'd taken to having a nip now and again. Something had to make it work again and the doc had said no Viagra on account of his heart.

He nuzzled up to his wife, his warm breath adjacent to her ear. Her white hairs tickled his nose. "Hi, sweetheart." What the heck, anytime was worth a go.

"Even with a truck, an ATV, or a Jeep, anyone would know they had plants on their property. What are they, blind? Pot farmers are criminals, Fred, and they're ruining our community. They should move the hell out." She felt a tickle near her ear, brushed away the fly and realized it was her husband. "I wish you wouldn't lurk so. Go get your own paper."

"It wasn't the paper I was looking for, Mildred," he said. "Thought maybe you'd like a back rub or something."

"Last time you rubbed my back, you tried to bend my bones with your thumb. Can't you feel the difference between muscle and bone?"

Fred thought all the skin on her back was nice, even her three moles, sort of in the sign of a star. "I could be more gentle if you like," he murmured, lightly touching her lace collar. She looked so sweet in lace.

"If they would have some proper discipline in the schools, they wouldn't have all these drug peddlers in our back yard. This is the third time this month I've heard about people growing dope out here. What do they think a National Park is for? Not supposed to be cultivated, with irrigation systems, chemicals, cutting down trees, and all that." She stopped her rant, looked out her window, scratched a mosquito bite on her arm, caught her breath. "Fred, Fred, for God's sake, what if they come here? You still have that twenty-two?"

This was more agitation than even Fred was used to. Her anxiety was getting to him, and now he didn't feel romantic at all. He filled the kettle from the tap over the deep farm sink, turned on a burner, and lit the stove. Blue flames came to life with a whoosh. "Want some tea? Something to calm your nerves?"

"Is it eleven yet?" Mildred patted her hair. "Time for Doris to give me a new updo. I'm feeling young again, Fred. How about a flip?"

Fred, feeling better now that his wife was more worried about her hair than pot growers, thought perhaps it would be a good time to feed the birds in the back yard.

Going outside into the cool morning, he stopped and looked back at her smooth white hair. It had been, he mused, so long. Time had become such a fog to him. He longed for a beer. "I'll take you to town in a minute."

"But what I don't understand," Mildred went on. "What do they get out of all this pot? Ruining our park and all."

"Money." He lifted her coat off a hanger. "A lot of money. Some people aren't as lucky as we are, dear. Ready for Doris?"

Mildred stared at the paper in her hand. "We didn't have any dope smugglers when we were kids; life was better then. Things were civilized."

"Oh yes. We had Al Capone, Tommy machine guns, child labor, the Triangle Shirtwaist Fire, and Mussolini."

"Fred, you're messing up history again."

"But still, Mildred, we had crime."

"Every year there's crime – but do they have to do it in our back yard?" She grabbed his arm.

It wasn't so much the holding he minded; it was the digging in with her bony fingers into the soft flesh between his thumb and his palm. "Honey, please, you're hurting me."

"Didn't mean to." She reached up close to him for a kiss, making his heart race. It felt so good to her; she tried another kiss, nuzzling his neck. She liked that fine and squeezed his hand ever so gently. The windows of the car were up and it was getting a little steamy inside.

She kissed him again. It was like high school, kissing him in the car, as long as she didn't feel his bulk under his jacket. He moaned softly.

"Shall we go inside?" he ventured, wanting, more than anything, to hold her.

"And disappoint Doris?" She buried her mouth on his.

"Times coming around like this don't happen very often," he murmured and stroked her whisper-thin hair.

"Nope, gotta go." Mildred put down his hands. "Missing an appointment with Doris would be criminal, Fred. Quit fooling around or I'll be late. Now, step on it," she said, while Fred, feeling like screaming, started the car.

SAN GERONIMO: At 7:54 p.m., a Red Boy Pizza delivery man drove into the creek and suffered a head injury.

The Pizza Man

"Can't you see I'm fine?" Thomas Freed clutched his head. He'd been late from doing his deliveries and pizza boxes had spilled all over the inside of the van.

Officer Linda Kettleman listened to the perpetrator complain. Blood was running down his nose, but not forcefully, so maybe she didn't need to call 911? She lifted her thumb off the call-back button on her radio.

"And how fast do you think you were going, sir?" She prepared for her accident report. First, assess personnel damage, then review the scene of the accident. Assess, report, make calls. She could do that.

Thomas blinked from blood running into his eye. He wiped it away with the back of his hand. The officer was – what, blond? He could barely make out her face with the goddamn flashlight she was shining in his eyes. "Do you mind?"

Linda sniffed for liquor on the young man's breath. All she could smell was garlic and pizza. She reached for her mother's handkerchief from the front pocket of her standard-issue blue pants. No. Use gloves. Whatever goop they have on them, don't get that goop on yourself.

"The light, please?" Thomas asked.

She flicked it on low. What should she do next? Call Cheda's for a tow? The white delivery van was head into a ditch, front wheels dropped into a bank of San Geronimo Creek. The van – and the guy in it – were up against a tree and not going anywhere. Satisfied, she crawled up the embankment to

11

the cruiser. As an afterthought, she put on her headlamp and adjusted it so that the light didn't spray the sky. Satisfied, she grabbed the first-aid kit and gingerly made her way back down the embankment toward the kid.

What the hell had he been doing? Speeding 60 in a 35? A 25? She didn't know the roads around here all that well – at least not yet – but she knew he was going way too fast. He was leaning over the steering wheel making gurgling noises with his throat. Gloves on, she came closer. Could she handle this one on her own?

"The wire for my braces slipped and one is sticking in my cheek," he mumbled, a trickle of blood heading for his lip.

With her hands full of gauze, Linda approached him. "Anything broken? Can you breathe OK? Any other problems?" she asked, trying to sound officious. Everyone had a first day, didn't they? Earlier, she'd been partnered up with Harold, but he had had to go home to a sick dog, so she was alone. "Your name, sir?"

"Thomas," he mumbled, fingers exploring his molars.

The door to the van had flown open with the accident, but Thomas, thank goodness, had been wearing a seat belt. People – families mostly – sometimes didn't wear seat belts, and the other officers told her some horror stories. Grateful this wasn't one of those nights, she checked on Thomas' posture, and released his seat belt. He fell forward onto the wheel. He looked a little pale.

"Thomas?" She pressed the button on her two-way radio. "You all right?" she asked, knowing he wasn't. Blood was everywhere.

"Just reaching for my iPhone, ma'am. It slipped under the seat," he mumbled and came up empty-handed, blood streaming down his face and his mouth a bit puffy. Ear buds dangled from his neck. "Can't be without my music, ma'am."

Was he drunk, on drugs, or just plain loony, Linda wondered, wanting to help him out of the van but not sure her 140 pounds would handle his weight. He was a big kid. Her radio crackled in her ear.

"You called for backup, Linda?" asked a dispatcher over the radio. "Your location, please?"

Linda had never actually seen Sarah in person, but sure loved her voice. "I'll get back to you as soon as I can," Linda said, then looked up and down the narrow one-lane road deep in the woods off of San Geronimo Valley Drive and wished she knew where they were.

She turned her attention to Thomas and pressed gauze all over his forehead. "Hold this," she said. "Apply pressure here. And here." The windshield was cracked and no glass protruded from his face, like she'd seen in so many movies. His lap was covered with chunks of green glass from a side window.

"Can you press the 'on' button, ma'am? I was just deep into "The Hand That Feeds" and want to hear the end," Thomas mumbled.

Knowing that all these kids knew their iPhones by heart, Linda pressed the talk-back button on her walkie-talkie. "Backup, now, Sarah." Something something burnt accosted her nostrils and it was not pizza. Brakes? Plastic? Something new? A car sped by along the road and Linda, needing help, cursed herself. She had forgotten to put on her flashers.

"Can you get down from the driver's seat and step out of the car?" she asked, her training coming in handy again. It seemed too easy for her to lose track of the situation. Thomas extracted one bare foot, and the other from the wheel well. He fell out of the van and onto her, throwing them both onto the ground.

"Mom!" he cried, his arms around Linda's neck.

Finding herself squished into the ground by the confused kid, she twisted her way free, adjusted the front of her shirt and jacket, and gently removed his arm from around her throat. "Thomas, I am not your mother."

Thomas, in the damp earth and leaves, was surprised. It was so cold and damp and had been so warm a second earlier. Now his face was covered in leaves, which kind of stuck to his cheeks, on account of the blood. "I feel like Puck," he said cheerfully, sitting up in the grass. The air still smelled of pizza, which was odd in Shakespeare. In his high-school class at Drake, they only had pizza after the show. And where was his mother? She was here a moment ago. "Mom?"

"She's not here," Linda answered. "You've had an accident and are bound to be confused." She stood up and straightened her uniform. Blood spots stained her jacket, but at least it wasn't vomit. Harold – who had been thrown up on numerous times – said it was hard to get uniforms smelling right after that.

"Now, Thomas, can you sit up?" She didn't want him to get dizzy. "Stand?" They were next to the van. Pizza boxes littered the damp earth between them and the driver's door.

"We need to get back! It's going to explode!"

"That's only in the movies, Thomas. You can relax." Linda wondered about her backup. If she left the perpetrator alone, he could flee the scene – or worse, fall into the creek not four feet below. But without her flashers, how would they even know where she was? Half-way into the woods, narrow road, shit. Her first call and she did not have the perpetrator in custody, yet.

She held out a hand. Thomas took it and rose. Still some bleeding, but minor. "Your head hurt?" she asked, offering some more gauze.

"Not as much as my cheek." Thomas felt a bit dizzy. He'd been having a blast listening to Nine Inch Nails, then blam, hit a tree and hurt his face – that was the order, yes? No? Lost his iPhone, fell out of the van, and thought he'd run into Mom. Not so good for his second week on the job. Mr. Friedman, he'd be pissed for sure. And now cops; soon there would be more. He'd leave quick, if he could find his phone. Was it still in the van? He staggered back, reached the door, and worked the wire in his mouth in a vain attempt to get it to seat. Damn thing hurt like hell.

"You'll have to come with me, son," Linda said, again with the officious tone. "Please step away from the vehicle." There was no reason to further contaminate the scene of the accident.

Thomas looked at her, at the van, at the faint touch of a moon peeking through the trees. "Ma'am, what did you say?" He pretended not to hear. He'd spent months paying off his phone – and from what he knew, once they hauled Mr. Friedman's van to the impound yard, he'd never see his phone again. That and his keys. Wallet? That was still in his rear pocket. Relieved, he pulled the keys out of the ignition.

She was upon him, her grip on his arm.

"Hey." He threw her hand off.

"The patrol car. Now," Linda said, using her bossy voice, the one she'd practiced so hard at the Academy.

"But my iPhone," Thomas complained, pulling free.

"You need to get in the car, son."

The sound of a car went by the road above. Linda, for a moment, felt better, but there were no lights, no voices, and the sound faded. Meanwhile, she had an uncooperative perpetrator. She flipped her headlamp on him and reached for her baton. She'd use it if she had to, but Thomas was such a nice boy. He reminded her of her little brother.

"Oh, for God's sake, you don't have to hit me," Thomas argued. "I'm a good kid." He moved just beyond the officer's reach. He'd get a DUI for sure; lose his license, his job, his girl, his chance to get out of debt. He bent down, searching between her and the van, his hands in soft earth, looking for something white, feeling for something smooth and white, but it was too dark to see. His fingers closed on something soft and squishy.

Above them, cars slid to a stop and blue lights flashed in the forest. Voices rang out as car doors slammed. This was Linda's last chance. She lunged at Thomas and threw him to the ground. He scrabbled away out from under her, picked himself up, and ran.

"He's in the woods!" she cried as other officers came down the embankment. Not to be outdone by the stronger, heavier men in her unit, she rushed on, following the crackles and footfalls ahead, as her perpetrator ran away on her first patrol.

"I'll cut him off at the road," said one of the officers who Linda knew from training. The hell he would, she thought, and kept moving. This one's mine!

"Thomas! Thomas! Stop! You don't want to do this!" She chased after the footsteps she heard. Her head lamp was useless, more or less, having tilted just enough to illuminate the tops of trees.

She heard a thunk just ahead and hard breathing. He'd run into something. She came upon him, easy, flipped her light, and saw him leaning against a tree. "It's OK, Thomas," she said, her hand on his arm, as she thought about whether she should use handcuffs or not. They always sort of hurt, no matter how gently she closed them.

Thomas was crying, his head against a tree trunk. "I lost my iPhone, my job, and now without any money, I'm going to jail and my mother's going to kill me." He stared at her handcuffs nervously. "Don't hurt me, ma'am, please. I hurt enough."

Gauging where the road above was, Linda held his arm, readjusted her headlamp, and led him back. Up ahead, three officers were waiting, lights flashing, voices crackling over the radio.

"Jeez, he's just a kid," said one of the officers. "Good job, Linda. Way to go," said another, suppressing a laugh. "Your first puny perp."

It had been hard as hell for her, but she wouldn't tell them any of that.

"Keep your head high, Thomas, and don't let them see your tears," Linda whispered.

"Tree down!" crackled the radio. "Blocking Drake. Entrance to the Park, East entrance. All officers." The deputies, noting Linda had the perpetrator under control, turned their cars around and sped off, leaving her and Thomas in silence and darkness.

Feeling better now, Linda opened the back door of the cruiser and helped Thomas inside. Noticing he'd started to bleed a little again, she applied some more gauze. There seemed to be an endless supply.

All she had to do now was get him back to the station, call Cheda's, do paperwork. First night alone; her sergeant would be proud.

Thomas looked sad in the back seat.

"Shall I go find your iPhone?" she asked, flipping on her big flashlight.

Thomas burst into a smile. "Oh! Would you?" he asked. "Oh God, thank you." It wasn't going to be such a bad night after all. He dabbed at his face with the gauze. The bleeding had stopped. Battle scars, he thought, history. Safe at last, he rested his head on the back of the plastic seat, relaxed a moment, and sat up with a start. Going home, however, that would be a different story.

FROM THE SHERIFF'S CALLS SECTION IN THE *POINT REYES LIGHT*,
SEPTEMBER 29, 2011

LUCAS VALLEY: At 12:23 a.m. inmates at juvenile hall were caught making love in the locker room.

Love in the Locker Room

"Oh my." Mildred caught her breath. "Oh my." She got up from her flowered couch and paced the house nervously. "Fred! Fred!" she called. He was sprawled on the other end of the couch, deeply offended about the end of the Giants' season.

"Hunh? What is it?" He sat up, dumbfounded.

"Animals, Fred, that's what they're like. Those teenagers. At Juvenile Hall." She poked at the paper as if it held a disease. "Those kids."

"Having another bad day, Mildred?" Fred shifted his weight and took his stocking feet off the coffee table. "You were upset last week with your sister. Now this."

"This is different. In the locker room. Fred, we were never like that."

Fred, reaching into his eighties, wished he'd been like that. Meeting Mildred when she'd been a teen, with her beautiful little rosebud mouth, her clear blue eyes, her vivacious spirit, if they'd had the chance, maybe he could've had fun with her in a locker room, but times were different then. Smitten, he had taken her out like a gentleman, driving his father's truck carefully from MM Ranch, getting her home on time, nervously asking her father for her hand.

With a bow tie on, too; Fred hadn't looked as sharp since. He looked down on his worn- out plaid shirt and brushed crumbs off his collar. He had promised Mildred's dad he would take care of her, and he had, hadn't he?

The house he'd built in Inverness Park hadn't come down yet. It sagged in the middle like he did. Big deal. He shuffled to the kitchen for another Bud.

"What are those kids in those places for anyway? Common criminals, I'd say." Mildred peered through her kitchen curtains. Mrs. Flanagan, a neighbor, was edging toward Mildred's garden again. Mildred rapped the window.

"Someday you'll break the glass, dear," Fred said with a sigh.

"She's stealing my gazanias," Mildred snapped. "First the kids, then this." She smoothed the front of her apron, adjusted her glasses. "Kids, these days, Fred, you'd think they'd have better things to do."

"Locked up in prison, I'm not so sure."

"I didn't ask for your opinion." Mildred eyed Mrs. Flanagan and wrapped her hand around the sugar bowl. "They have no sense of propriety, no sense of shame." But she thought better of hurling the sugar. They'd had a big problem with ants, and even though Fred had vacuumed them all up, she still felt they were in the vacuum cleaner, eager to get out.

Fred thought it was kind of interesting, those kids. They had moxie. He couldn't remember the last time he'd had moxie. Speaking up two years ago in church? Recalling his trip to the cardiologist, he eased himself back on the couch, in the warm spot he had left. Comfy and spread out, just like he was. A spring was winding its way up through the cloth. He pushed it back in and covered it with Mildred's afghan. She'd never know. She never sat on his side of the sofa.

"Fred, don't you see?" Mildred said. "Now that I think about it - these kids – they have something. They have passion, Fred. When was the last time we had passion?" She came to sit down next to him, her bony little body pressing on his ample belly.

She felt like a bird, but passion, he thought, no. "Mildred, please, you're squishing me," he complained, gently relieving the pressure and hoping to avoid her landing on that spring.

Spinning on her heels and coming down on the opposite side of him, resting herself on the arm of the couch, she lifted her horn-rimmed glasses. "Oh Fred, kiss me. Kiss me like those movie stars. Let me feel that passion. Forget about the baseball game."

Fred, awash in feelings of trying to remember if it was one out or two, felt his body want to respond, but how. Why? Mildred was playing him like a fiddle but he was a drum - wrong instrument, wrong day, wrong goddamn decade. He couldn't remember the last time he'd kissed her, kissed her fully. Now he looked at her thin lips, with just a brush of coral lipstick. She'd missed her mouth again, just a bit, nothing new there, but she smelled so, so Mildred-like. If he could close his eyes, envelop her, they were on the couch, comfortable even, they had a right, didn't they? He puckered up.

She rose quickly, turned on the lights, marched into the kitchen again, flipped back the curtains. "I can't, Fred. That goddamn Mrs. Flanagan, she's into my tulips again."

INVERNESS PARK: At 1:37 p.m. a woman said the father of her son or daughter was threatening to take the child.

A Bad Day for Doris

"What I don't understand," Mildred took a sip of chamomile tea from the Bovine and put down the paper, "is this simple question. Doesn't the woman know if the child is a boy or a girl?"

"Of course she does, Mrs. Rhinehart." Doris' hands danced around the elderly woman's head. It had only been a week since her last do, but her hair had lost all of its life. She'd used almost every product they had, and still Mrs. R.'s hair lay loose and lifeless in her hands. More spray – everything worked better with more spray. "Close your eyes."

Mildred tightened her eyes until she saw stars. "But that mom!" she cried, agitated, worried about her own daughter Janet. She'd not called in a week. "For heaven's sake, Doris, quit spraying, I've got to open my eyes, I need to think."

Doris put away her spray and her scissors and held up her biggest blow dryer. One way or the other, she was going to get the older woman's hair to behave. "They don't say what gender the kid is in the paper for security reasons, Mrs. Rhinehart." And, she supposed, to keep people out of everyone else's business. But this father worried her. He was threatening to take the child. How old was the kid? Was the mother beside herself with worry? What about Barry? What if he came and tried to take Joshua?

"If I was the sheriff, I'd go right up to that man and tell him to stop scaring the mom and the kid. A mother and child need each other. Grab my cell phone, Doris, and I'll put a stop to this nonsense. Dial nine-one-one."

Doris pulled her own cell phone from her pocket. "Nine-one-one's for emergencies, ma'am, but I'll put in a call to the sheriff, to Officer Kettleman, if you like."

"She's the one who chased after my Fred last Thursday. Don't you dare!"

Oh dear God, I'm losing my mind, Doris thought, and handed over the phone. "If you feel that strongly, go ahead, just dial whoever you like. I need a break." She walked away from the chair, away from Mildred, away from all the other women baking their heads under dryers. Outside, it was a simply gorgeous day and didn't smell like preservative or hair spray or the sour little old lady smell she endured most of the time.

The door to the store was open and instead of stopping, she crossed the street, to Toby's, to the collection of people shopping, waiting for coffee drinks, normal people thinking normal type things. A stack of *Point Reyes Light* newspapers were in a rack. Doris thought of stealing them all and throwing them away. Then Mrs. Rhinehart, Beatrice, Hortense, and all the other ladies would have something else to complain about. Something normal, like mortgages, or recalcitrant children, or overdue books at the library.

Pausing in front of the newspaper rack, Doris tasted freedom for a second. Surely they would all be moving around in there like anxious hippopotamuses or rhinoceroses, creaking and worried and knocking everything about. She had to go back.

Instead of waiting for a truck to go by, she dashed across Route One. A BMW, a black one, driven by a woman from San Francisco who was talking on her cellphone with one hand and putting on her lipstick with the other, screeched to a stop.

"Oh dear God!" Doris, one hand covering her mouth, spun in a circle and fell.

The driver, an unnatural blonde, got out of the BMW, cell phone wires dangling from her ear.

Doris wasn't sure where she was but the ground wasn't as soft as her bed at home. Why was she lying in the street? She would hear voices in the distance a little more clearly if there wasn't such a ringing in her ears.

"Is she hurt?" Beatrice asked, a glob of shampoo dripping from her cheek.

"You upset her again, Mildred," Hortense said. "I told you not to tell her what's in the paper."

"I did no such thing." Mildred pulled off her smock and was about to lift Doris' poor head off the sidewalk.

"Don't touch her." The voice of authority rang out. It was Officer Kettleman. "Someone called nine-one-one. How long has she been down?"

"Oh thank God, thank God." Mildred clapped her hands. "Please help her – she's our hairdresser." She peeked into Doris' eyes. "Doris, honey, you all right?"

Linda called into her radio. "Ambulance needed. In front of Cheda's. It's …" and before she could finish sirens punctuated the air.

"Officer, oh please, do something. You've got to save her!" Beatrice urged.

"I'll call my doctor," the woman from the BMW said.

"We don't need any help from you, you stupid cow," Mildred hissed. "You killed Doris."

Linda left Doris to the paramedics. Her face looked a little pale but there was no blood, and her vital signs were good. She listened to their patter, corralled the BMW driver, and hustled the women back inside the salon.

"Now, what am I going to do?" Beatrice asked. "I'm covered with soap."

"I can rinse." Mildred steered her toward the basin. "Now, do you like your water tepid or really hot?"

Beatrice settled into her chair, and bent her head back. "Nice."

"And I have foil in my hair," another customer said.

"I can take it out for you." Hortense felt official. "Have a seat." She drifted a smock over the rather large woman.

"So, I guess we can do without Doris." Hortense pumped up the chair and picked at foil.

"No, we can't." Mildred sprayed water all over the wall. "No, we just can't." She burst into tears.

Giving it all up, they walked to the front of the salon and looked out onto the empty street. The BMW was gone. So were Doris and the EMTs.

Hortense fumbled with a cell phone someone had left on the counter. "Shall we call nine-one-one?"

"We'll just go down there, all of us." Mildred stuffed the *Point Reyes Light* into a trashcan. "What do we want someone else's stories for, girls, when we have our own? Everyone ready?"

And the contingent, in various stages of dress, marched down the street to the sheriff's department, their purses at their elbows, eager and ready to take care of their own.

From the Sheriff's Calls Section in the *Point Reyes Light*, October 20, 2011

WOODACRE: At 11:46 a.m. a caller said, "Yeah, my husband..." before hanging up.

An Open Road, a Blue Sky

Mildred was angry. Fred had not taken out the trash, cleaned the refrigerator, or started her car. She paced the kitchen nervously. He was being lazy, still staring at the TV long after the last game of the World Series ended, his head in his hands, muttering continuously.

So she called the cops.

"So? Anyone can call the police, any old time," she said to her friend Beverly, who had come over for some freshly baked chocolate cookies. Mildred stirred the batter. "They call about cows in the road, why can't I call about Fred? He hasn't left his chair all day."

"You didn't have to call the cops." Fred sat up with a frown.

"You have a husband. He does stuff, Beverly." Mildred greased up a cookie sheet. "Fred, do something, be useful."

"Hey." Fred stood up, all six foot two of him. Tall and heavy, he towered over both women. "Don't you think you're being a little unfair?"

"After all these years of being married to you, I have a right to be unfair." Mildred shoved the cookies into the oven.

Beverly reached for the back door and left, making the doorbell jingle.

"You didn't have to scare her," Mildred sniffed.

"Me? I don't scare anyone," Fred said with a sigh. "'Cept on Halloween." He loved all those little kids coming to the door, their costumes hidden under their jackets, eager for candy. Mildred, however, hated the sound of them, their eager chatter, their high voices, the incessant ringing of the doorbell.

"What is it that you want me to do, now that you've made such a fuss?" There was no placating her. She had her ways. Her ruts went deep and they just got deeper. He considered himself an easy-going man. "Honey?"

He found her staring at some beauty magazines in the living room, her hair askew, the hairpins that once held up her beautiful white hair now sticking out at odd angles. "Sweetheart?"

"Brad Pitt is not coming to Point Reyes Station after all. He said he would."

"Olema's a long way north of Hollywood, Mildred," Fred said, hoping he could escape to the garage where he could put the finishing touches on his reassembled bicycle, his long-term project.

"I'm disappointed," she said.

Disappointed in him? Fred felt a little bad. He was always short-changing Mildred one way or another, according to her. But he tried, didn't he? Wash the dishes once a week, vacuum every month? Or was she disappointed in Brad Pitt? That thought made him smile. He headed to the garage.

"Not so fast, buster. The woodpeckers are poking holes in the house. Sooner or later, they're going to knock the place down. Fred?"

He closed the door behind him.

"Fred?"

Holding a wrench in one hand and a can of WD-40 in the other, Fred figured if he could just oil the chain and adjust the brakes he could take off on Route One and go on a long ride like those guys he saw dressed to the nines on their road bikes, thin, strong guys with power, with youth, with energy he'd never had. Ignoring Mildred, he flipped his bike back over on its wheels, tested the tires, put away his wrench, and pressed the button opening the garage door.

The day beckoned. A blue sky, an open road, and all the time in the world. Being careful, he mounted the bike in the garage, set his weight down, shoved it into high gear, and took off down the street. Fifty feet past the driveway he hit a crack in the pavement. His tire hung up for a moment, and not having quick enough reflexes, he went down in a flurry, hitting his shoulder, but not his head. He was thankful about that, the one good thing that happened today, and he eyed the pavement in front of him, the asphalt glistening with stars, the mica reflecting the sun.

"Fred!" Mildred ran after him. "Are you okay?" She peered down, saw that his eyes were open, open but not looking at her, staring, staring at something.

She grabbed her phone, dialed 911. The sheriffs came on the line, fast, drilling her with questions, as she panicked for a sec, forgot her name, her address.

"Fred? Sweetheart?"

He opened his eyes, focused on her for a moment. "I was trying, dear, to be that movie- star husband you always wanted."

"Oh Fred, you don't look at all like Brad Pitt," she said, and walked back into the house.

From the Sheriff's Calls Section in the *Point Reyes Light*,
November 3, 2011

BOLINAS: At 3:35 p.m. a woman who had called several times in the last few days reported that someone had broken into her home, stolen $120 from her purse and returned a missing set of keys.

Missing Keys

"What I don't understand, Fred, is why anyone would want to return the keys." Mildred snipped her diseased roses in her yard on Dream Farm Road. "Isn't that weird?"

"Isn't what weird?" Fred was having his own time of it adjusting his patio recliner. Every time he set the back up, the bottom of the chair, where he was about to put his legs, fell to the ground. Two times already it had folded itself in thirds, as if it was eager to get back in the box. He opened it up and bracing his arms and legs, looked back at his wife. "Mildred, someone broke into a house and returned keys?"

"My cousin Bertha had a tenant problem too. But she changed the locks when she threw old Mr. Thompson out. He smelled." She snipped off the buds of five coral roses. She didn't like the color.

"But why didn't this gal change the locks?" Fred asked. "Did the woman have a girlfriend?" After he realized what he said, he stopped talking.

"Girlfriend, for a woman? What is the world coming to? Why can't girls marry boys the way they're supposed to?"

"I don't know," Fred said. He had no idea what she was talking about.

"But if you're going to take money, why return the keys, or vice versa?" Mildred continued. "Doesn't make any sense to me." She put down her shears and wiped her brow with her apron. Gardening was hard work – she could hire some of those people who did yard work, but she couldn't explain stuff to them, and she was a gal who liked to explain.

"I know what it was. It was her sister. Telling her not to call her again," Fred ventured, finally making the lounge chair behave. He eyed a pile of half-assembled lawn chairs in the corner of the garden. Satisfied he'd finally figured it out, he sat down, eager for a nap.

"Are you making a crack about my sister?" Mildred asked.

The lounge chair collapsed under him. "No," he growled. "I'm making no comment at all. On anything." He picked up the lounge chair and threw it on top of the others.

"But don't you want to hear how it comes out?" Mildred cut off all the odds and ends of the coral rose. It was springtime and they were unruly. She caught a thorn on her wrist. "Ow!"

"What else is in that paper that gets you so upset? You seem to be crying," Fred asked, one hand on the back door.

Mildred, who was not crying in the least, sniffed. If it would get Fred to do the roses, it was worth a go. "I'm bleeding. How can you go inside when I'm bleeding all over my dress?" When he was looking with dismay at the pile of lounge chairs, she wiped her wrist on her apron. "It's such a mess, Fred. Could you do it?"

Fred, still trying to understand the proper workings of his lawn chair, came over to see what she had done to the roses. They were all cut, the same height, all exactly twelve inches above the ground, not a twig or branch at all, just stalks. "What have you done, dear?"

"Look at my hands." Little scrapes and thorns and smears of blood covered her tissue-thin skin. And on her apron, great smears of blood. "It was a jilted lover, Fred, someone who wanted to insult her. Steal her money, then throw..."

"She didn't throw."

"Of course not. But can you imagine if she was there? Right. In the kisser. Pow. Here are your goddamn keys." Mildred tossed the shears up and down in her hand.

Fred wasn't sure how close he wanted to come to those shears, and if he talked to Mildred about her sister again, she'd surely throw the shears at him. He paused, hands on the fence. "So it was a finality, wasn't it, Mildred?"

"I guess." She hummed softly and handed the shears to him, handle first, the way her mother had taught her to pass tools. "An ending."

"So, are we going to end that way, dear?" Fred bent down and picked up coral rosebuds. There were so many of them.

"I'll never leave the keys," Mildred said, coming to put her arm through Fred's. He was so manly like, cooing and sighing to the roses.

Fred patted her hand. "No, of course not. And I'd never steal from you either." He wondered about the locks on their own house. They'd been out all afternoon, and he always locked the door behind him, letting Mildred go first. The shears felt heavy in his hand. "I forgot my keys," he said suddenly. "We're locked out."

"Shall we call the sheriff?" Mildred asked, taking his hand and leading them to the door.

FOLLOWING ORDERS: At 10:42 a.m. deputies called for back-up for a "pedestrian who was not following orders."

Following Orders

"There's no crosswalk so I can cross anywhere," Fred Rhinehart told the officer. There was no traffic, it was a sunny day; what were they hassling him for?

"Sir, make up your mind," Officer Anderson requested.

"But nobody's here," Fred complained. He needed to buy a steak for Mildred, but everytime he headed across the street, he couldn't remember which kind or if it was a head of lettuce she wanted? He didn't want to go home empty-handed.

"Sir, you're slowing up traffic."

Fred was in the middle of the road and a hay truck and Cheda's tow truck were stopped, waiting for him to cross. Mildred had been in the kitchen clucking her tongue and threatening to write down a list and pinning it to Fred's shirt. Now Fred sort of wished she had. "Okay, okay, officers," for now there were two of them. He walked back to the relative comfort of the sidewalk and sat down on the bench in front of the Bovine.

He went through a list in his mind. Milk, check; bread, he remembered a big cheese loaf on the counter; coffee? He'd seen Mildred's five-pound bag in the pantry. That left, that left, he sighed, everything.

Five minutes later the officers were gone and he started across again. The sun was in his eyes. It bounced off a windshield coming up the street and Fred wasn't in Point Reyes Station at all. He was in a field, courting Mildred, pressing a dozen fresh-picked daffodils into her hand, and her face was radiant, her blond hair shining in the sun, a soft breeze fluttering her sunflower-yellow dress. He put out his hand and she took it, those lovely soft fingers, and she was his, all his, right there on a Sunday afternoon in Ferguson's field and someone sounded a horn, not a sound he would consider romantic, and she looked at him with a dazed expression on her face and he went down.

Mitch Fontloy, of Dillon Beach, had seen the man step off the curb and had anticipated him going all the way until the man paused and Mitch had to slam on the brakes of his white F-150. Mitch jumped out of the car, panicked he'd killed a man.

Deputies were already on the scene. Mitch felt terrible. Was the man on the street okay?

"Third time today," Officer Anderson said to his partner, the vivacious and thrilling Linda Kettleman, who'd joined the force only months before.

"You'll have to stay here and give a statement," Officer Anderson told Mitch, while Linda checked on the downed man. She took off her jacket, laid it under the old man's head, and cooed.

At least Fred thought she cooed. He had a good view down the front of her blouse and he wasn't going to say anything to change the situation. From this view, she looked so Mildred-like, Mildred like she was younger, Mildred when she used to run in the grass and make him laugh.

By the time they got to the police station, Fred had come to the realization that no, this cop was not Mildred, which disappointed him, but when the real Mildred came into the police station he wasn't so pleased either. Her hair, once blond and luscious, was now white, and braided tight next to her scalp. She looked like a very busy squirrel. She marched right in and elbowed her way to Fred, who was sitting in the captain's chair nursing a cup of coffee.

"We're glad you're here, Mrs. Rhinehart," Linda said.

"I sent my husband to get chocolate and next thing I know, deputies are at my house, ringing my doorbell and disturbing my ironing."

"You can't send him out alone, ma'am." Linda tried to get Mrs. Rhinehart to understand. "He almost got hit by a car."

"But I wasn't, was I, Officer ..." Fred couldn't remember her last name, and calling her Linda just sounded too familiar.

Officer Kettleman sighed. "He can't stay here, ma'am. We've got other calls."

"Ready then, Fred?" Mildred offered her bird-thin arms to his rather heavy body. Light as a feather he was, holding onto her. He waved any help away.

"Shall we go get the steak?" he asked eagerly.

"It was chocolate, you forgetful old thing," Mildred clucked, as they walked into the sunshine.

It all seemed the same to Fred. He held his wife's arm proudly as they crossed the street. She felt light as the day they met, years ago, his hands full of daffodils, her soft hands reaching for his.

FROM THE SHERIFF'S CALLS SECTION IN THE *POINT REYES LIGHT*,
NOVEMBER 27, 2011

POINT REYES STATION: At 10:42 a.m. deputies
called for back-up for a "pedestrian who was
not following orders."

Their Timing Was Perfect

All afternoon Kelly Dunlap, 45, of Point Reyes Station, had been watching the old guy trying to cross the street, and was about to help him when he saw deputies coming to the man's aid. Satisfied, he turned his attention back to his work, refinishing the rebuild of a 1979 cobalt- blue Pontiac Trans Am. The car was as smooth as a tub under his practiced hands.

It was a busy morning at the garage. Five cars and two tractors were lined up, and the orders on clipboards flapped in the breeze from the open garage doors. That Trans Am looked great – it wasn't the usual kind of car they serviced and Kelly was proud. It had taken over a month, fitting it in here and there. He couldn't wait until the owner saw it.

Wiping his hands on his monkey suit, he headed to the office. It was time he made that call to his ex-wife. He'd put it off for hours, but wanted to call her before she called him. Otherwise, one of the wise guys would holler over the loudspeaker system: "Kelly, Betty is on the phone," his laughter rising to the rafters, which would make Kelly cringe. The worst part of it was that everyone out on the street in downtown Point Reyes Station would hear the same thing.

Kelly picked up the dusty rotary phone in the office with grease-stained hands. No matter how much GoJo hand cleaner he used, the creases in his fingers were always black. He listened as the phone rang at the other end. Maybe Betty was in the yard with the kids, with dour Charles who hated his name or pretty Mary who liked to bring home the wrong kind of boys from school and while away the afternoons while Betty was stuck in her office, providing paralegal help to a bunch of rich guys from Petaluma. Kelly kept telling her to move to West Marin, but she wouldn't hear of it.

In the middle of the fourth ring, someone walked into the shop bay and he put down the phone. It was Deputy Linda Kettleman and she was a knockout. He wondered if she'd been a model before she moved into his little hometown.

"Hi, Linda, can I help you?" Kelly asked, wanting to wipe his hands cleaner than they were.

"Cruiser's got a dent, Kelly. Came around a blind corner last night, in dense fog, hit a deer."

Kelly, a venison lover, started asking her about the deer. Was it hurt? Stunned? Dead on the side of the road? He was just about to ask where it was when he realized, with a start, he hadn't asked her how she was. "I could come pick it up, Linda, save you the trouble, and quarter it for you." He was used to butchering meat: it was in his family's blood. They had a ranch along Chileno Valley Road and he'd still be there if he hadn't taken body shop in high school, turned his back on the family business, and pissed off his father for life. He looked at Linda eagerly.

"Kelly, we don't do that. We call the Humane Society." She liked venison too, but she was a rules kind of gal. And she was new. At the station, the guys talked about hunting, but none of them ever did. She was a much better shot than all of them.

Kelly ran his hands over the cruiser's crumpled fender. "As for the cruiser, three days, a thousand dollars, unless ..." He stopped there. The boss wouldn't be too happy if he found out Kelly bartered sometimes. He winked.

"I haven't got all day. Can I have the car tomorrow afternoon?"

"So, you didn't answer my question," Kelly said.

"Oh, yes I did." She adjusted the grip on her standard-issue holster: damn thing dug into her hip and still, after six months, she wasn't used to the weight of the belt and all the equipment. Twenty pounds on her too-heavy hips was unnecessary in this cow town. "Just fix the cruiser. Forget about the deer." She tossed her keys to him and headed to the door.

"Hey Linda," Kelly called. "Paperwork." He headed toward her with a clipboard, pen and form. His hands didn't work right. He kept focusing on her front. He knew better: women like Linda were way beyond his world. But what the hell, worth a try. "How 'bout a beer, you know, like, after work?" he asked. He had no way with women but was fascinated by them.

"You asking me out, Kelly? You know I'm not supposed to date perpetrators."

"Perpetrator? What'd I do? Conspiracy to clean up road kill? Dating you, it's legal, don't you think?"

"And after the beer?" Linda asked, teasing him. She had a bit of a cruel streak, and sometimes didn't feel like tempering it.

"Dinner?" he asked, not believing his luck. He came closer. "You know where I work," he said, trying not to appear overly eager. Was she this easy? That's not what he'd heard from the other guys in town.

"And after dinner?" Linda asked, knowing the answer already.

Kelly wasn't going to say anything. He had a nice view from here. What would it be like when she took off her uniform? His hands were getting sweaty, and the pen kept slipping from his fingers.

"Kelly, Kelly," Linda sighed. Not six months on the force and everyone hit on her. "I'm not going out with you."

His face fell.

"I was teasing you – bad habit of mine." Her manipulation of men was nothing to be proud of. She liked putting bad guys behind bars, but she had trouble being around the good ones. Too many years being chased by her two older brothers and they had been relentless. She'd been taught too well to fight back and had lost her gentle side.

Kelly, his face clouded, scratched his head. Twice denied in less than two minutes. He could understand the venison, and the date, but there'd been no call to tease him like that, to turn on him. Maybe he'd take two weeks to fix her cruiser, and fill the bumps and hollows with Bondo.

"The heck with it." He threw a wrench into a tool chest. He'd been too forward, Betty was about to call, the guys were back in the office, and he'd been shot down. Not a good day so far.

"I'll get to the cruiser today, ma'am," he said, putting on his best business-man voice.

Linda felt bad for him. He did have a nice head of chestnut brown hair and eager, light- blue eyes. She could, she supposed, do something nice to make it up to him. Her dad had told her she'd never get a husband if she didn't lighten up. But a husband like Kelly? Well, definitely not him. But she could at least. "How 'bout that beer?"

Kelly brightened, but guardedly, so as not to let her see it. He wasn't go-ing to be fooled again. "Say, six?" he asked, teasing her this time. He'd be long gone out of Cheda's by then.

"While you're working on the car, check this address." She wrote some-thing down on a piece of paper. "Use a flashlight. Shouldn't be too hard to find. See you later." She handed him the paper and walked out the door.

Kelly looked at the address. Just where Samuel P. Taylor Park began, where the redwoods closed in over the road. He knew the place. "See you then," he called after her. He could go get the deer with a friend and be back by six.

Linda was halfway down the block and out of earshot when the loud-speaker over Kelly's head crackled to life. "Kelly, Betty is on the phone." It was followed by the unmistakable sound of laughter from the wise guys in the office. At this point, and forever after, Kelly was thankful to the gods – wherever and whoever they were – for their timing was perfect this time.

FROM THE SHERIFF'S CALLS SECTION IN THE *POINT REYES LIGHT*,
DECEMBER 1, 2011

TOMALES: At 8:10 p.m. a woman said she saw
a car full of costumed people, possibly burglars,
on her ranch.

The Night Visitors

"They're out there, I just saw them," Mildred said, letting the kitchen curtains fall. "Burglars, Fred."

Fred, whose eyes had been glued to the football game, sat up with dismay. Third time today Mildred was all worked up.

"If there's one thing I know, it's burglars. There were right there, Fred." She peered out the window.

"What did they look like?"

"They were not farmers. One was wearing all black, another was wearing a red and gold shirt," she said.

Forty-Niner colors, Fred thought. Can't be all bad. "Just two?"

"They were four sneaking around."

Fred sighed. They were staying at his cousin David's 200-acre ranch just outside Tomales. Farmworkers there helped out, but they were gone for the day. So who was out there? He had a wife goddammit, a wife to protect, and he didn't want her to think he wasn't up to the task.

Bring back the burglars, he thought, and I'll be ready. He took up a seat on the porch. He kept his rifle by his side, but unloaded it first. Last time he'd handled the gun, he'd shot his niece's pet rooster by mistake. He sat there through bedtime, through the lights going out in the house, through Mildred's reminders to come to bed.

Around midnight his feet and his backside had gone to sleep and he rose, creaking, and slammed the screen door on his way in, bringing Angel in too. Some help she was: she'd slept all evening.

Up in the bedroom, Fred carefully changed into his pajamas, brushed his teeth and climbed into bed, making the springs squeal. Mildred moaned a little and turned over.

That was when he heard it, a wheel rolling on gravel, the sound of boots hitting the ground, an engine ticking cool. Then it was silent. Silent except for whispers. Fred slipped out of bed and peeked out behind the bedroom drapes.

Mildred sat up.

"Lie back down, sweetheart," Fred said, pulling his rifle closer. He opened the window slowly, letting cold air rush in. Mildred tucked deeper under the covers. Angel, well into her teens, crawled under the bed.

He saw them first, two burly men wearing dark clothes, just like she had said. Fred paused.

Watching the men, Fred climbed down onto his knees, reached into the bedside table, placed a shell in the chamber, aimed for the trees, and pulled.

The recoil of the rifle knocked him back on the floor. Angel barked and jumped on the bed. Mildred rolled away from her side and onto the floor, taking all the covers with her.

Fred heard yelling and was about to load again when a flashlight came on in the woods outside.

"Son of a bitch! Someone is shooting out the window!"

It was time Fred went outside to see. Putting on his bathrobe, filling his pockets with shells, and with Angel at his side, Fred bounded down the stairs to the front door. He flicked on the security lights. The front yard, his own Buick, and the woods exploded with light. One cop was leaning against a patrol car, talking into the radio. Another was in the back seat, hunting for something. Angel got to them first, barking for all her might. Fred followed, as clear and tall as John Wayne, walking to meet his maker.

"You didn't have to shoot!" the officer yelled. "We're on patrol!"

"We thought you were burglars," Fred said.

"Maybe it's time you went into the home after all, you crazy old coot," said one of the cops. "Please, hand over your weapon."

"But it was my grandfather's," Fred said, not at all happy with the turn of events.

"And the shells, sir," the cop asked.

"You scared the shit out of me – and the wife!" Fred cried. "Take it then, take the whole damn thing. Satisfied? Now, go away." As it was, they had too many weapons anyway; Mildred was still buying them over the Internet.

"Ready, Bert?" one of the cops said.

"Last time we swing around this ranch," the other said. "We were lucky this time."

Fred thought so too. After watching the cruiser drive away and satisfied that all was quiet, he gathered Angel and went back inside the house. Now, with the coast clear, he could get some sleep. Mildred was upstairs, waiting for him, her body nice and warm and the bed freshly made.

FROM THE SHERIFF'S CALLS SECTION IN THE *POINT REYES LIGHT*,
NOVEMBER 22, 2011

POINT REYES STATION: At 11:16 a.m. deputies
got a call in which they first heard a woman
saying she needed to go to sleep and then
heard a baby talking.

The Talking Baby

"Fred, read it to me, again," Mildred demanded. "A baby? Talking? About
sports, news, the weather report?" She stared out the window at Mrs. Flanagan cutting off the tops of her dead daffodils. Stupid cow, they'd never come
back now.

"I'm sure the baby wasn't talking that way, dear." Fred watched his wife
flip through the pages of the *Point Reyes Light*. "Maybe the deputies don't
know the word 'babble'."

"Maybe the deputies don't know anything." Mildred ran a rolling pin
over some pie crust. She was a pie-type girl, it was Thanksgiving, and she
was on her third. "Now," she gestured with one flour-covered finger, "what
was this about a woman calling the deputies because she needed to sleep?"

"Maybe she dialed nine-one-one by mistake." Fred settled into the af-
ghan-covered couch to watch the football game. Mildred just went on so.
He knew better than to argue. He smiled to himself, remembering that he'd
learned that trick a week after their wedding. He reached for the remote.

"But if it's a mom needing sleep, then the baby would be too young to
be talking." Mildred pressed the soft pie crust into a glass pie pan. She had
enough crust to weave a top, but she'd kind of forgotten how. Everything up
or everything under? Didn't make sense to her. She dug her hand into a bowl
of apples. "I swear I don't know what the world's coming to, Fred, talking

babies and goofy moms calling the cops. Don't you think it would be better the other way around?"

Fred, deep into watching the half-time show and wondering how those girls kept those scanty uniforms on, couldn't figure out what his wife was talking about. If it wasn't one thing it was another, and if her sister Phyllis wasn't coming over for Thanksgiving, he could spend the whole day watching half-time shows, flipping channels. "Don't you think all babies are kind of goofy?"

"I cracked a joke, Fred, and once again you're not listening. Still, why would this mother call the police? Do you think she's in danger?" She sighed, grabbed her rolling pin, and peered out the window. "They should have printed her address in the newspaper. I could go help her."

"Maybe it was a crank call – you know, talking baby and such." Fred flicked the channel and tried to find another half-time show. "I'm sure somebody made a mistake."

"That poor mother." Mildred slid the pie into the oven and slammed the door closed with her hip. "I should know. We had four."

Four, Fred thought, and now only three. She had to bring that up, today, a holiday, and he'd been having such a good time watching the girls in their red and gold glittery costumes. Now the action on TV seemed crass and cheap. He turned it off, rose his bulk from the beat-up couch and walked over to the tabletop where Mildred had placed Peter's picture. It was dusty. She hadn't wanted to touch it, even though the rest of the house was sparkly clean. Peter had been a baby, too, when they'd lost him. Sitting up, with a Santa hat on, his warm brown eyes looking at the photographer, eyeing some teddy bear the Sears photographer held in his hand, just above the lens. Peter had loved teddy bears.

"Peter talked, Mildred. He talked all the time – sometimes to the animals in the forest, sometimes to his imaginary friends, sometimes to the new baby he'd met from next door."

"He didn't really say all that." Mildred pulled some more flour from the shelf. If she kept baking, she wouldn't feel anything. It took all the concentration she had, counting the cups, stirring the fruit, setting the timer. "Oh Fred. Five years, ten, fifteen, twenty, it's all the same. It feels like yesterday."

"The little ones are so sweet." Fred counted their children on his fingers, "Matt, Janet, Hattie."

"Janet's not little anymore, Fred. None of them are." Mildred recalled Janet's college graduation. "She's not going to sit in your lap and listen to you tell a story."

"But they all love us," Fred said, wanting to comfort Mildred, but not sure exactly how. Nothing worked, lately, not since what would have been Peter's 45th birthday. "It's a nice day. Let's go for a walk." He felt desperate. Phyllis would be coming over within the hour and he couldn't start drinking just yet.

"My pies, Fred, I can't leave my pies." Mildred smoothed the front of her apron.

"Janet will be here soon. She always makes you laugh."

"She's the only one who can come," Mildred sniffed and pulled off her apron.

"Do you think she's the deputy who got the call?" Fred asked, curious. "You know, the one about the talking baby?"

Mildred clasped her hands. "You think it was a message from Peter? He always had so much to say." She rubbed her sore arthritic knuckles, and put on a coat.

"Maybe so." Fred slipped on his jacket. "And that mom – she was tired, and called the cops by mistake. Peter was always talking to us, and I sure was tired all the time. He was such a busy little baby."

"Many days I felt like calling the cops." Mildred took his arm.

"Me too," Fred said, buttoning his wife's coat and leading her out the door.

FROM THE SHERIFF'S CALLS SECTION IN THE *POINT REYES LIGHT*, DECEMBER 29, 2011

POINT REYES STATION: At 9:36 p.m. an elderly man drove onto someone's front yard and became lodged in the septic mound.

So It Was You

"It wasn't me!" Fred was outraged. "I'm a better driver than that!" He paced through their 1930s' cabin which sagged in the middle like he did. "It's some other old fart."

Mildred, who had been baking chocolate-chip cookies all afternoon, took a look at him. "Then why are your boots all muddy?"

"All the frigging deputies are mistaken." He carefully took off his boots and set them on a mat by the front door. "I was heading to the dump, the other direction."

"Harrumph." Mildred shoved the oven door closed with her hip. "Your driving has been leaving a bit to be desired lately, Fred Rhinehart."

"Oh brother." Fred dropped into his recliner. It was a big game day, and he had his potato chips and one beer, which he would savor all afternoon. Later, maybe, if she'd let him, he'd drive down to the Western and have a few more, at least for the second half. Mildred had decided years ago that he was an alcoholic, but Fred knew he was nothing, *nothing*, like his old man. Who could argue about an old guy like him having a pop or two in the morning, just to get his joints lubricated and his eyelids open? He cracked open his beer.

"So," Mildred strolled out of the kitchen and smoothed her apron, "just who was it that drove into that septic mound, Fred?"

Her little eyes were trying to bore through his fuzzy mind. He couldn't remember all of it. "Henry, the Palace Market stock boy. Looks just like me."

That much was true, except Henry drove a sedan and Fred drove an F-150 Ford pickup. But the paper hadn't mentioned which kind of vehicle, and he'd scrubbed the wheels and the fenders clear of all that muck. The truck, uncharacteristically clean, stood proud like a ghost in the barn. First bath it had had all year. But Mildred would notice. "Hey sweetheart," he crowed, "I washed the truck."

"Well, what about my car?" she spat. "Come on, I do favors for you all the time."

Right, thought Fred, favors like overheated dinners and indigestible meat. He had mentioned cooking classes to her once, but she'd thrown the College of Marin Adult Education brochure at him. He could smell the cookies from the oven, about to burn. "Your cookies, darling." He settled back to watch the game.

"Keep yourself to yourself and out of my cooking," she scolded and set the timer.

"Oh, Mildred." Fred sighed, more to himself than to her. For months now, she hadn't been able to handle the oven, and as for him, his problem had been the truck. He couldn't see so well beyond the windshield, and his feet hadn't been able to differentiate between the pedals. There were just so many of them, so he had pressed them all.

"First down!" The football announcer's voice broke out, followed by a burst of applause. Mildred's trouble with the oven, and his sight – they weren't enough to make them move into an old people's home, were they? He loved this house with its crooked windows, rumpled carpets, and slanted floors. He extracted himself out of his chair, stood by the big picture window, and looked out on the rain coming down Inverness Ridge. He'd lived in this place forty years, since he'd been a young man and Mildred had been a princess, wearing flowers in her hair on their wedding day, and he'd planned on having and holding her forever, and he had, hadn't he? He heard a cry from the kitchen and ran in.

"Damn it all." Mildred held the oven door open and stared at a dozen blackened blobs. "I set the timer for ten minutes, and it didn't go off. It's not my fault, Fred; the stupid oven needs to be calibrated."

"You've told me that before," he sighed, "I'll call the appliance man." He led her away from the hot oven, turned it off, and removed her oven mitts. He checked the timer; it had never been turned on. "Maybe it's time you stopped baking for the church."

"But it's my job." Eyes brimming with tears, she dropped her head into her hands. "Thirty years – I used to be able to do it easy."

"And I used to be able to see well enough to drive, sweetheart," he cooed, holding her.

"So it *was* you." She eyed him with her bird-like gaze.

"I didn't say that I didn't say anything like that," Fred said. His sweetheart looked so sad. "So, Mildred, would you like to watch? It might be safer than baking."

"I hate sports." She threw her apron on the floor and marched toward the back of the house. Halfway there, she stopped and turned. He looked so lonely, sitting there, by himself. "Well, okay, just this time." She tucked herself next to him and fluttered her handmade afghan over them. "Just this one time, Fred."

FROM THE SHERIFF'S CALLS SECTION IN THE *POINT REYES LIGHT*,
JANUARY 12, 2012

POINT REYES STATION: At 12:23 p.m.
someone reported that a mentally unstable
man who might be armed with a bow and arrow was camping out on the northeast corner
of a piece of property, in a eucalyptus grove.
Deputies took down the man's tent.

Sweet Wally Lamb

Meadow, satisfied, put down the phone. That fool – thinking he could set
up camp on her property. And that thing about the bow and arrow worried
her. Whatever, she got him to move.

Grabbing a leash, Meadow called her hound Wally Lamb. She named all
of her animals after authors, and when she was lonely – which was much of
the time – she called their names and felt she was at a literary event. When
they didn't answer her, that was okay. Talking amongst themselves was en-
couraged at her place.

She strolled through weeds chest high. The fire department had told her
to clear brush at least thirty feet away from her house, but Meadow wouldn't
do it. She didn't have the tools, but that was only part of it. The tall grass
held butterflies and bees and spiders and mites and all kinds of critters and
she didn't want to hurt any of them. She felt the same way about homeless
people, poor guys who had no place to hang their hats, so she brought them
home. After a few days, though, they wouldn't behave. They wanted things
- they wanted her, her car, her clothes, her clean dishes, her credit cards, her
food - and then they had to go.

Hawks circled overhead. Twenty acres was a lot of ground to cover. As
she walked the narrow pathways through the tall grass, she swore she heard

a sound. A moaning through the slight wind? A group of crows, perched in the top of a Monterey pine, took off in a rush of wings.

Ascending a small hill with a view of the sparkling ocean beyond, she sighed. Her favorite spot. In the silence of the wind and rushing grass, she heard the moaning, louder now. The guy she'd thrown off her property? Damn! She'd have to call the cops again. As she followed the sound, she entered the coolness of the eucalyptus grove and entered a clearing. There, sitting on a log, was a boy. A real boy. A boy of thirteen, maybe. A boy with a shock of blond hair. A boy digging at the dirt with a stick. Nearby was the tent, collapsed by the sheriff's deputies.

"You didn't have to call them." He shot her a glance. "We would have left in good time. Now you've destroyed the only home I've ever had."

"Where's your dad?" Meadow asked. She'd remembered the guy, full beard, dusty worn-out blue jeans, a blue watch cap, and a ragged jacket. She didn't know he'd had a son. "Surely you have a better home than this?"

"He's gone, you know." The boy pitched rocks at a tree. "We weren't hurting you or your property."

"I heard the noises at night and they scared me." Meadow had had all kinds of homeless people on her land. Why had this one bothered her so? "You had a bow and arrow, boy. What were you trying to do, kill me?"

"Game, ma'am. Haven't you ever heard about the recession?"

Having inherited money from her dad, Meadow couldn't remember ever holding a job, much less worrying about losing one. But she did her part, didn't she, taking care of the homeless? Just not this one. "When did your dad leave?"

"How the hell should I know?"

"You in school?" It was Tuesday, wasn't it? "Why aren't you in school?"

"What do you think?" The boy kicked over a can of old cigarette butts.

"I'm going to have to report you for defacing private property," Meadow stated. Usually, the homeless guys left quickly and quietly – except for the one who'd died in her backroom. But that hadn't been her fault. "Your dad know you're here? How 'bout your mom? Shall we call her?"

"My mother?" He laughed. "Where's your mother? How 'bout I ask you questions for a change? Why'd you call the cops?" He lifted up a corner of the tent and threw one of the broken poles on the ground. "You think I'm staying out here for fun?"

"Not someone who likes camping so much, I guess." Meadow tried to assess the situation. If she hadn't smoked a doobie before she left the house she could make more sense of things.

"You call it camping a weekend a year. I call it hell every night of the week. Hey, can I come in and take a shower? I feel grubby as a toad."

Meadow gazed at the boy, skinny, narrow face, strong cheekbones, long neck, and fine dancing fingers. Maybe she could help him out. Maybe she'd blown it with his father. But shower inside? Never. She'd give him the hose.

He followed her back to the house. His name was Eric. Not entirely happy with the situation, she showed him the hose and a bucket.

"I'm not a car, lady. I'm a person. I need shampoo, towels, and a shower. A private shower."

"I don't have to help you at all," Meadow shot back. "You can march right on out of here if you're going to have that kind of attitude."

Wally Lamb, her hound, went up to Eric and wagged his tail. Eric looked from the dog's round sweet eyes to Meadow's, back to the dog again, then to the house. "I'm only thirteen, ma'am. Bet this dog has a better home than I do."

"Oh for Christ's sake." Meadow sighed and led him toward the back bathroom. She would have locked the French doors between the back and front of the house if she could, if she'd had a lock. Shit, she didn't even have a lock to the front door. When she heard the water running, she went outside to talk to Wally Lamb.

Five minutes later, she heard a crash come from inside the house. What the hell? She ran in, half-expecting to see a naked kid trashing the place, but there was no one in the front of the house. She heard scuffling behind the French doors. With Wally Lamb at her side, she opened the double doors and sent him through, sort of hoping he would be the watch dog her father said he was. She heard a squeal, opened the door again, and Wally ran past her, bleeding.

Meadow found the dog cowering, in a closet, splattered with blood. She grabbed his head and, forcing him to be still, checked for a wound. The closest vet was in Point Reyes Station, thirty minutes away. Grabbing his muzzle, she saw two scratches above his nose. Wally was wide-eyed, all hopped up. Whispering to him, she checked him over. A handful of Kleenex tissue and she'd staunched the bleeding. Now to find out about the kid.

Coming to the glass French doors, she carefully opened them and listened. Who had scratched Wally? The cuts weren't that deep. A raccoon perhaps? A bobcat? The back door was closed. Had Eric hurt her dog? Incensed, she grabbed the fireplace poker and, sidling up to the wall, crept up to the rear bathroom door. Instead of hearing something crashing, she heard singing. Singing?

"The long and winding road …" trilled Eric against a fountain of spray. "When I'm sixty-four …"

Meadow was thinking hard about her next move when the bathroom door opened and she was enveloped in a blast of steam. Eric walked out, a towel around his middle.

"Sweet." He licked his lips. "My dad would like you. And your place. Thanks." He stepped up to her and kissed her on the mouth.

Meadow jumped back.

"You want more?" he asked. "I bet you want more."

Meadow wiped her mouth with the back of her hand. "You have a lot of cheek."

"That's what they all say," Eric mentioned and slowly, without effort, buried a razor in her neck.

They found Meadow two days later, in the forest by the collapsed tent. A broken arrow lay across her body, and the dog, sweet Wally Lamb, was discovered later that afternoon, rambling amongst the other strays, out in front of Smiley's, looking for a home.

FROM THE SHERIFF'S CALLS SECTION IN THE *POINT REYES LIGHT*,
JANUARY 12, 2012

POINT REYES STATION: At 9:02 p.m. someone heard a young woman, who was upset by a phone call with her boyfriend and had gone for a walk to calm down, yelling.

She Felt Like Hattie

"What do you think she's yelling about, Fred?" Mildred stood by her yellow kitchen curtains, trying to see what was going on outside on Mesa Road.

Fred, who had just cranked the handle back on his recliner, was feeling comfy. "What is it that you're saying, sweet thing?" He churned through the channels on his remote. There had to be some football on somewhere.

"Oh no! She's coming this way!" Mildred closed her curtains and turned off the lights. "I told you we should have installed police locks. Fred, do something."

Fred, stuck in his chair, jammed the handle on the way up and had to climb out. It would have been easier but for two problems. The chair was an extra cushy one and he was, as his doctor put it, a tad overweight. He caught up with Mildred in the pantry, where she slammed a heavy flashlight into his hand.

"Go see who it is, Fred."

Jesus, it was cold outside. He took a step. Then another. Heard the crunch of gravel. "Is there anyone out there?" he called. His flashlight danced against a barn door, their old Buick and a dirt road.

Hearing nothing, he turned to go back in when he heard someone crying.

"Hey you. Can I help you?" Fred was trying to determine the source of the noise, but he wasn't wearing his hearing aids, so couldn't be sure. He squinted into the fog.

"I'm not going to hurt you." He came a little closer to the sound. "I'm eighty-two years old, an old man." He winced at the word; he never liked that word 'old'.

More sniffles and something sparkly showed through the bushes.

"Who's there?" he asked gently. Mildred would be peeved if he left a young woman outside in the fog. The sparkles moved and so did he. That was when he saw her; she was what? Eighteen, twenty, thirty? All women looked young compared to Mildred. He winced. She wouldn't like him thinking like that.

"You okay?" he asked.

More sniffles. "My boyfriend – he left me," the girl said.

As small as Hattie, Fred thought, light and wiry like she was, but this gal's eyes were bigger. "Are you hurt?" He shoved his hands into his pockets. "It's chilly tonight."

"There's no place I'm warm, Mister." She lit a cigarette.

And so young, Fred thought. "Are you lost? Did your car break down?"

She stubbed her cigarette out on the sole of her army boot.

Fred saw her sparkling jacket, skinny blue jeans, backpack, and army boots clearly as she stood under his newly installed security light. A thin wisp of a girl.

"He left me, at the Station House. We were on a date, I came out of the ladies', and he was gone. Didn't even pick up the check." She pulled a tissue out of her pocket.

"Did you wait for him?" Fred waved her closer with his flashlight.

"An hour. Jeesus. That's a hell of a way to treat a person."

"Did you walk here?" Fred asked. They were at least a mile out of town and well off the main road.

"Oh, I hitched a ride with the tow truck driver, and he was going to take me to Petaluma." She chewed on a fingernail. "Where the hell is Petaluma?"

"Where do you live, then?" Fred asked, suppressing the urge to say "honey".

"East Bay. We came out here to go hiking – and we had a really nice time." She eyed his house. "You have a really nice place."

"Maybe I should call the sheriff," Fred said. "They're real good with run-aways."

"Oh no, don't call the cops. Please. They'll call my parents." She paused. "I should never have come."

"So I see." Fred's bunions were killing him. "Now it's dark, you're stranded, and went out with an older guy," he guessed.

She sniffed. "He didn't hurt me or anything, and he was real nice ... until ..."

"That's the thing." Fred paused. "No manners."

"Could I come inside? Use your phone? I would call a cab, but there's no reception. Just take a second."

"I can take you to the sheriff's office," Fred answered, thinking for a moment how much she looked like Hattie, and if it had been Hattie, how he'd have her inside, warm her up, then give her the third degree. Late-night dates with older men; she should have known better.

"Please Mister, don't leave me stranded. People, they just dump me everywhere. I'm society's garbage, then, is that it?" A flash of anger in her blue eyes, eyes like Hattie's.

"No, nothing like that." Fred felt bad. He could bring her inside, but Mildred was too fragile, and he couldn't leave this girl out here either. His neighbors' houses were dark. His feet were cold, he'd forgotten his cane, and the zipper on his jacket was broken.

"I just can't go on." She sobbed, ran up to him, and buried her face in his shirt.

Fred stepped back, feeling awkward and clumsy. His arms enveloped her. She smelled like Hattie, felt like Hattie, Hattie who hadn't talked to them for over a year, and he couldn't help it: this one could've been one of his own children, she was so bony and cold. Muffled sobs came from his chest. Staggering a little, holding her close, he brought her toward the house.

The back door burst open in a fountain of light. It was his wife, beckoning them in. Fred released the girl; she went toward Mildred.

"Oh God, thank you, thank you," she said.

Mildred moved quickly and brought up her shotgun. "Not so fast, sister."

The girl looked from Mildred to Fred, back at Mildred again. "You must be confused, ma'am, I'm unarmed, I've been left out here, stranded, my boyfriend ..."

"Stuff it, girl." Mildred pulled the hammer back.

"Mildred, please," Fred urged. "She's all alone, no car, no way home, just as she says. You know how you get sometimes, sweetheart."

"If you're going to be that way, Fred, you can go stand by your new girl-friend and both of you can go down. Now, hands up."

"Oh come on," Fred coaxed, "not me too. Did you take your meds to-day?" He heard tires cross the dirt road behind him. The neighbors. Help at last. He turned.

"Fred, no!" He ducked. Mildred's shot rang out. The girl hid behind him, safe behind his bulk.

"You stupid fool." Mildred held a bead on them. Nearby car doors opened. "Keep them away. She's mine."

"That's enough, Mrs. Rhinehart," Officer Kettleman said. "You've done well; we can take it from here." The other deputy clasped the girl in hand-cuffs and led her to the sheriff's car.

"She didn't do anything wrong," Fred said, feeling at a loss. "Mildred! You almost shot me."

"Did you load it with rock salt like I asked, Mrs. Rhinehart?" Officer Kettleman asked.

"But rock salt still hurts!" Fred felt like he'd been left out of the parade.

"I read about her in the *Light*," Mildred said with a swagger, as Officer Kettleman took down a report. "That little girl robbed the Palace Market, Fred, and she would've gotten away with it too, if I hadn't called it in."

"You were lucky this time, Mr. and Mrs. Rhinehart," Officer Kettleman chided them. "Next time just call the cops, and Mr. Rhinehart ...You have a sweet and loving heart, sir, but this time you could have been killed."

"By my wife," Fred said, keeping his eye on Mildred. "By my wife."

From the Sheriff's Calls Section in the *Point Reyes Light*,
January 19, 2012

POINT REYES STATION: At 7:36 a.m. someone reported that a woman who had moved to town a week before was not letting her boyfriend see their child.

The Good Mother

"Isn't that just terrible, Doris?" Mildred said, holding her purse tight and taking a seat in the hairdresser's chair.

Behind her, Doris pumped up the chair until it was the right height. It was an early appointment and she was still tired from being up half the night caring for her ten-year-old son Joshua.

"For the mother or the father?" Doris pulled out her scissors.

"What was the mother thinking, moving away in the first place?" Mildred sniffed. "Things weren't like that when I was younger."

"Maybe this mother came to West Marin so the kid could see his dad," Doris suggested, running shampoo through Mildred's hair.

Mildred moaned while Doris rubbed her temples.

Doris wrapped Mildred's head in a towel and sighed. She would have done anything for Joshua to see his father, but Barry hadn't been interested.

"Mothers should stay with their children and fathers should be responsible." Mildred hunted for her compact. Where had it gone? It had been in her purse yesterday.

"Same as usual, Mrs. Rhinehart?" Doris ran her hands through the older woman's thinning hair.

"If the mother just moved to town, why wouldn't she let the boyfriend see their child?"

Doris, her hands poised over Mildred's head, had her own thoughts. "Maybe the boyfriend is a jerk, and doesn't return the kid when he's supposed to. Or maybe the dad has a new girlfriend and the mom is jealous. Maybe the boyfriend is a bum, Mrs. Rhinehart."

"Of course he's a bum, Doris. Not marrying the woman, running off, having lots of girlfriends. Just where was this dad when she needed him, at the Western, having a drink?"

Maybe he was hell and gone to Idaho, Doris thought, twisting Mildred's hair a little too tight.

"Ease off a little, girl, would you? In my day, fathers were at home or at work, Doris: they were present." Mildred grasped the sides of her chair, grabbing so tight the skin of her hands went white. "All this irresponsibility has got to stop. That poor mother."

"Now, Mrs. Rhinehart, please, calm down," Doris said, scissors poised in the air. The lady was as agitated as a squirrel.

The door to the salon burst open. It was Officer Kettleman.

"You heard about or seen that woman with the baby?" Linda raised her voice so all the elderly ladies in the salon could hear her. "She's run off with the baby and the boyfriend, the dad, he's beside himself."

"Well, that's perfectly all right with me." Mildred touched her heart. "She's a mother, it's her right, and it's her child. Officer Kettleman, forget about it and go find some real criminals."

"We haven't seen anyone, but we'll keep an eye out," Doris said, eager for that dad to find his kid.

"You wouldn't be so complacent if it was your son's child, Mildred," one of the other customers argued.

"Not your business, Hortense. Go back home – it's too early for you to be out," Mildred snorted. The old biddy was always trying to stick her nose into everyone's business.

"Now, girls," Linda said. "Mrs. Elliott, please, I'll get to you in a minute."

"That mother should be arrested." Hortense rose out of her dryer chair and threw her smock on the floor.

"I saw a mom and kid heading to the gas station," said another customer. Beatrice was kind of small and liked to stay out of the fray. She didn't like crowds and had come to the salon early hoping for quiet. Now it was as busy as a farmer's market Saturday.

"When did you see them last?" Linda asked.

"Beatrice doesn't know anything," Mildred said. "She talks to bees."

"Bees are animals too," Beatrice said and sidled up to Officer Kettleman.

Doris tucked her scissors and comb into a pocket. "Mrs. Darcy, please, sit back down."

"Go check them out," Beatrice uttered. "They're on Route One. She was hitching – and on such a cold day, too." Beatrice, well into her nineties, pointed to the door with a trembling hand.

"Can't you leave the poor mother alone?" Mildred grabbed her purse and threw it at Beatrice.

"Ladies, please," Doris urged.

"I've got to find her, thanks, Mrs. Darcy," Linda said, shifting the weight on her equipment belt.

"I just know she's a good mom," Mildred said.

Beatrice gave her a dirty look.

"She's a drug addict, Mrs. Rhinehart," Linda replied. She didn't like giving out police secrets, but these ladies tried her patience. "Now, if you'll excuse me."

"I'm still sure she's a good mother." Mildred climbed back into her chair. "Cops don't know everything."

"If you say so, Mrs. Rhinehart," Doris said, trying to decide how to cut her fine, thin hair. When she got home she'd try Barry again. No matter what, a child still needed a dad.

From the Sheriff's Calls Section in the *Point Reyes Light*,
January 19, 2012

BOLINAS: 1:39 p.m. Resident reported a transient she befriended possibly absconded with her cat.

Mr. Twinkles

"I can't chase after a transient, boss." Linda shifted her belt. Even with her saddle-bag hips, she still felt bruised at the end of a twelve-hour day. "And I'm not chasing after a goddamn cat."

"You don't like animals, much, do you, Linda?" Walter tapped his pencil on his desk. "She's called five times in the last hour. Go see what you can do."

"But boss," Linda replied, eager to go after real criminals.

"But nothing. Get yourself over to the Mesa. I don't care about the cat." Walter knew cats could get by, especially on the Mesa, where there were plenty of rodents. "Do your job, report back – and Linda," he frowned, punching in some numbers on his cell phone, "keep your phone on, your radio on, and call in. No more monkey business, is that clear?" He slammed his palm down on his desk. Losing Harold in a hit-and-run had hit him hard. He'd loved the young deputy like a son.

A few minutes later, Linda shoved the cruiser into reverse and backed out of the parking lot. She took the back roads. On a day like this, sunny and warm, the whole town was crawling with tourists, people who couldn't drive worth a damn. They'd stop in the middle of the road, dumbfounded. They needed a cop downtown just for them, and she had to go to Bolinas, hippieville, and placate some woman. Her cat, a transient – what the hell was the woman thinking, befriending a transient, taking him home, thinking he was another lost cat? Christ. Linda braked for a bevy of bicyclists, who had been warned, fined, pulled over, and arrested fifty times for blocking the road and still they came, a silent hoard of brightly dressed maniacs, ready and willing to take over the road.

She dropped the car into low when she came to Mesa Road, taking the turn slowly. A coyote disappeared into a thicket in front of her, and despite her cranky mood, wild animals always made her smile. She checked her iPhone for a map to the woman's house, and after driving down three wrong dirt roads on the Mesa, finally found the right dead end, a ramshackle cabin, two metal storage containers, a beat-up VW from the sixties, and three mangy dogs. From the looks of them, she should call the Humane Society. She made a note of it, and stepped up to the painted red-front door, redolent of patchouli and painted with flowers. Another hippie who refused to believe that the sixties had ended decades ago.

She pressed the bell and, hearing nothing but the music of the Jefferson Airplane, pushed it again. No answer. About to turn back to her cruiser she noticed that the front door was ajar. Was this resident too confused to keep her door closed and locked? Or had something happened to her? Linda pushed the door open and hollered hello.

A garland of flowers decorated a mirror over a fireplace: bouquets of spent daffodils leaned over in coffee can vases. The sweet smell of paperwhites hung in the air.

"Hello? Hello!" Linda called, feeling uneasy. She held her hand up to her call-back button to report in when she heard a shout and went down.

When she came to, she was lying on a poor excuse for a sofa, thick foam over plywood with lots of pillows. A weight pressed on her chest. Looking down, she was pleased it was only a cat. But there was more than one. The place was crawling with them; four or six were on top of her. She sat up, scattering cats, checked her gun and her radio. Her head ached from the blow.

"Oh, you're awake," a young voice said.

Linda looked over at a girl – barely out of her teens – with long blond hair parted in the middle. She sat in a lotus position, a paisley blouse billowing around her and wearing a long skirt covered with tiny mirrors.

"You didn't have to hit me." Linda rubbed a thick egg on the back of her head. "Assaulting a police officer is not a good idea."

"You broke into my house."

"The door was …" Linda tried to stand, trying to take control, but the room spun a bit. Better to sit than to fall. She held herself together the best she could. "Did you give me something?"

"Nothing I didn't give myself. It's nice. Smooth, hunh?" The girl rose on thin bare legs stuffed into tall and clunky cowboy boots. "I made it myself – a concoction. You like it?"

Linda pulled a notebook and a nub of a pencil out of her pocket. Licked the pencil for some reason. When she placed the pencil lead on the paper, it made marks. Cool. Her hands trembled.

"It's a combo of LSD and well – I don't need to tell you nothing. Want some tea? We weren't properly introduced. I'm Ardys."

"And you drugged a police officer, Ardys. Not a real good thing to have to report in a court of law."

"My friends like it. You're my friend, aren't you?" Ardys came closer to Linda and read her nametag. "Nice name, Linda, just rolls right off the tongue."

Linda bristled and tried to remember how to operate her cell phone, her walkie-talkie, her radio. All the equipment had rules and she couldn't remember any of them. Her hands fluttered from pocket to belt to radio.

"You'll be okay in about twelve hours or so," Ardys crowed. "I didn't even have to force you. You just opened your mouth and down it went."

"What are you, fourteen?" Linda forced the words out through what she assumed were thick puffy lips. Late-afternoon sunlight coming through the picture windows was edged with borders of red and green.

"Twenty-seven. Everyone thinks I'm a kid and I hate it. How would you like it if no one thought you were a grown-up, Linda?"

Linda, having troubles of her own, had mastered the pencil-and-paper thing. If she pressed hard enough, she could make lines, sometimes circles, but the pencil kept wandering off the paper. She cleared her throat, trying to organize her mind. "So, you met some transient, who took one of your cats?" What would it matter, one or two missing? There were so many of them, sleeping in the sun, on the back of the couch, on ledges, on top of cat scratcher posts. One long-haired black cat stared at her with intense yellow eyes, stretched its claws, then jumped into her lap.

"Oh, that wasn't me. That was my neighbor, batty Mrs. Henderson. You think old ladies would know better," Ardys whispered, proffering a cup of tea. "Drink. It will make you feel better."

Linda shook her head. More magic drugs from Ardys and she would never find her way home. As it was, she knew she couldn't drive the cruiser. What would Malcolm think? She stared at the ceiling, a lazy fly making sharp turns in a slight breeze. That was his name, right? Her boss? Malcolm?

"Got any bottled water?" She forced herself to sit still. It was all she could do. The world was soft and dreamy-like, and she felt like she was floating. "So, Ardys, can you lead the way to Mrs. Henderson?" She lifted the cat off her lap. He'd been purring. Now it stood, back arched, hissing.

"Mr. Twinkles prefers a gentle touch," Ardys said. "And now you've gone and made him upset. Oh dear."

Linda eyed the cat watching her. It suddenly seemed like all the cats in the world were staring at her. "Mrs. Henderson, ma'am?" She slurred her words and sounded like the drunk they'd brought into the station the night before. She rose, wanting to take the tea, so thirsty all of a sudden, but once on her feet, she could make out the open front door, and beyond, the cruiser. No houses nearby at all.

"So there's no Mrs. Henderson, is there, Ardys?" She turned to face the girl.

Ardys' face fell. "I sure as hell didn't call the cops, Miss. Maybe I gave you too much? Next time, just ask. One tab, not two. Remember it."

"What about the transient?" Linda asked, looking for evidence of another person in the place. She thought of consulting the manual of police procedure she kept in the cruiser, but reading it at the moment could present a challenge. Something else was wrong. Was there pipe smoke in the air? "Was somebody else here?" she asked through a thick fog. That's what she was here for, the transient, not the cats. The cats mewed and circled around her feet. "Where'd he go?"

"If you want money, I don't have any." Ardys opened her wallet. "I thought we were friends. I was helping you out."

Linda nodded. There was something funny about the place, and this time it wasn't her. She tried to remember the code for a crazy person. Was it 5170? 999? 5150? She'd call it in as soon she could operate her radio right after her eyes focused and her head stopped spinning. "The transient?"

"I don't know anything about any transient." Ardys crossed her arms.

Remembering some of her training, Linda got up, slowly. Four doors stood off the living room. She peered in each open door. One was a bedroom, redolent of patchouli. Another was a meditation room, empty except for candles burning down to their saucers. The third was a bathroom full of lime-green towels reeking of mold. That left door number four. She let out a giggle, forcing herself to concentrate.

Ardys followed her, flitting her hands and talking rapidly. "Cats live in there. Please don't open the door. They're all FIV positive. Can't have them mix with the general population." She flattened herself against the closed door.

"Miss ... miss." Linda tried to place the odor through the door. Dead fish? Rotting seaweed? Dirty cat box?

"You're not very bright, are you?" Ardys said.

"I need to check it out. Now, please, step away from the door."

"But my cats."

"Catch them." Linda pushed the door open. Inside the steamy closed-in room there were no cats. There was just a white wall, white floor, white bed, with a figure on it, a man. Holding her hand over her mouth from the smell, and with an eye on Ardys, Linda crab-walked over to the man.

"Who's this? Husband? Boyfriend? Lover? The transient? A loser?" Maybe unprofessional, but Linda was pissed. "Hello? Hello?" she called out. No movement.

"That's my brother," Ardys replied. "He's tired from hitching across the country. He came all the way from Des Moines. Poor guy."

The man did not move. The acrid smell Linda noticed was stronger. He looked kind of pale.

"No, please. Don't touch him!"

Linda turned on her. Out of focus or not, the girl had to go. "Should I cuff you or are you going to be quiet? You understand?" Linda hoped she sounded forceful enough. Couldn't be sure for all the weird sensations flowing through her body.

"You don't have to be so mean," Ardys pouted.

Linda made her sit on the floor and snapped on her gloves. Two rights but that would have to do. She bent over, one hand on the man's carotid artery. Slow pulse, any pulse, some pulse? Ardys kept bawling. "Hush, now."

She kept two fingers on his neck and waited. Nothing. Lifted his hand, and, feeling nothing, let it drop. "How long has he been dead?"

"I didn't kill him, if that's what you mean. Mr. Twinkles did it. The man didn't want to leave. Mr. Twinkles said he had to go."

Linda pressed all the buttons on her walkie-talkie and her radio while keeping an eye on Ardys. She couldn't be sure, but it seemed like the girl had come a little closer. Three cats were at the door, then four. "5150, 999, Dolores, 1054, possible dead body, and hurry." That was the dispatcher's name, wasn't it, Dolores? "Hello? Hello?"

Ardys was now sitting on the bed.

Linda wasn't sure she had moved, but why would she have allowed her to sit at her hip? Voices came into the room through the air, and Linda, confused, kept calling. "You better hurry, Dolores, I'm alone here." Linda shot a look at Ardys, who was now less than two feet away. "Dolores, please, answer, Dolores I don't think I can drive." She kept calling as the room filled up with cats and someone took hold of her hand and slowly put down her radio.

From the Sheriff's Calls Section in the *Point Reyes Light*, February 2, 2012

BOLINAS: At 7:11 a.m. someone called about a Mustang with its top down.

Ardys Loves Chocolate

"So, was it raining or something?" Linda asked Walter. They were sitting in his office at the station. She took a bite out of her bear claw. "Was someone in the car, or was it just abandoned?" She'd always loved Mustangs, the older the better.

"Bernard went to check it out." Walter sipped his coffee. "Don't worry, it's taken care of." It had been three days since they'd found her tied up out on the Bolinas Mesa. Her eyes still looked a little strained. "You okay?"

"Right as rain," Linda lied. When she went to bed, she had nightmares about cats, cats purring, cats sharpening their claws, cats coming after her. She sure as hell wasn't going to tell him any of that. "Was the car ruined?"

"Now, again, why didn't you call for backup right away?" Walter chewed on the stub of his cigar. He smoked only outside and this one had never been lit, so no one could complain that he'd been smelling up the place. "Tell me exactly what happened after you entered the house."

"I told you, boss. The door was wide open." The fact that she'd lost control was not something she wanted to discuss. To have on her record that she was bested by a five-two 105- pound hippie from Bolinas was too much. "Where's the car? At Cheda's?" She couldn't tell him how confused she'd felt. At lunch maybe she'd check out that Mustang.

"Forget about the car." Walter took his soggy cigar out of his mouth. His tongue felt like he'd been chewing on rags. "Are you going to the counselor like I asked?"

"Are there any calls? I'm ready to go on patrol."

"Did you follow correct police procedure?"

"Of course." She thought she had.

"Robbery in progress, at the Palace Market." Deborah's voice came over the intercom.

"I'll check it out." She rose, strapped on her belt.

"You stay here. I'll go," he added, not wanting to let his greenest deputy out of his sight. "I'll drive over."

"It's a block away. I'll be there before you start the car." She didn't need a goddamn babysitter.

Clinking and clanking her way down 4th Street, Linda hurried to the market where a few tourists were peering through a window.

"Go back to the station. We have all the cops we need," Bernard said as soon as Linda walked in.

Beyond him, crumpled by shelves of chocolates, was Ardys.

"But I know her," Linda replied.

"Oh, it's you." Ardys wiped away tears. "I knew if I prayed loud and long enough, you'd come." She read his nametag. "Told you so, Officer Bernard."

"She's half your size. Come on, give her some air," Linda requested.

"All points bulletin, Linda." Bernard smirked, blocking her way. "And she's such a puny little thing."

"You look so tall now that you're not sitting down, Officer," Ardys cooed, her brown sweater hanging loose over her shoulders.

"Having a bad day, Ardys?" Linda asked. "Come on, open your pockets."

"How's that thing you have with cats?" Ardys asked.

"Show me what you took – or do you want to go back to Unit B?"

"That's where they keep the crazy people, Officer Kettleman," Ardys giggled.

"And you're not crazy?" Linda grinned. "Pockets empty, now, if you please." Not her most demanding voice, but surrounded by two cops, she knew Ardys would cave.

Ardys, looking at the floor, brought out a Clipper Card, two quarters, three packs of Juicy Fruit gum. "I didn't steal the gum, if that's what you're thinking."

"All your pockets, Ardys."

"Shit." Ardys pulled out three bars of Dagoba chocolate, a ragged tissue, her Social Security card, and a ten-dollar bill. "I could've paid for the chocolates. I'll pay for them now, okay, Luis?"

But Luis, the cashier, his eyes blank, backed away from the register.

"Book her for stealing." Linda reached for Ardys.

"My dad's going to sue you for battery. And harassment." Ardys tried to fight them off. Bernard backed her into a corner, where Linda slipped on zip ties and pulled them tight. Ardys looked her in the eye and filled her mouth with spit.

"Oh no you don't." Linda placed her hand just in front of the girl's mouth. "Bernard, how long has she been out of the hospital?"

"Everything in control over here?" Walter growled, marching into the market. "You like being locked up, Ardys?" He eyed both Bernard and Linda. "Good job."

They led the perpetrator out of the store. Linda felt proud. It was high time she got a compliment for her good police work. At last she'd done something right. Now she had a real chance to make captain.

"Linda." Walter pulled her aside. "I didn't give you permission to come here. Bernard had it in hand."

"He was being too hard on her. She was all crumpled on the floor. He hadn't cuffed her or anything."

"He was the officer in charge. You had other things to do."

Like filing? Hell, no. "But boss. She's the one, you know, who ..." Linda felt like screaming.

"Officer Kettleman." Walter watched tourists wander into the Station House Café for breakfast. "Next time, try following orders, would you?"

"I'll do my best, boss." She held her back as straight as she could, kept pace with him down 4th Street. His hip was still bothering him, and she could run circles around him, easy.

Across the street, with a big smile, Bernard, back in his cruiser, turned on his siren and peeled away.

BOLINAS: At 10:49 a.m. someone who deputies decided was not making sense called to speak with officers named "Jeff" and "Sheldon."

The Boys at the Beach

Thomas giggled into his chocolate milk. He was way too old to drink chocolate milk, but it made him happy.

Justin played with his cell phone. Both boys were leaning against a wall outside the Olema store, next to the big map and one of the last few public telephones in West Marin.

"That'll make 'em confused." Justin laughed and reached for his ice-cream sandwich. It was starting to melt in the unseasonably warm weather. "That'll get the Sheriff's Department."

Thomas wasn't so sure. Since he'd been popped by Officer Kettleman, he'd spent one night in jail, endured lectures from both parents, lost his job, and had his license suspended. Now he and Justin were driving around in Justin's thirty-year-old Toyota Celica, bored silly on a Wednesday morning. They'd both skipped school.

"So, what else do you want to do, Justin?" Thomas hadn't been doing anything wrong either on the day when he'd been delivering pizza. He'd just pressed the wrong button on his cell phone and, trying to correct it, had run the van down an embankment and into a creek. He had thought the arresting officer had been decent about it at first, until she'd thrown the book at him.

"Shall we find out where the officer lives?" Justin asked, a wry smile crossing his buttery soft cheeks.

"You can. Not me. I'll take the bus home."

"Spoil sport." Justin picked his teeth with a fingernail. "You just dabbled in a pool of trouble. What – water's too hot for you?"

"Shut up, Justin, just shut the hell up." Thomas had a court appearance next week; he'd plead guilty. What else did they want? Blood? As it was, they'd promised the accident would go off his record, but he couldn't trust them. He felt like a wanted man. "Hey Justin." He watched some hawks overhead. "Don't you think we better move? They'll trace the call."

"They don't have time for that kind of bullshit. My dad was a cop and he was busy all the time."

"That stupid arrest probably ruined my chances to go to Cal," Thomas said. His parents, who had saved all his life to put him through college, had been disappointed. Now he felt guilty. He thought of lighting a cigarette. He'd just started and the taste did not yet agree with him.

"Felony. It's a felony. And it's on your record, not mine."

"Go to hell, Justin. You'd feel differently if it was you."

"Cool your liver. Chill. Now that we're here, let's go to Limantour. I'll get some brew." Justin headed into the market.

Twenty minutes later, with the car's springs squealing down the last stretches of Limantour Road, and with the beach in view, Thomas felt like crying. He'd made such a mess of things. A junior, facing the prom, and with no money, no prospects for a date. He was a loser. As for Justin, his future seemed assured. Early acceptance to Harvard, damn him.

At the beach, it was quiet. It was a stupendous day, with a glorious sun, a few high clouds, and small waves breaking like diamonds. They took a long walk down the spit, Justin voicing his opinion about the best gear for rock climbing, while Thomas, lost in his own thoughts, let him babble on. Afraid of heights, there was nothing that would ever make him leave the safety of the ground like that.

The boys both took off their shirts and lay down in the sun. Getting too warm, they decided to wade in. Justin, the better swimmer, went out, farther, faster, while Thomas, ever cautious, went in up to his knees and froze.

"I'm getting used to the cold!" Justin threw water in the air. "I'll be ready for Boston!"

Thomas, who was watching some birds take off in the dunes, looked back toward his friend. Justin had disappeared.

"Justin? Justin!" Thomas scanned the water where his friend had just been. He scanned the water looking for splashes. Waves crashed against his knees. He paused. Justin was always fooling around. Maybe he'd swum down shore and was hiding under the surface only to explode in a flurry of laughter? Or maybe he'd been caught in an undertow and taken out to sea?

"Justin! Justin!" Thomas called again and surged into the freezing water. When it hit him below the waist, his breath caught. Up ahead, in the low waves, there was still no sign of his best friend. Thomas even looked for reddened water – a bite from a great white was a possibility – but out here? "Justin!"

Not a good swimmer himself, Thomas dove under and opened his eyes: they stung. He surfaced and wiped them hard. The waves surged against him as he waded in, deeper and deeper, while keeping an eye on where Justin had disappeared. There were no sounds but the cries of gulls.

"Jesus! Justin!" he cried, his poor excuse for a crawl carrying him forward. Justin had been standing right here, hadn't he? Or there, twenty feet away? Waves crashed over his head: a sea of foam obliterated all other disturbances at the surface. The sound of his voice disappeared into the sound of waves.

"Justin, where are you?" Thomas felt the pull of the undertow as he reached deeper water and the bottom disappeared. The weight of his blue jeans pulled him down. He swam farther, just a little farther. He was well beyond the breakers now – further than he knew he could swim. There, beyond his reach, he saw something floating in the water. Ignoring his freezing feet and now numb hands, he went for whatever was floating. Halfway there, it moved. Could it be Justin? A tarp? Someone's backpack? For a moment he looked toward shore, toward home, toward safety, then turned back to see that floating thing, and picked up speed, his sloppy legs in his bell-bottom blue jeans feeling like slugs.

Ten feet away from the floating thing, Thomas dropped into a trough and lost his way. Coming up, he saw it again, something blue, dark blue, in the dark water. He reached closer. The thing did not move. He grabbed for cloth – and pulled. The shirt moved, but not the body underneath.

Breathing hard, Thomas searched the blue for Justin's head, finding and grabbing his hair. He could feel the undertow pulling them away from shore. Holding his two hands under Justin's shoulders and rolling him over, Thomas prayed he wasn't too late. Mouth slack, eyes wide open, skin a slight tinge of blue.

"Justin!" Thomas gathered his body under the heavier boy and tried to figure out how he could get them both to shore and fast. Too much time out here in the cold water and they'd both die. Forcing his own nose and mouth above the water, and knowing nothing else to do, he slapped Justin across the cheek. It wasn't a hard slap.

The cold water had sapped all of his strength. He didn't have much time. The shore was sliding away. He grabbed Justin by the shoulders and keeping his mouth to the sky, Thomas angled toward shore. The crest of each wave brought them up so he could see the beach, and the next trough hid everything so he had no idea which way to go. He had to keep moving. While kicking hard, he checked back on Justin's mouth, feeling for breath, and not being sure, slapped him again. No response.

Rising and falling with each wave, Thomas continued to drag his best friend toward the beach. His parents would be furious and Justin's parents would kill him. At last, he felt bottom and held still a moment, catching his breath, Justin still under his arm. Thomas kicked just a bit farther to get both feet steady and with one arm holding Justin's shoulders, he blew into his slack mouth while holding his nose, breathed again, then pushed them toward shore.

About to slap him again, he heard the intake of breath. Then a huge breath in. Justin coughed, and Thomas, worried he would choke, turned Justin sideways as best he could. But his body was heavy and he couldn't hold him up. Justin sputtered, choked, and panted for breath. Thomas turned his friend's face to the sky and continued to move toward the beach. "Help!" he hollered a few times into the sound of the water and the waves, while Justin moved and turned, his body heavy and sloppy in Thomas' arms.

Coming to, Justin climbed over Thomas, pressing him down in an effort to get more air.

Thomas held onto Justin with an iron grip until they were waist deep in water, then, together, they staggered to shore and collapsed on the sand.

After a few minutes of catching his breath Thomas threw up.

As soon as they could, they retrieved their belongings and started for the car. But Justin collapsed again. Thomas, exhausted himself, felt like sleeping too, but knew that their wet clothes would kill them. Not being able to stand on one leg, he had to sit down to strip to his skivvies. He went to take off Justin's pants. Justin flung his hands away until Thomas pulled harder. Leaving their soggy pants on the beach, the boys staggered to the bridge, with Justin leaning on Thomas like a drunkard. Once or twice both boys collapsed in the sand and rested for a bit, but each time Thomas kept thinking about the clock in his head, a timer, ticking away the minutes of their lives.

That walk from the beach was the longest walk Thomas had ever made. By the time they got to the car above the outhouses, Thomas was completely beat. Justin immediately passed out in the passenger seat. Sitting in the car, trying to make his frozen fingers work, Thomas finally pressed the phone number he had so willingly pressed before – the Sheriff's Department.

"Please, please come, and hurry," he said over and over, and covered his friend's bare skin with his jacket and a spare blanket he had in his car.

Fifteen minutes later, he heard the unmistakable sound of wheels on gravel. It was one of the rangers, pulling up in his white truck. Thomas' teeth kept chattering and Justin, not knowing what he was doing, kept throwing off the blanket.

An hour later, once the boys had warmed up in the ranger's house on Limantour, their bodies wrapped in blankets and hot tea in their hands, a deputy sheriff came in. It was Officer Kettleman. She recognized Thomas.

"You okay, Thomas?" she asked, checking on Justin at the same time. "You boys had quite a scare. You were lucky."

"I'm sorry, Officer, I'm so sorry," Thomas said, feeling like his relationships with everyone had gone to shit. "I shouldn't have teased you – or the department."

"Tease all you want, kiddo." Linda threw another blanket over him. "You were a real hero today, Thomas, a first-class hero."

The Dinner Party

"What I don't understand, Fred," Mildred spritzed napkins on her ironing board, "is how could the baby know that."

Fred, stretched out on his recliner, gave his wife a look out of the corner of his eye. He was knee deep into a new mystery, and the large-type edition pleased him no end. He was close to guessing who the perpetrator was, and didn't answer her right away.

"Fred! Did you hear me?"

"Dear God, woman, are you trying to kill me?" He grabbed his chest. "What's the matter? Is everything okay?" His doctor had told him to take it easy, on account of his heart, but his doctor didn't live with Mildred.

"The baby dialed nine-one-one, Fred. How would a baby know how to do that?" She projected her voice loud, so he could hear. Crazy old coot, he was hard of hearing, but way too proud to admit it. He would always say she talked too fast, so she kept her sentences short and to the point.

"The baby didn't mean to." Fred reached for the book he'd dropped.

Mildred smoothed the corners of her napkins and folded them over, making a sharp crease with her spray starch. She loved ironing. She knew no one did it anymore, but they didn't know what they were missing. She had a stack of fifty linen napkins in her closet, and except for the occasional scorch marks, they looked great. But there were too many of them. They didn't have the dinner parties they used to have; Fred didn't like to entertain much anymore.

"Hey Fred, let's have a dinner party!" She stacked a clean napkin on top of the others. The warm smell of ironing filled the air.

"What is going on with you, dear? First babies dialing nine-one-one and now dinner parties? You think maybe you're losing it?"

"Well, you don't care about what I say anyway, so who are you to talk, Fred Rhinehart?"

Fred sighed, memorized the page he was on, and then, thinking he was going to forget, thumbed the corner over, and put the book down. Every time he got to a good section, she started to ask him questions, and it seemed as if all she did these days was talk.

"Dinner party?" he asked. And have to clean up the place? He admired his stacks of *Wall Street Journals*, his piles of *Motorcycles Forever*, his twenty years of *Sunset*. He hadn't cooked for years, nor did he garden like they did, but he loved the photographs in *Sunset*. Always looked like someone had a better life than he did. "Company? Here?"

Mildred spritzed another napkin and gave it an explosion of starch. She had become used to the spray starch, but in a way, it still felt like cheating. She set the iron on low. "We could get rid of a lot of junk." She brushed a wisp of hair away from her face. "And I have a killer shirred- beef recipe."

Oh brother. Fred rearranged his pillows. He rose, and holding his bulk steady with a cane, an appendage he'd come to hate, gazed at his wife. She couldn't cook for beans. "You want to do all that work?"

"I'll have it catered, then." She strolled to her kitchen window to check on Mrs. Flanagan. The old bat kept poking her nose into her roses.

"Hey you!" Mildred shouted out the window. She rapped on the glass. "My roses, Mrs. Flanagan. Those are *my* roses, not yours!"

Not again, Fred thought, stumbling toward the front door. He peered out. No one in the front yard, no one at all. And Mrs. Flanagan's place, the yellow one with white shutters, was closed up tight. She was away on holiday, visiting her son in Carmel. He walked around the house and stood in front of the kitchen window, looked in, and waved at his wife.

"Oh my God, no!" Mildred screamed.

Fred hadn't planned on startling her like that. He ran inside the house as fast as his weak legs would allow.

When he found her, she was holding up the kitchen scissors in one hand, her hot iron in the other. He could smell burned cloth.

"There was a man in the garden, Fred. And he's coming this way!" Her eyes were wide and her hair loose from her usual tight little bun.

"It was me, sweetheart. It was only me. Please don't worry so," he said.

She dropped her scissors and picked up a butcher knife. "Don't come any nearer, you big lunk!" She slashed at the air between them.

Fred backed away from her, muttering. "What a day, what a day." He contemplated going back to his chair, but doubted the wisdom of that decision. From the living room, he eyed her carefully.

"Someone's gone and taken my husband – and left you behind. As if I couldn't tell the difference!" She backed up to the kitchen counter.

"Shall we call the sheriff?" Fred eyed the distance between himself, her and the front door beyond. He wasn't quite close enough. He sidled over a little.

"Don't move, you sniveling big oaf." She held out the knife in a trembling hand.

"If you hurt me, darling, we can't have that dinner party you want," Fred said softly, not having quite enough courage to put out his hand for the knife. She still had a bit of a wild look in her eye.

"What dinner party?" she asked.

"Would you like me to help you with your ironing, sweetheart?" Fred felt that maybe it was time, now, to call Eleanor at the home. He hadn't been ready, not yet. Janet had been bugging them to move for years.

"Why in the world would you put a sharp knife in my hand? They're not used on cloth. Meat, Fred, think, knives and meat. Can't be that hard."

From the relative safety of the bookcases, Fred watched his wife put down the knife, tuck the scissors in a kitchen drawer, and carry the iron over to her stack of linens.

"I swear, Fred, you're losing it more every day." She touched her finger to her mouth and tapped the iron. A slight hiss filled the air. "Perfect." She smoothed another napkin.

"Shall I call nine-one-one?" Fred asked.

"Fred, Fred, Fred," Mildred muttered. "Calling nine-one-one is for emergencies. We have no problems here. Now, while you're up, would you mind passing me the other hamper?"

From the Sheriff's Calls Section in the *Point Reyes Light*, February 23, 2012

TOMALES: At 9:20 a.m. a 15-year-old girl had a recurrent attack of something, although this time she was not bleeding.

Alice

"You okay, Alice?" Mrs. Hartman asked.

"Fine, right as rain, no problems here." Alice felt weird. She didn't like being the center of attention, and this was the second time someone at the school had called the authorities about her in the last month. Last time she'd had a bloody nose. Big deal. Everyone got a bloody nose sometime, didn't they?

A circle of kids hovered over her. Mrs. Hartman asked them gently to back away. Alice was sitting against one of the lockers. Her head hurt, but she wasn't going to tell Mrs. H. about that. She picked at her shoelace. She wanted to feel like the rest of them; she looked like them, dressed in tight-fitting blue jeans that cost a fortune, a handmade bracelet on her wrist, and long hair, halfway down her back.

"You want to go sit in the nurse's office, Alice?" Mrs. Hartman murmured. "You want me to call your parents?"

"No, no, and no. Thank you." Alice stood up and grabbed her backpack. Damn thing had weighed a ton ever since she started chemistry. Another thing she did that made her different. Mary and Beth Ann, girls she hoped to become her BFFs, had told her that boys were intimidated by girls who were brainiacs, but she loved the symbols, the way the molecules danced on the page.

"Steady now?" Mrs. Hartman cooed.

Alice nodded.

"Ready to go back to class, dear?" Mrs. Hartman was a forty-something assistant dean. She held her eyes on Alice's, making her feel like an oddball.

Alice nodded, and entered room 14B, algebra. When she stepped in, all the students started whispering. She took the central front-row seat, the only empty one, but the one she'd take even if all the chairs were free. She liked to see everything. Even with her thick glasses, some things, at her peripheral vision, were still just a smidge fuzzy. It was the best the doctors could do.

As Mr. Friedman lectured, he circled and dotted and starred the word "factor" on the board. All the kids snickered. Friedman tried to make games out of algebra, Alice knew, and she liked him and his sense of humor, but for all the other kids – who would become farmers like their parents - algebra was a dead end. They passed notes, shot spit balls, and texted each other, giggling whenever Friedman cleared his throat.

Alice doodled on her page. Math was easy to her; she always paid attention, completed her homework, and did well. She stared at Mr. Friedman's clothes and wondered who'd dressed him. His belt went around his waist one and half times. Did he shop at Goodwill? REI? TJ Maxx? Marx Brothers? Brooks Brothers? She fell asleep.

She came to with a start. The classroom was empty and she was suddenly scared. She felt trapped by her chair with the little desk. Hadn't she heard the scuffling of feet? The rise of voices as the kids were suddenly freed by Mr. Friedman's "class dismissed" rallying cry? Had she had another one of those, what they called, spells?

Confused and out of sorts, she staggered to the door, not quite ready to go to her next class. All she knew was that it wasn't chemistry. The hallways were deserted. She checked her nose. It felt wet, but wasn't blood, thank God. Were her parents worried? Did they know about her, uh, spells? Her loss of reality from time to time? It wasn't epilepsy: she didn't shake or anything like Marta, a senior. She read the door numbers, concentrating hard. Was it 121 or 122 or 132 that she had to find? All the doorways and lockers and hallways looked the same. She opened a classroom door and, hearing French, closed it. She leaned against the outside wall and tried to think, next class, next class, PE? Where was Mom? Mrs. Hartman? Anybody?

"Perhaps it's time to go home, dear." Mrs. Hartman's soft voice came through Alice's consciousness. She felt her hand being patted and an arm on her shoulder, leading her somewhere. Where? Her next class? Alice froze, trembling.

"I'm not ready; the kids can't see me like this." She tried to make sense of her upside- down world.

"Even the most confident kids have days like this, Alice," Mrs. Hartman said. "College prep is hard, full of pressures, confusions. Add to that hormones, and you have a potent mix."

"Most days, I'm fine." Alice eyed the door to the administration office, the parking lot beyond, and home, two miles away.

"Most days I'm fine too, honey." Mrs. Hartman led Alice inside the office. "Why don't you just sit and rest in the nurse's office, while I call your parents."

The black cot in the nurse's office looked inviting, but it was a one way street. Once Alice lay down there, she'd be sent home in disgrace, and the kids would never think she was normal.

"I'll take your backpack," Mrs. Hartman said kindly, and lifted the weight off Alice's shoulders.

Alice sat on the edge of the cot, her back straight. She wasn't going to let them win, see her fall victim to the spells and the enormous fatigue that made her want to sleep all the time. Instead, sitting there, ears and eyes focused on every sound, she overheard Mrs. Hartman's voice on the phone.

"Second time today. Yes. Lapses in and out of reality. No, no bleeding. Some intrinsic helplessness."

Who the hell was Hartman talking to? Mom? Dad? A doctor? The sheriff? Alice studied the door, the open window, the grass beyond.

"Yes, please, come and get her. I can't stay with her. There are other students. And," Mrs. Hartman's voice had an edge to it, "please hurry."

Alice couldn't wait, not for the authorities, not for the doctor, not for her parents. She looked at her backpack – too heavy to run with it all. She grabbed her chemistry book, cell phone, and wallet, and ran. She'd be home before lunch if she was lucky - that is, if she didn't start bleeding again.

FROM THE SHERIFF'S CALLS SECTION IN THE *POINT REYES LIGHT*,
MARCH 1, 2012

OLEMA: At 12:52 a.m. four young men were
standing around a white sedan, looking suspi-
cious.

Billy Boy

"I didn't do anything, I swear, Officer Kettleman." Thomas stood up
straight and faced her.

"You boys are too young to be out this late. Anyone been drinking?"
Linda asked. They all looked Thomas' age, in high school, certainly none old
enough to drink legally. She recognized Justin, the kid Thomas had saved at
the beach. "Boys, hanging out here isn't helping your future any."

"Officer, I can explain," said a taller boy. "I'm a Christiansen. They were
helping me at the ranch. So much to do. My father's ill. I know it's a school
night."

Justin looked at Thomas and Thomas looked at his feet.

"Uh-hunh." Linda shone her light in their faces. Their eyes grew wider
but it looked like no one was high, not yet, anyway.

"Go back over the hill. Go home to your parents. And stay out of trouble."

"But I don't live over the hill," said Billy – the smallest boy. At fifteen, he
looked more like twelve.

"Hush," Thomas whispered and kicked him in the shins. "Wait for her
to go down the road."

"Thanks for checking up on us, officer." Justin flashed his million-dollar
smile.

When the sheriff's tail lights disappeared around the corner toward Point
Reyes Station, the boys hopped back into the car.

"Jesus, that was close." Justin kicked over the engine and headed north. "Back to the plan, boys. Everyone ready?" He gunned it toward Bear Valley Road.

They reached Limantour about one-thirty in the morning. Justin carried two twelve packs, Thomas the briquettes, fuel, and matches, while Billy tagged along behind with the dogs and burgers. Andy Christiansen led the way. It was a cloudless night and the sky was full of stars.

"Yes, that's the place, that's where Thomas – " Justin trailed off. He was grateful. Good God, he was grateful.

"I'll get the fire started." Billy set out the grill. He knew fires were not allowed on the beach but what did they care? It was almost summer, all their parents thought they were at each other's houses, and they were safe enough. If they got blasted, big deal. They had sleeping bags.

"Thomas, Jesus, what can I say ..." Justin whispered.

"That's okay." Thomas felt weird. All of a sudden, he was a hero. He didn't feel like anyone's hero. He'd been feeling tired ever since the incident. He stretched out on the sand, hoping he wouldn't fall asleep. A cold beer would help.

"So, what's it like, then, back East?" Billy took a long slug of beer. Not quite used to the taste, he choked a little as the liquid went down. Someone lit up a doobie, and the red glow from the joint and the red glow from the little fire made Billy feel like he belonged. It had been forever since he'd felt like he belonged anywhere. The boys – all older than him – told stories, passed around joints, and Billy wasn't there on the beach anymore, he was in college, following Justin, his hero, down across a green lawn in between brick buildings. It was his first day of college and he was ready.

He followed him into a big hall. A professor paced across the stage, markers in hand. He swiftly filled up board after board with numbers and formulas, talking into a lapel microphone as everyone took furious notes. Billy was with Justin, an hour later, at a bar, and all the women in the room looked at him when he walked in. They were beautiful and bright and all making google eyes at him. Billy was glad he'd studied so hard in high school, studied so much he'd missed all the barbecues, the dances, the parties with his friends. It had all paid off. A blond, with straight hair and an appealing deep V-neck sweater, sidled over to him.

"Billy?" Her voice was smooth as honey. She touched him on the shoulder and cooed into his ear. "Oh, Billy."

He held out his arms for her beautiful body. "Jennifer?" he asked, "Jennifer, is that you?"

Billy heard laughing and opened his eyes. He sat up on the beach, sand in his hair and his fingers gripping his own shirt.

"Tell us about Jennifer, Billy Boy," Justin taunted. "Blonde, brunette, redhead – or beanpole?"

"Cut it out, Justin," Billy said. He wanted, more than anything, to go back into the dream and be the star at the bar, Jennifer's boyfriend.

"Time to go, Billy Boy," Thomas murmured.

Billy stood up in a hurry, stars flying in his eyes. The fire was still smoldering. The rest of the boys were already high-tailing it back up the beach to the parking lot.

Billy looked around in a rush, and felt for his wallet in his back pocket. At least that was there. A pale dawn was breaking over the distant cliffs down by Sculptured Beach, a place Billy had heard about but had never seen for real. Just like the beautiful girl in his dream.

"She was a knockout, Thomas." Billy kicked at beer cans and brushed sand out of his hair. "Don't you think we better pick up the mess?"

"Put the heat on, Billy Boy, or we'll all be late for school," Thomas urged.

Thomas and Billy headed inland, all the time hearing the rush and crash of waves behind them. A flock of sandpipers hopped down the shore as seagulls greeted the dawn. Billy felt good that the guys had been good-natured about his dream.

Their Reeboks crunched sand as they made their way up the path beside the outhouses. The sun brightened the world, all washed clean, rosy and tinged with pink.

There was another car in the parking lot, its engine ticking cool, a car neither of them wanted to see. It was white with bright green letters, Park Ranger painted on the doors.

"Looking for someone?" Officer Kettleman asked as she nudged Ned, the local Limantour ranger. "The other boys are gone, Thomas, and that leaves you two." She shook her head. "Thomas, Thomas, Thomas, why can't you ever stay out of trouble?"

"I didn't do anything …" Billy muttered.

Thomas elbowed him in the ribs.

"That's what they all say," Linda stated. "Bet there's trash all over the beach, boys. Now, march." She held out a bunch of plastic bags which smelled faintly of coffee.

Before Thomas took them, he noticed something out of the corner of his eye. It was Justin's white sedan, cresting the hill, just leaving, on its way to freedom. "Shit."

"Not your lucky day, is it, Thomas? Now, go on. I'll take you to the bus stop when you're done. And while you're at the beach," she studied their crestfallen faces, "think about who your real friends are. Now scoot."

FROM THE SHERIFF'S CALLS SECTION IN THE *POINT REYES LIGHT*,
FEBRUARY 23, 2012

DILLON BEACH: At 1:14 p.m. a woman reported
that her gardener had entered the downstairs
of her home while she was showering and had
then come into her bathroom and French-
kissed her while she was blow-drying her hair
and wearing only a towel.

Sisters

"That's what happened, I swear." Alice tugged at her sleeves.

Mrs. Hartman slipped her reading glasses down her nose. "I find that hard to believe, Alice."

"But Mrs. Hartman, he did that. It was horrible. Beth Ann, she said, 'Tell Mrs. Hartman. Tell someone. That's sexual abuse, Alice,' she said."

After twenty years as assistant dean at Tomales High, Mrs. Hartman thought she had heard it all. But this Alice, she had a new twist. "Want some coffee? Tea? Something to calm your nerves?"

"Red Bull," Alice replied, looking at a skiing poster on the wall. "Can I go back to class, Mrs. Hartman? There's no need for me to stay here and be humiliated."

"I'll be just a few more minutes. Now, Alice, you were at home. Your grandma was visiting. And your parents?" She raised an eyebrow.

"Skiing. And I would've gone with them if that Mr. Friedman hadn't failed me in history. He's ruining my chances to go to college."

"We'll discuss that later. Now, why didn't you lock your bathroom door?"

"Why should I? Grandma can't make it up the stairs. And the gardener was outside working. How the hell was I to know he was going to come in and kiss me?" She rubbed her mouth raw with the back of her hand. "Gross."

"Accusing someone of sexual abuse is a serious matter, Alice. What was his name?"

"He was all slimy and sweaty. He was disgusting."

"I see." Mrs. Hartman tented her fingers. "I wouldn't have liked that either. And he came into your bathroom?"

"That's what I said. Want me to write it down for you?" At school, she was already a pariah for her bloody noses and her spells. Now this?

Mrs. Hartman narrowed her eyes. "And you'd seen this man before?"

"He's one of my mother's gardeners – she goes through them like soap. It's a big place. Mom loves pansies. You love pansies, Mrs. Hartman?"

"You want to file a report, Alice? Get the police involved? Make sure this gardener never works again?"

"He walked into my bathroom and stuck his tongue in my mouth while I was naked, Mrs. Hartman. That okay in your book?"

Mrs. Hartman tapped a pencil on her desk. "Going to court all right with you?"

"I was defiled in my own bathroom," Alice sniffed.

"Testifying in a courtroom with a judge, bailiff, your parents, me, and the perpetrator present will be tough. And point him out? Swear you're telling the truth?" Serious charges against a gardener by a girl who fainted at school, was a little weird, and had paranoid delusions?

Mrs. Hartman lined up her pencils on her desk. "And if they don't believe you?" She knew the gardener wouldn't say a word. "Tell you what. Go home and think about it. Talk to your Grandma …"

"My Grandma talks to trees, Mrs. Hartman. If she listens to me at all, it will be a first."

"Then we will need to contact your parents. Do you mind waiting here a sec so I can reach them?" And with that, Mrs. Hartman left.

Alice bolted. She left the office, the administrative wing, climbed on her mother's ten- speed bike and took off for the woods. She didn't return home until well after dark.

When she got there, Grandma was in a tizzy in the kitchen, two cops at the house. Alice stepped inside wary; had Mrs. Hartman told on her?

"Well, here she is, Mrs. Rhinehart," the policewoman said. "You must be relieved."

"We thought you'd been kidnapped, Alice." Mildred reached out to hug her. "Where have you been?"

"Would everyone please leave me alone?" Alice ran up to her bedroom. How could she prove anything? There was no DNA kit in her backpack, and no one - not her teachers, not her Grandma, and certainly not her parents - would ever believe her. There was no possibility of proof. After settling in to her fifteenth viewing of "Sex in the City", season two, episode four, she dialed Beth Ann.

She didn't answer. Nor did two or three other girls she barely knew. Alice stared at the flower wallpaper her mother adored and looked out the window. The sea looked black and inky under a half-moon. From downstairs, she heard people calling her name. The policewoman came to the door a moment and knocked. Alice answered that she was in the bathroom and eventually the cop went away. At long last, the house was quiet and she came downstairs.

She found Grandma digging into her mother's linen closet.

"Tssk, tssk, tssk," she muttered, peering in, and resting her hands on her knees. "Your mother doesn't iron, Alice, I thought I'd taught her better than that."

Alice watched her take something out of the freezer and put it into the oven.

"And she doesn't cook either. For God's sake, child." She surveyed the messy kitchen, noticed Alice looking a little pale.

"What's got into you? Sweetheart, you look seriously perturbed."

Alice sat down on the window seat and ran her fingers in circles on the yellow vinyl cushion.

"You came home so late, we were worried about you, honey." Mildred was clearing out the refrigerator and throwing food, good or bad, into the trash. It was time her daughter learned to keep house properly.

"Hey! That's my lunch," Alice cried, noticing her day-old sandwich and week-old yogurt heading to the bin under the sink. "Please, Grandma. Mom didn't leave me any lunch money. That's all I have."

"I'll drive to the store. This food is old."

"But Grandma!" Alice went back to the vinyl seat under the rotary phone. Now, what? All Mom said about Grandma was don't let her drive and don't let her cook.

Feeling ignored, Alice threw the drapery cords away from the window and heard them hit with a resounding clink. She was jolted out of her reverie when Grandma returned with a cup of tea and a piece of cinnamon toast, her favorite.

"Tell me what happened today, dear," Mildred cooed. She took a seat and sipped her own tea. It didn't taste quite right so she added some more whisky from a flask she had in her purse. "We were worried about you. Was it a boy?"

"It wasn't a boy, Grandma. It was a man." Alice stirred her tea and, feeling for sure Grandma would tell her she was lying, slowly and in bits and pieces, told her the story.

"Uh, hunh. I see. And when you saw Mrs. Hartman?" Mildred downed her second whisky-tea combo drink. When Alice was done she shook her head. "This is disturbing, very disturbing, indeed."

"And no one believes me. Not you, not Mrs. Hartman, no one."

"But I do, dear." Mildred patted her tight little braids. "I'll go see that Mrs. Hartman in the morning. She did a terrible thing, not trusting you."

"Oh, Grandma." To Alice they felt like sisters.

"Vince should never have come inside, much less touched you." Mildred brushed a wisp of hair from Alice's forehead. "I'm so sorry. He was looking for me."

FROM THE SHERIFF'S CALLS SECTION IN THE *POINT REYES LIGHT*,
MARCH 1, 2012

MOUNT TAM: At 9:52 p.m. a group of hikers
reported that a 75-year-old man had fallen into
a pool near Cataract Trail and was sitting on
a cliff above the water where they left him an
hour ago.

Cataract Canyon

Thomas waved down Officer Kettleman, who was making her rounds at the Pantoll Ranger Station on Mount Tam. "There's an old man out there. He wouldn't come back. He's still in the woods, down Cataract Canyon," he said, leaning on the cruiser window.

"Thomas, someone is out there in the dark?" Linda asked.

"We went out about four, kinda late, I know," Thomas continued. "Sarah and I saw him sitting on the ground. We kept asking and asking, but this old guy, named Fred, he just wouldn't budge."

"And when did you see him last?" Fred? Mildred's Fred? What the hell was he doing hiking in Mount Tam in the dark? "Where was this, exactly?" Linda asked.

"We were on our way back. It was dusk and he was soaked," Sarah said, working her hands.

"He's still there? Alone?"

"Justin's with him," Thomas stated. "They're deep in the canyon, on the rocks, above one of the pools."

"Man down! Cataract Canyon! Close to the ridge," Linda barked into her radio. She turned back to the kids. "How's he holding up?"

"His face was kind of pasty, and he kept asking for his wife. He'll never make it if we don't ..." Sarah's voice trailed off. "He didn't look so good."

"Any volunteers?" Linda eyed the small crowd in front of her. Five kids, no one over the age of eighteen. "You guys did the right thing, coming here." Fred was lucky they'd been out there.

Linda gathered her first-aid gear and gave instructions to the kids to stay together. They had to hurry. It was getting cooler by the minute.

A moment later, their flashlights splashed a narrow path across Rock Springs meadow. Linda heard the thump of Thomas' boots at her heels. This was the easy part, then the meadow, and then the real challenge, Cataract Canyon Trail. How would they get Fred to walk back up in the dark?

When they entered the woods, branches pulled at their faces and clothes. The path dropped fast and soon turned into an uneven rock staircase. Below crashed Cataract Creek, two feet from their own shoes. In a few minutes, it would be well below the slick, moist steps they were descending in the dark.

"We left them so long ago," Sarah said, hesitating at a root.

Linda almost knocked her into the creek. "Don't stop like that, please."

"Sorry."

Linda could hear the tremble in her voice.

They slowed as they descended the stone steps with a twelve-inch drop from one to the next. The trees seemed to close in, the rocks on the side of the trail cold, sharp, and covered with moss. Sarah called for Justin and Fred.

"Hush," Linda said, and the three of them, close enough to touch, stood on an outcropping. Between the crash and dripping of the creek, they heard someone calling.

Was that the rangers coming down behind or the kid and the man below? Linda wasn't sure. If they could just keep moving, they'd find the pool; from her memory it couldn't be that far. Despite their desire to hurry, the three of them descended slowly over slick rock faces and steps that seemed to disappear into inky darkness.

"Down here!" a voice cried, and they drew closer. Rounding an impossibly thick redwood and scanning the woods with her flashlight, Linda could finally link voices to faces. She found Fred leaning against a tree, holding a handkerchief to his chin. There seemed to be something dark and wet on his face.

"He's losing heat; I can't keep him warm for much longer." Justin rubbed Fred's shoulders and hands. "I gave him my jacket, my hat, and all the water I had. He stopped talking thirty minutes ago."

Linda assessed Fred's condition, gave Justin his jacket back, and tucked Fred into her own thick regulation coat. She relayed his condition to the paramedics over her radio.

She placed Justin and Thomas on each side of Fred, with their arms under his shoulders and around his waist. Fred collapsed the moment they tried to make him stand.

With a great deal of persuasion and two failed attempts, they finally got him to put some weight on his feet. Now for the trail, slick, steep, and in the dark, hard to see. Linda asked Sarah to stand above the group and point her flashlight low and across the stone steps as they rose. It seemed like a Herculean effort to get Fred to come up the stairs. He moaned with every move.

The five of them struggled a step at a time above the crashing creek. Linda heard nothing but huffing and puffing, while commanding Sarah to keep moving ahead of them with the light. Fred shivered and trembled, losing his footing from time to time. Thomas took leg duty, and, standing below them, placed Fred's shoe on each stone step, calling ready when they could go higher.

By the time Linda, Fred, and the kids gained the woods above the steep rock stairs, everyone was drenched in sweat. When the rangers arrived, everyone helped Fred onto a stretcher. The rangers strapped him in and took off at a run.

Linda, Justin, Thomas, and Sarah race-walked the rest of the way. They reached the well-lit ranger station and, a moment later, watched a helicopter fight its way to the parking lot. There was a flurry of lights, the thwoop-thwoop of helicopter blades, lights illuminated the forest, and then they were off. It was well after two in the morning when Linda saw the kids' drawn-out faces clearly for the first time. "Call your parents, tell them you're safe, and if you want to wait, make sure it's okay with them first. You guys have been great."

They all stayed there, until morning, until the dawn light flooded the forest and the radio crackled and they found out that Fred was going to be okay. A whoop went out over the crowd, and Linda thought for a moment that maybe it was time to call Fred's wife.

Mildred answered the phone on the fourth ring.

"Your husband's going to be okay, Mrs. Rhinehart," Linda said.

"What do you mean my husband's going to be okay? He's in the next room, sound asleep," Mildred snapped and slammed down the phone.

It Could Have Been You

"That could have been you, Fred Rhinehart." Mildred banged her rolling pin on the table. "What the hell were you thinking, hiking out, late like that, alone? Cataract Canyon? Have you lost your mind?"

Fred, back at home for two days and ensconced in his blue recliner, felt like he was in heaven. "Scold all you want, you old bag," he whispered under his breath. He tucked her handmade afghan closer to his neck.

"And?" She rolled out her sugar cookie dough.

"Stienstra listed it as one of the best hikes in Marin County for waterfalls. It was in the *Chronicle*."

"Stienstra, my ass. Did he recommend old farts like you climb rock-strewn canyons? Did you see enough water, then?"

"It was awfully cold." Fred took another cup of tea from his wife, the fifth she'd given him in the last hour, and it was having an effect. He'd have to get up and soon.

"And how'd you get there?"

"The guy from Cheda's – he was going to give me a ride but he got a call." Fred hoped he could doze off. If she would just stop talking, and if he had already gone to the bathroom. He lurched out of his chair, unsteady on his feet. He would have a jar nearby if Mildred wasn't home. She was such a tidy little thing.

"You stood on Sir Francis Drake and hitchhiked?" What a fool he'd been, what a lucky old fool. As soon as he disappeared into the back room, she tidied up around his chair. Magazines, newspapers, and endless coffee mugs. Tissues. Dear God, he had been lucky.

When Officer Kettleman had called for the second time and been insistent, Mildred had argued with her for a little while, then went to check on her husband. She'd just about fainted when she'd seen his bed empty; now, two days later, she still hadn't recovered from the shock.

She listened to sounds from the bathroom. No crashing, just normal noises this time. Hearing him come down the hall, she headed to the kitchen to hide. He didn't like her fussing over him.

Fred felt satisfied. He was really tired and still cold. He was wearing long underwear, sweatpants, and the fine wool sweater Hattie had given him. Rabbit fur and wool made him feel special.

"You promise, promise, never to go hiking alone again, Fred?" Mildred turned on the kitchen fan. Cookies just got a little too dark this time.

"I got a ride from a guy at the bottom of the road. He thought it was cool."

"The guy was an idiot." Mildred placed her cookies to cool on the counter. When she'd finally arrived at Santa Rosa Memorial with Officer Kettleman, at four a.m., Fred had been pale as a piece of paper, with tubes and all kinds of junk attached to him. He was sleeping and didn't recognize her at first. She straightened that out in a hurry.

"Those boys were wonderful to stay with you, Fred," Mildred said. She'd had to stay in Santa Rosa for two nights to be near the hospital. The hotel had had lumpy beds and coarse sheets – and the food had been horrid. "Let's invite them for dinner to thank them."

"Not again."

"What'd you say?"

"No. No dinner parties. No company. No nothing."

"You sound awful tired, Fred. Or are you just Mr. Cranky-Pants?"

Fred's head hurt and too much tea was calling him to the back of the house again. "You and your dinner parties, I swear Mildred, you've gone off your rocker. Send them a note."

"I already sent them a card. Made it myself, too." She'd had to break the heads off two dozen purple pansies to cover the whole card with flowers. The yellow dotted centers had made her smile.

"No more parties? No more socializing?" Mildred loved seeing the kids – her grandchildren - and especially that Alice. Reminded her of herself. "Now that you've been brought back from the dead – from people you don't even know – you're going to thank them by becoming a recluse?"

"You don't have to be so negative, Mildred. Please, I've had a shock."

"You've had a shock? What about me, having some sheriff call me at three a.m. and tell me you're all right? What about if she'd called and said you'd succumbed?"

Fred rolled his eyes. He didn't want to tell her how close he'd come. He hadn't seen any white light or anything like that, but when the kids had come, and Justin had sat with him, he'd been so thankful. "Can you please, honey," he pushed his afghan onto the floor. "I'm freezing."

"You're like a little kid, Fred, throwing off your blankets." Mildred tucked the blanket all around him, especially around his feet.

He would've asked for a massage but didn't want to press his luck. He looked up. "Sweetheart?"

"Yes." She smoothed her apron. "You want some more tea?"

"Oh, God no," he said and fell asleep.

FROM THE SHERIFF'S CALLS SECTION IN THE *POINT REYES LIGHT*,
MARCH 8, 2012

SAN GERONIMO: At 5:31 p.m. a resident
reported two teenage girls who were in the
creek, muddying the water and "killing off the
salmon."

Muddy Waters

"There's somebody out there." Alice peered at a figure staring at them
through the trees. She pushed another wad of gum into her mouth. Her
parents wouldn't let her chew gum at home, but what the heck. She wasn't at
home. She was at Beth Ann's for the weekend.

"My Grandma says Mrs. Willis lives out here. Bet that was her," Beth
Ann said. "Nosy old bat." She let the branches drop.

Alice crouched down in the creek a sec. They would have been able to
see the fish, but they'd been jumping in the water and now it was brown and
her legs were peppered with mud. "So, you think your parents will wonder
where we are?"

"Nah." Beth Ann threw a rock into the river. It made a nice splash. She
decided she needed a bigger one, and stepped to shore.

Alice watched sediment drift over her toes. A frog – a tiny frog, a little
green guy, no bigger than a quarter - was all tucked inside a leaf. It was the
cutest thing she'd ever seen. She bent down and reached for her iPhone. Still
good enough light for a photo. Grandma Mildred would be delighted.

"Hey you! Get out of there!" screamed a voice above her.

Alice's hand jerked in surprise. The phone fell onto the leaf. She reached
for it, but the leaf wouldn't hold the weight and the phone disappeared into
the creek with a plop.

"Damn you! You've ruined my phone!" She started to charge out of the creek. But when she saw Officer Kettleman standing right there, holding onto an old lady's arm, she stopped fast.

"I'm going to report you to SPAWN*," Mrs. Willis yelled. "You're killing all the fish!"

"I'll take care of this, Mrs. Willis," Officer Kettleman said. "Please calm down."

"It's ruined. Completely ruined. I spent all last summer cleaning houses for that phone." She choked back tears.

"I told you they were trespassing, Officer Kettleman," Mrs. Willis argued. "I told you."

"Now, Alice, you know you were trespassing," Linda stated.

"I was not."

"She doesn't know much, does she, officer?" Mrs. Willis piped up.

"Just come out of the creek, and we'll figure this all out." Linda reached for Alice's hand.

Alice knew better than to go up there alone. "Beth Ann!" she shouted. "Beth Ann!"

"Trespassing and killing salmon," Mrs. Willis scolded. "There's a hefty fine for that."

"And there's a hefty fine for making me drop my phone!" Alice wanted to go after Mrs. Willis. The old lady was holding an alligator bag on her arm, just like Grandma Mildred. "You startled me. I almost peed my pants."

Linda tried to figure out what to do with the two of them. "Mrs. Willis, please."

Mrs. Willis scowled.

"They're wet through," Alice complained, lying a little. Jesus. All her contacts and photos and music – all ruined. She heard footsteps coming through the woods.

"Oh hi, Mrs. Willis, Officer Kettleman. You guys on a nature trip too?" Beth Ann asked. "Something bothering you, Mrs. Willis? You're looking a little pale." Beth Ann grabbed her hand. "Good to see you."

Mrs. Willis shrieked. Beth Ann had dropped a tiny snake on her palm.

"It's a baby garter snake, Mrs. Willis. No reason to be afraid." Beth Ann held up three tiny snakes that slithered through her fingers, one trying to get away. "Whoops." She caught it with her other hand. "They're not poisonous, and they certainly can't smother you or squeeze you to death like a python. You like pythons, Mrs. Willis? I've got one in my bedroom, but he's only four feet long. The vet says Jerome could grow to sixteen feet. You want to come over and meet Jerome, Mrs. Willis?"

Mrs. Willis let out a shriek, backed up, and ran.

Linda stood there with the two girls and no one to file a report. "Beth Ann," she chastised. "You didn't need to scare Mrs. Willis. Now, would you girls please get out of the creek, and stay out. You're covered with mud." She headed back to her cruiser.

"We didn't start out that way," Alice giggled. She was glad she'd picked Beth Ann as a friend. Beth Ann was cool. "Can I touch one of those snakes?"

"Of course." Beth Ann dribbled the snakes into Alice's palms. "They're plastic," she said and burst out laughing.

SPAWN: Salmon Protection and Watershed Network, a powerful salmon protection organization in West Marin.

From the Sheriff's Calls Section in the *Point Reyes Light*, March 8, 2012

MUIR WOODS: At 12:09 p.m. someone saw several young adults drinking beer in a car; a woman got out and approached the caller to ask if she wanted one.

Out for A Drive

"It wasn't me if that's what you were thinking, Fred Rhinehart." Mildred stared out the window of their 1967 red convertible VW bug. They were driving back to Point Reyes after visiting family in Mill Valley. "You know I don't drink." She patted her purse holding her flask. What he didn't know wouldn't hurt him.

Fred, hunched over the wheel, wasn't sure just what was ahead, a big family or a mother with two large dogs. He slowed just in case, making the engine lug.

He swerved around a few trash cans, screeched to a stop, and pulled into the first parking space he could find. "Man, that was close." His hands were shaking. "What is this place, a nature reserve? Jesus Christ, I almost killed them all."

Mildred fanned her face with her handkerchief, waited a few seconds. "Are we going home or not, Fred? We've been sitting here for hours."

Fred hadn't thought he'd been there that long. He started the little car – the car they'd had since he was forty. It had been a dream once, all cherry red and shiny. Now it was like him, bumps and scratches and a slump in the hood from where Alice had sat on it.

"So, how did my sister seem to you?" Fred asked, laboriously turning right at the 2 a.m. Club and starting up the mountain. It was the bar, that was the short cut to the mountain, wasn't it?

"I swear, I don't know what that woman does with her time," Mildred clucked. "Her house is a mess."

"You don't have to be so mean," Fred grumbled. So what if his sister Miranda wasn't as neat and tidy as Mildred was. Big deal. He was about to say something about that, but stopped. He knew better than to argue with his wife about anything. He searched for a safe subject. "Hey sweetheart, wouldn't it be nice if time stood still, and nothing would change, not even us?" He maneuvered the car around a series of turns and felt lucky he knew the way. Still, his hands began to sweat.

Mildred wasn't so sure she wanted to be young again. She'd finally gotten the hang of him. "Don't try to change what we can't change, Fred. I've discussed this with you a thousand times."

"But we can dream, can't we?" he asked, pulling up to Four Corners. It looked familiar enough. He had no idea which road to take to Point Reyes. He hesitated, then descended.

"Fred, no! You're taking us to Muir Woods!"

"It's such a pretty day," he replied, feeling happy. "Thought we'd go for a ride."

"Fred, no, no, no. Please don't take the coast route. Turn around! Turn around!"

Fred, negotiating a tight switchback, had no room to turn, much less around. On this? Was she crazy? The road dropped straight down. "I have no choice, sweetheart. You should've told me where to go back there."

"Just stop the car! You'll kill us both!"

Fred couldn't concentrate with her screaming in his ear. He pulled into a turnout, slamming on his brakes then killed the engine. The smell of hot brakes permeated the little car. "Now, how are we going to get home, Miss Smarty-Pants?"

Mildred fumed.

"If we really stopped time, sweetheart, I could drive you anywhere and never get confused. I would be strong again, if I tried."

"Don't be foolish." Mildred rolled down the window and waved down a car. It looked familiar. It was the same Chevy Cavalier she'd seen in the woods. Four kids looked at her. One of the boys stepped out and strolled over.

"I remember you. We met on the valley floor, ma'am," the boy said. "Car trouble?"

"Husband trouble," she sniffed and got out of the car.

"Hey!" Fred croaked.

"He keeps riding the brakes, he went the wrong way, and he's in no position to drive us – or me – to Point Reyes."

"I can help you, ma'am."

"But you've been drinking."

"No more than you," the boy smiled. "I saw the way you nursed your flask. And really, I haven't had enough to drink. I'm with my friends – and need to get back to Inverness. That where you live?"

Mildred eyed him with a scowl. "Maybe."

"Well, what do you want? Him or me behind the wheel?"

"Thomas, let's get going," the kids yelled.

"She reminds me of my Grandma," he said. "Give me a sec, will you?"

Mildred looked from the VW where Fred was dozing, to this young kid, to the road, dropping fast.

"You live in Inverness Inverness or Inverness Park?" Mildred asked and put out her hand. "I'm Mrs. Rhinehart."

"I'm Thomas." Thomas waved the car full of kids away. "Glad to help." They woke Fred up and ushered him into the backseat.

Thomas made himself comfortable behind the wheel. "So, tell me how to drive a stick, if you will," he said, starting the car, "and we'll be all set."

MOUNT TAM: At 6:22 p.m. a passerby reported that a passenger was performing a sex act on the driver of a Nissan pickup.

Gossip Girls

"Did you see that, Doris?" Mildred poked at the paper.

"Yes, I did, Mrs. Rhinehart." Doris floated a smock over her customer and pumped up the chair. Oh yes, she'd seen that entry.

Hortense, Beatrice, and the other ladies in the salon shifted their eyes from deep within beauty magazines, adjusted their glasses, and stared at Mildred.

"What did you see?" Beatrice loved gossip – the more the better. "Is it about a movie star?" Oh, how she loved movie stars, that hunk Marcello Mastroianni, Paul Newman, dreamy Cary Grant.

"Well, Mildred," Hortense hissed. "Now that you've got my attention go ahead, spill the beans."

"I can't read it aloud." Mildred flushed a hot pink. The women stood up, set up their walkers or grabbed their canes, and crowded around her.

"If you could all please sit back down," Doris ordered. They could break something, but worse than that, they could fall. They were all well into their eighties. "Then I'll pass around the paper."

"What is it? What is it?" Half-dead Beatrice was the first to put out her hand. Doris passed over the paper, pressed her finger to her lips, and led her back to her chair.

Hortense looked over Beatrice's shoulder.

"Quit snooping." Beatrice yanked the paper away.

After Beatrice read the entry, her face flushed. "That's disgusting." The paper fluttered from her hands.

Mildred couldn't figure out what had affected Beatrice so. No one would be so foolish as to do it in a car. Either the kids or the cops were lying. Stupid old fools would believe anything.

Hortense scooped the paper off the floor and turned to the Sheriff's Calls section. "Oh my." She touched her heart. "Oh my." Her eyes rolled to the ceiling and she fainted.

Ten minutes later, after the paramedics had come and gone, Hortense sat up in one of the beauty chairs nursing a cup of chamomile tea, her hands still shaking.

"I told you it was a lie, Hortense. Why didn't you believe me?" Mildred barked. No one in the salon had any sense.

Doris put her scissors down and comb and stared out the picture window at Route One, out onto the pouring rain. Once, a long time ago, when she'd been a teen, she'd had fun in the car – and Barry, bless his heart, he'd enjoyed it too, and one time he stopped the car ten feet before they would have gone off the road. For them back then, their car had been their only private place, and they'd kiss for hours, the tiny Datsun parked deep in the woods, well away from the prying eye of parents or cops. Doris looked at her girls, grandmothers and great-grandmothers all, they had children, they'd been loved, they'd had sex. And they'd all forgotten that driving desire that used to make them wild.

It was getting late in the day and the light was fading. Hortense, Beatrice, and the other ladies got a ride from their driver Frank from Hill House and headed home. Mildred went to see her cousin Bert, who worked at Cheda's next door. The ladies had spilled their tea, dropped tissues everywhere, and left the beauty magazines upside down on the floor. Doris wondered whether she would ever become like them, have that slightly sour odor, and be afraid of nearly everything. She was counting the money in the till and looking forward to getting home to take care of Joshua when she heard a knock on the door.

"Are you still open?" a man asked, making the door bells chime.

"I'm about to close," she said, and hesitated. The voice was familiar. "Barry," she whispered. She hadn't seen him in five years.

"I could use a bit of a trim." He let the door close behind him.

She couldn't believe it. Same sandy hair, cleft chin, dimple in his cheek, sweet blue eyes. Still holding the scissors, she wasn't sure she could control her hands. "Where the hell have you been?" She tossed her scissors into a drawer and slammed it shut behind her.

"I've been living in Texas." He smiled and stepped just a bit closer. Doris leaned back against the counter.

"They don't have phones in Texas?" Doris asked. She remembered the day he'd left, out for a cup of coffee and he'd been gone ever since. She'd stayed up all that night, wondering what she'd done to make him leave. Josh had been a baby.

"I've been hard to reach. Sorry about that. How's Joshua?"

His voice still had that honey tone to it. And he smelled good. God, he smelled good. She couldn't remember the last time she'd been held, much less kissed. Damn it all, if it hadn't been so long. She willed her body to behave.

"So, what brings you to Point Reyes?" She kept an eye on him and picked up newspapers and magazines awkwardly, so as not to turn her back to him. The only way she could get out, aside from the front, was the back, which opened into the Western. She hoped that Marlena had unlocked the door.

"Great to see you, sweetheart." Barry took a seat in one of the salon chairs and pivoted it around.

"Barry, what do you want?" Doris asked, feeling a mixture of heat and anger. Wearing a leather vest too, her favorite. She was ashamed she felt so attracted to him.

"How's our boy?" Barry cooed.

Standing up and coming closer with that slow lope of his, his blue eyes grasping for hers, Doris could feel his pull on her. "You deserted us." She leaned back against the counter and felt for the drawer, that drawer, the one that held all those recently sharpened scissors. Behind her, she could hear the clink of glasses from the bar next door. Would Marlena hear her if she yelled?

Barry swaggered, leaned toward her. "Sweetheart, come here. Come here and kiss me. Kiss your love hello, Doris."

"You'll do nothing of the sort," snorted a voice behind Barry.

"Mrs. Rhinehart!"

Barry, momentarily confused, stepped toward the front door, toward Mildred.

Doris opened the drawer, pulled out her sharpest scissors, held them behind her back.

"All under control, Mrs. Rhinehart," Doris called out, hoping that Barry wouldn't hurt Mildred. She was half his size and three times his age.

"You look like my Grandma, Mrs. Rhinehart. Now, go back home. Doris and I, we go way back. We're family."

"This Joshua's father?" Mildred snapped, sizing him up and down. "Not much to look at." She shoved her hand into her housedress pocket, tried to remember which button was preset to call 911. Holding her trembling hand as still as she could, she pressed all of them.

"Ma'am, we're all set here. Just go on home now. You don't want to be part of this."

"Deserting your wife and child is a terrible thing to do." Mildred slapped him across the face. "You should be ashamed."

"Hey, lady, what the hell?" Barry reached for her.

Doris opened up the scissors and stabbed him in the neck.

He turned, hurt and bleeding, and shoved Doris into one of the chairs. He was slipping his belt from his jeans when the door opened with a ring.

"What's going on here?" Linda drew her sidearm.

"Jesus Christ, they're trying to kill me!" Barry wailed and held his fingers to his bleeding neck.

"Mrs. Rhinehart, Doris! You okay?"

Mildred felt faint but excited. This was better than the soaps any old day.

Doris, trembling hard, didn't want to go to jail. "He tried to accost Mrs. Rhinehart, Officer Kettleman," she cried as the paramedics rushed in.

Linda watched them leave with Barry, then sat for a moment with Doris and Mildred. She gave Mrs. Rhinehart a glass of water.

"Thank you, Mrs. Rhinehart." Doris planted a kiss on Mrs. R.'s soft cheek.

"It was the newspaper. Fred wanted a copy," Mildred said, flushing a little. "He said, he said he always thought we were the only ones who had tried ... not just tried ... to have fun in the car. So I had to show him proof." She picked up the paper. "He's next door at the Western," she said and stepped back out into the rain.

FROM THE SHERIFF'S CALLS SECTION IN THE *POINT REYES LIGHT*,
MARCH 22, 2012

POINT REYES STATION: At 5:11 p.m. the
Station House reported that a customer, a gray-
haired woman, was refusing to take a dog off
her lap, and the animal was laying its head on
the table.

Supper at The Station House

"Did you see that?" Mildred tugged on her husband's arm.

Fred, pleased they were at a restaurant, didn't really care about the dog. He was digging into his meatloaf, and it made him happy. So did the popover, warm and covered with butter, sitting on his wife's bread plate.

"Fred, it's wrong. It's just plain wrong." Mildred eyed the Westie, its muzzle resting beside his owner's fork. "It's unsanitary, that's what it is."

Fred stared at his meatloaf. Covered in gravy, it just looked so tasty. "Mildred, please, you're making a scene." He took a quick bite.

"It's that wacky Mrs. Willis. The old bat who called the cops on Alice. I'll show her." Mildred reached for her cane.

"Leave her be!" Fred barked. "The restaurant can take care of it."

Mildred, unsatisfied, turned her back on Fred and stared at Mrs. Willis.

The restaurant owner whispered to Mrs. Willis, who would not budge.

"But Albert is all I have in the world." Mrs. Willis patted his curly head. "With David gone, how can I let my puppy suffer? Can you stand to see animals suffer, Miss Evelyn?"

Miss Evelyn smoothed her hands on her long V-neck dress. It wasn't just the Rhineharts who were staring at the woman with the dog. "I can sit you both out in the patio, ma'am, but even there you can't have your dog's head on the table."

"He's not just any dog!" Mrs. Willis cried. "He's Albert."

"Then perhaps you can put him in your car."

"Alone? Never."

"Ma'am," Miss Evelyn pleaded. "Dinner's on us. Now, if you will, take your dog and go home. I'll make up a doggy bag for the rest."

"Oh good, a fight." Mildred grabbed Fred's arm. "I love a good fight." She pushed back her chair. "I'll tell that Mrs. Willis what's good for her." She stood up and held her cane over her shoulder. "Mrs. Willis, you crazy old bat. Take your mongrel and get the hell out of the restaurant."

"Help! Help! I'm being accosted!" Mrs. Willis shouted and grabbed her dog. "Get her, Albert, get her!"

Albert, on command, bared his teeth and growled.

"I'll take care of your ugly cur, Mrs. Willis." Mildred banged her cane on the floor.

"It's a free country. I can stay here," Mrs. Willis spat. "And Albert can stay here. But you, I don't think so."

Fred debated pulling Mildred out of the fight, but she seemed to be having so much fun. He took another few bites of their shared meatloaf and the rest of her popover. Let her pick on someone else for a change.

Some of the patrons pushed back their chairs and pulled out their wallets. Miss Evelyn, rushing around to placate them, wasn't about to comp everyone's meal, and she certainly wasn't going to lose her whole evening service either. The place was packed with a long waiting list, and Mrs. Willis wouldn't listen. She called the sheriff and went back to manning the front door.

When Officer Kettleman arrived five minutes later, half the dining room had cleared out. Fred was finishing up the rest of the meatloaf and it had gone down real well. He was contemplating bread pudding for dessert when he heard his wife yell at Mrs. Willis again.

"That's enough, Mrs. Willis. Now take yourself and your dog outside," Officer Kettleman commanded. Despite her voice of authority, Mrs. Willis wouldn't move. "Now!" Linda placed her hand on her sidearm.

106

"Help! She's trying to kill me!" Mrs. Willis shouted and she grabbed her purse, Albert, and fled out onto the patio.

"Good riddance." Mildred headed back to the table. "Hey, you ate all my potatoes, Fred." She sat down to a nearly empty plate and a nub of meatloaf. "There's nothing left."

"That's what you get when you don't pay attention." It was the best meal Fred had had in months and he hadn't had to share any of it. He watched Mrs. Willis drive down Route One, Albert's head half-way out the window.

Within a minute they all heard a crash. Mildred stood up to look: she loved a good accident.

Fred watching her go, felt bad he'd eaten all her supper. "If you go out there, I'll get all the bread pudding."

"Don't you dare," Mildred answered, sat down, and picked up her fork.

From the Sheriff's Calls Section in the *Point Reyes Light*,
March 29, 2012

OLEMA: At 3:31 p.m. someone reported a black Prius that had become embedded in some shrubs.

It Wasn't Me

"I wasn't the one behind the wheel this time." Thomas stood beside the car. Three- quarters of the sedan was buried inside a mound of manzanitas.

The cop scanned his driver's license.

"Officer Kettleman, come on, I'm a good driver."

"We'll see about that." Linda ran his license. "So, if it wasn't you driving, then, Thomas, who was it? Your grandma?"

Thomas shifted his feet. "It was Justin. Justin was behind the wheel."

"Well, let's see. This car is registered to your father. Perhaps he knows you're out here in the middle of a school day? That would make him happy, don't you think? Do you wake up in the morning looking for trouble, Thomas, or what?"

"Julie was here too. They took off."

"So where are they?" Linda tried to determine if it was worth it to climb into the bushes. She'd just had her uniform cleaned. The kids had to come out somewhere. She walked through the parking lot, saw the creek beyond. Trails led all over. Alone, she'd never find them.

"Well, Thomas." She pulled out her ticket book. "Let's start at the beginning. Tell me everything, so I can help you."

"Like the last time? You threw the book at me, Officer Kettleman." Spending the night in jail had not pleased his parents in the least. "I'll prove to you Justin and Julie were here." He opened the car door.

"Don't touch anything. Sit on the bench, stay still and I'll do it. Unless you want me to call for backup?"

"No, ma'am." Thomas sat down, hands in his lap. Justin had been behind the wheel, because Thomas couldn't take a chance of being pulled over again. It had only been a month since he'd run the stupid pizza van into the creek.

"Find anything?" he asked a minute later, until he'd remembered they'd smoked a doobie, and he couldn't remember if they'd put the stub end in the ashtray or thrown it out the window. Dear God, why, oh why, did he do such stupid things?

"This yours?" Linda held out a yellow sweater with lace trim.

"A girly sweater?" he asked. Silently, he thanked Julie.

"Kids your age, they can go either way."

"Officer Kettleman, please, don't make this worse than it already is." If the other kids heard what she'd said, oh my God.

Behind him, he heard a movement in the bushes. A squirrel? A bird? He peered into a mass of branches.

"Pssst, Thomas. Is she still there?" Justin asked, his face obscured by leaves.

Thomas had a half a mind to stand up and let Officer Kettleman know that Justin was there – right there! Just like I said, ma'am. He paused. Ostracized at school for being a rat would not be good. He stayed silent.

Linda watched Thomas carefully. She walked around the outside of the parking lot and found two pairs of tennis shoes sticking out from under the bushes.

"Waiting for a bus, kids?" she asked, trying not to laugh. "The bus stop is out in front, by the road, not here." She grabbed each foot, one large, one small, pulled hard, and knelt between the kids. "You move, I cuff you. I cuff you, you go to jail. Clear?"

"Clear," replied Justin.

Julie, her mouth full of dirt, refused the urge to spit.

"You want to talk to Thomas, talk on. I've got all day." Linda let them up. "Going to get your story straight? Or do you want to talk to me first?"

Justin shook his head. "You've got it all wrong, Officer Kettleman."

"Shut up, Justin," Julie said. "Just shut the hell up."

"Proud of your friends now, Thomas? Didn't I tell you? With friends like these, you don't need enemies." She crackled instructions into her radio.

A minute later, two cruisers come down Route One. Two cops interviewed Justin and Julie and took them away. Linda stayed with the car and Thomas. When the parking lot was empty, she gestured for him to get in the back of the cruiser.

He looked at the pathetic hard-plastic seat, the rifle by the windshield, his father's black Prius stuck in the bushes.

"My dad's going to kill me."

"No, he's not." Linda watched Cheda's tow truck pull into the parking lot. "Ever heard of rubbing compound? Wash the car, polish it good, and scrub it like hell. This will be our little secret. And Thomas? Stay the hell out of Point Reyes. You're making my job a real pain."

"You bet, ma'am. You're right. I've never even heard of West Marin."

OLEMA: At 6:03 p.m. a passerby reported that a man in white pants was wheeling a suitcase down the middle of the highway.

The Lucky One

"Are you stopping for me because I'm wearing white pants? I know it's not summer," Henry said. "These were the only ones I could find."

Linda maneuvered her cruiser over and killed the engine. "Sir, the white pants don't bother me a bit. But you walking in the middle of the road does. Someone could come around the corner and hit you."

"So?" Henry answered with deep-set sad eyes. "I don't have any reason to live. Frances told me not to wear white pants after Labor Day, and yet, here I am."

Linda tried to steer him toward the side of the road. He kind of danced around her a little, until he made a beeline for the solid double-yellow line. "Nope, I'm happy here." He touched the paint with his toe.

A few cars saw the two of them, slowed down, and sped up again as soon as they went by.

"Sir, may I call your wife?" Linda asked, worried as much for herself as for him. Maybe she should put on her flashers. But that would mean leaving him out in the street alone. "Sir?"

"Frances left me long ago. She's with the angels." Henry held his suitcase close.

"Then she won't mind you wearing white pants," Linda suggested. "But maybe she wouldn't like it so much with you in the middle of the road."

"What does she care? She's dead!" Henry crossed the road in front of the Olema campground. Once, a long time ago, they'd camped there – back when Frances liked camping, back when she loved everything Henry did. "I'm bereft."

"I know, sir." Linda waved traffic to go slow. "Perhaps I should take you home."

"I don't like it there." Henry watched cows munch grass on their side of the road. "I feel so empty, so wrong without her."

"Sir, perhaps I can help you, then. Have a pastor?"

Henry scowled. "Pastor said nothing but lies when we buried Frances. He didn't know her. You going to follow me all day, or what? Don't you have work to do?"

"Ensuring your safety, sir, that's my job. What's your name, then?" She eyed his threadbare suitcase. "Can I at least carry that for you?"

"Jesus Christ, why can't everyone just leave me alone?" Henry dropped his suitcase and marched into the campground. This was the place, wasn't it, under the stars, where they'd set up their pup tent and she'd smiled as he'd put out his hand?

Linda grabbed the suitcase, set it by a tree, and read the nametag.

"Henry Rhinehart?" she asked. He looked a little like his brother Fred. "Got any friends or family I can call, take you home?" He lived alone, up Drake's View Drive, way up on top of the hill in Inverness Park, if his tag was current.

"I was young once," he muttered.

"Want some supper, Henry? You hungry? Tea? Beer? Whisky? The bar's not far."

Henry sat at one of the picnic tables, and searched a long time until he found it. Initials – their initials – barely readable in the chipped and marked redwood. For all those years, Frances had gone camping and canoeing and hiking, doing all the things he had loved and she'd never complained. When she got home, he could see the relief on her face – yet he still made her go.

Was it the last trip – when she was so cold – that had done her in, caused the pneumonia that killed her?

"Henry, please, let me help you."

Henry said nothing, just put his head down on his hands. Frances Ann would still be here, if he hadn't been so stubborn.

Linda called dispatch. In a few minutes a squad car rolled up on the gravel, followed by a '67 red VW Beetle, Fred hunched over the wheel.

"I told you we shouldn't have let your brother live alone," Mildred scolded.

"Mildred, hush, leave me be," Fred said softly. Second time this month they'd found Henry strolling down the middle of Route One. Now Fred had to do something he'd always decided he would never do: make Henry move into a home. Living with him and Mildred was not an option. He found his brother sitting at a picnic bench, tracing letters in the redwood.

"Henry," Fred asked, "what are you doing?"

"She's been gone six months, Fred, and I'm still not over her." Henry pulled out his pocket knife. "She'd be disappointed her name's all messed up." He dug into the soft wood.

"Henry," Fred asked, "and who might that be, bud?"

"My wife, Frances Ann. You never liked her much, did you?"

"You were never married, Henry. Frances Ann was a girlfriend you had in grade school." Fred could say she had died years ago, but he wasn't sure. What the hey. "Shall we go home and see if we can find her on Facebook?"

"She should have married me." Henry let his fingers trail the letters on the table.

"You were eight, bud, in third grade."

"But I loved her." Henry stared at the trees swaying in the wind.

"Of course you loved her, Henry. We all did. She was beautiful."

"Uh huh," Fred said.

"And you were the one who was the first kid invited to her birthday party, remember?"

"I was the lucky one," Henry said.

"That's right. You were always the lucky one. Now, shall we go home, Henry?"

"Nah," Henry said, resting his chin on his hand. "I'll wait for her here. She said she'd only be gone a minute."

From the Sheriff's Calls Section in the *Point Reyes Light*,
March 29, 2012

BOLINAS: At 11:45 a.m. someone reported a missing black man, tall and slim, who had driven a rented white Ford Escape to town to go surfing the day before.

The Surfer

"Missing person you say?" Linda asked. It was hard to hear with dispatch shouting over the intercom. "When did you see him last, ma'am?"

"He was here, just a while ago," Ardys replied. "We were on Brighton Beach – by the naked lady sculpture – and he went into the water, then I didn't see him again."

"Maybe he went around the corner?"

"If he did, he never came back. And he left his car. Why would he leave his car?"

"And this is a friend of yours?" Linda wondered.

"Before he went surfing, we watched a shark eat a seal. Just there."

Linda sighed. She put down her bear claw and fresh cup of coffee from the Bovine. "I'll meet you. Stay there." It had been a slow day so far, but surfers being eaten by sharks, that wouldn't be so good.

Twenty minutes later, she met Ardys at the end of Brighton Road.

"See? See? His car is ... still there." Ardys pointed out the white Ford. "And it's a rental. Why would someone who rented a car just leave it? You think he got eaten?"

Linda had perused the record before she'd left the station. No one in Bolinas had seen a great white, but Stinson, across the way, that was a different story. She examined the car, finding nothing there but sweats and city clothes. "So, Ardys, describe him to me, if you would."

"About six feet, toffee-colored skin, thin, tiny beard, and he was wearing a wetsuit and hood. I've just been so worried. He went so far."

"I'll call the Coast Guard."

In a cottage not far from the beach, LeVaundre Phillips reached for a cup of water on the bedside table and yawned. Man, he'd had a great night. The woman next to him snuffled, turned over in her sleep, and snuggled next to him. He'd been out in the ocean, paddling his board, trying to find at least some semblance of waves, when he'd seen the blonde on the beach, drying her hair and giving him a big wave.

What the hey, he was a city boy, and maybe country life wasn't so bad after all. He surfed on a wave that hardly reached his knee, ground out on soft sand, and walked over to her. She was in Bolinas for the weekend, trying to decide whether she should stay with her boyfriend in the city – or move on. This was her "cooling-off" weekend. LeVaundre couldn't believe his luck.

He'd chatted with Nell all afternoon. They'd watched children play, birds fly overhead, sandpipers chase waves, until it got chilly and she'd invited him in. Now, satisfied, LeVaundre reached his arms over his head, looked at the blonde hair cascading across his chest, and promised himself he'd visit Bolinas more often. The girls were looser here than in the Mission where he lived, and he'd always liked loose girls.

He extracted himself from the covers, careful not to dislodge her, and disappeared into the bathroom. He hadn't been wearing much, just his bathing suit, which was now cold and clammy. With his wetsuit over one arm and his surfboard under the other, he strolled back to the beach. It hadn't been a far walk the night before, but now, in his bare feet, the nubs and stones of the road hurt his feet.

About a block from town, he heard the sirens before he saw the fire trucks and EMTs. He wondered what the problem was. It was a cool morning, and he shivered while he walked, goose bumps prickling his skin. It wasn't too far now to the car.

A small crowd had gathered at the entrance to the beach. Parents grabbed their children's hands tighter and ignored their plans to play.

When LeVaundre found his car, a cop was looking inside it and he stayed still. A black man in a white town; he couldn't take any chances. He waited a moment until the cop left, dug out his spare key from the wheel well, and climbed inside. Turned on the heat. The crowd nearby made it impossible for him to change completely, but he was able to slip on his sweats and flip-flops. Feeling much warmer, he left the car and stood by an elderly white man and his wife who were squabbling at the back of the crowd.

"Move forward, Fred, and let me see," the woman insisted. "I can't see diddly-squat from here."

"Ah Jeesh, Mildred," Fred sighed and helped her move forward.

LeVaundre made his way around the crowd.

Out on the beach, deputies checked for footprints and clues, while in the water a cutter with a red stripe across its hull crisscrossed the waves. Overhead, a helicopter beat the air, its foop-foop sound conferring an intensity to the once-quiet morning.

Ahead of the crowd LeVaundre saw a woman, a thin white woman following an officer like a shadow. He was trying to decide whether he should go back to Nell's or head into the city when they turned around.

"It's him!" the woman shouted. "It's him!" She ran toward LeVaundre, her little feet pounding the sand, the cop at her heels.

Thinking they would pin him as a thief, LeVaundre took off and reached the Ford long before they gained the road. Without bothering to change, he gunned it, leaving Bolinas in a huff. As he made the right turn onto Route One and headed home, he threw Nell's phone number out the window. He wouldn't be back. He couldn't take the chance of going to jail again.

FROM THE SHERIFF'S CALLS SECTION IN THE *POINT REYES LIGHT*, MARCH 29, 2012

INVERNESS: At 4:34 p.m. a man was seen lying on the side of the road, babbling.

At the Coast Café

"I'd never do anything like that." Fred eyed Mildred across the table. "And my brother wouldn't either."

"By the way you've been acting lately, Fred Rhinehart, I wouldn't know."

"You must be joking." He took the basket of bread from the server. Second night this month they were out to dinner. It felt like recess.

"So, who was it?" She adjusted her hat. She'd taken to wearing hats lately. She thought they made her look smart.

Fred was looking out the window at a shapely woman crossing the street. A sight he always loved. "Hunh?"

"The man, or boy - I bet it was a boy - babbling by the street. Bet he was on drugs or something."

"I wouldn't know." Fred watched the woman get into a red Porsche and tug on her too- tight yellow skirt. Nice.

"So, what do you think the cops did?" Mildred asked.

The cops wouldn't do anything with a woman with a too-short skirt, Fred thought: they'd be staring too. The Porsche sped away. He sighed.

"Are you listening to me at all, Fred Rhinehart?"

Her voice was like a buzz in his ears. "Of course," he lied.

"I bet." Mildred dug into her bread. "This kid, he could have been someone's son."

"Of course it was someone's son." The party at the next table burst into laughter as Fred watched his wife open her mouth and didn't hear a word.

Mildred, onto her husband's little game, was telling him a story about his sister – his dull- as-nails sister, the one who couldn't clean house, the hussy, who'd run off after having two kids. Her husband had been a dolt. Mildred spoke a little louder, " … and all the kids have a potty mouth, just like you, Fred."

Fred's ears perked up at the sound of his name. "My what? What did you say, dear?"

"Thought so. You weren't listening."

"You said something about my sister that wasn't very kind."

"Not me." She scraped the rest of the butter onto her bread. "I was saying we were invited to a party and we should bring nuts."

"You didn't say anything about a party."

"They're having a party to welcome our new pastor. I told you yesterday."

Fred was confused. The words hadn't sounded like party. He mumbled into his soup. "So, what about the kid? The one on the side of the road?" Their server brought him their fish. They usually shared dishes. Mildred ate fast and she'd eat everything if he didn't get a move on.

"One of Bolinas' finest, I would think, Fred." Three minutes later Mildred dabbed her mouth with her napkin and put down her fork.

"But if it was someone's kid, some poor parents are worried sick. Remember the problems we had with Hattie, dear?" Fred asked.

"I told you you were too soft on her." Mildred waved the waitress away. "If you had kept her at local schools instead of sending her away to that fancy private school."

"Nevertheless, Hattie did great there. She's a science teacher. Can't be all bad."

"She won't talk to us, so what difference does it make?" Mildred looked out the window at a lightly falling rain. Hattie always loved rain. "We weren't the successful parents you hoped we'd be."

"We did our best." Fred watched a man stagger down the street. "At least none of our kids are like that."

Mildred drummed her fingers on the table. "So, what will the cops do about him? Do you think he's a fifty-one fifty?"

"You watch too much TV." Outside the guy stumbled over a curb. "At least the kids are all healthy and happy."

"So what will the cops do?"

"Take him to Unit B, I guess."

The door to the restaurant opened with a jingle.

"Well, he's back now," Mildred said.

The stumbling man took a seat beside them. He was wearing three jackets, torn pants, and tennis shoes covered with duct tape.

"We could've been like that." Mildred took Fred's hand.

Surprised by the turn of events, he felt her fingers on his and gave them a squeeze. He hadn't felt that kind of warmth for years.

"It's because of you and your hard work that we're not like him." Mildred had always been afraid she'd end up a bag lady. "You've not been so bad, Fred, despite all your faults."

"Not so bad? What do you mean, not so bad?"

"Got any spare change?" the stranger asked. Hearing no response, he took a deep breath. "How 'bout fifty grand?"

"We're done here." Fred helped Mildred from her seat. If she had thought he was a hero before, she'd sure think he was one now. He felt her lean on him as they made their way out the door. Snuggled together against the drizzle, her unfamiliar warmth made him feel giddy. If they could get home in the next few minutes, they could do what they used to do, years ago. He laughed. How many years had it been?

"What's so funny?" she asked.

"Nothing. Nothing at all. Everything's right as rain." He opened the passenger door to the VW bug and guided her in.

"Fred?" She touched his arm as he squeezed inside. "Let's call Hattie when we get home."

"Let's call them all," Fred said and started the car.

MOUNT TAM: At 12:25 p.m. a car was sliding down a ravine, its passengers safely outside it, on Fairfax-Bolinas Road.

Nice Wheels

"Shit!" Thomas held his hand over his mouth. He was standing in a bunch of scotch broom, when his father's car, a 2010 BMW 535i, started sliding off the road.

"Oh my God! Oh my God!" his girlfriend screamed.

Thomas had parked the car, admired the view, and thought he'd set the parking brake. And he would have if Debbie hadn't breathed in his ear. He'd gotten his license back and Dad, trusting him, had handed him the keys just last week. Now the car was slowly smooshing bushes on its march to the sea. Thomas looked over the edge. The car, still perfect, was picking up speed. "Justin! Grab the other door!"

Justin grabbed the left hand mirror but it sprang loose under his hands. He reached for the door handle, while Debbie pulled back on the bumper. They braced themselves. Beneath their feet, off the nonexistent shoulder of the road, a steep cliff opened onto the same road a few turns below. The car kept sliding.

"Shit, she's going to go!" Thomas grabbed the handle as hard as he could, shoved his heels into grass, and leaned back.

The car rolled on a few more feet, then slowed to a stop, one tire over open air.

"Call the cops! Call the cops! I can't hold it forever! Get the goddamn phone!"

"I left it in my bag!" Debbie panted. "It's in the car!"

"Go in and get it. Carefully, carefully. Then call nine-one-one and get your ass back here. Justin and I can't hold it forever."

Debbie tiptoed to the edge, pulled open the door, and grabbed for her purse. It looked so scary, the car hanging there – the boys she hardly knew; the ground at the side of the road so slippery. She ran back to the road, heard something crunch, and saw the taillights disappear over the side.

"Get the police! Get them now!" Thomas yelled, making her feel more afraid of him than the situation. Frozen, she held the phone out in front of her like a disease, until Thomas, disgusted, grabbed it and punched in 911.

"You didn't have to yell at me like that." Who cares about some stupid car. "That hurt my feelings."

"Sometimes you really are a ditz, Debbie Mae." Thomas stared at the taillights. The car had come to a rest about twenty feet down. The slope was steep as hell, and he sure wasn't going to go down there and make it secure. With what? His belt?

"Should we call your dad?" Justin shoved his hands into his pockets and peered over the side.

"No, no, and no." The phone just rang and rang. Had Debbie programmed it wrong?

He called Cheda's. "Oh shit," he murmured, looking at the car. At this angle he couldn't see any damage, not yet anyway, but the front could be smashed. "Hell's bells!" he yelled, then heard someone finally pick up the phone. "Got a little problem here," he said to Jerry, and Jerry, having a hearing problem and the phone on speaker, shouted into it. "Thomas, that you, again?"

"Hurry! The car could kill someone!" Thomas leaned over the side to take another look.

A small crowd had gathered by the time Cheda's bright yellow truck came up the road. Jerry pulled over, climbed down, surveyed the scene, and climbed back up. "Thomas," he scratched his head, "do you smoke so much dope you don't care where or how you drive?" He extracted his hook and a tow wire from the winch.

"Don't start," Thomas pleaded.

122

"Nice wheels, eh?" Jerry whistled. "And a Beemer too. Good going, Thomas. Your dad's going to be delighted seeing this, don't you think?"

"Jeez, don't you start. You think we can save it? Put me to work. I'll climb down there before the cops arrive."

"No to the first and no to the second." Jerry set up orange traffic cones. "Besides, they're already here."

Thomas heard the sirens before he saw the sheriff's cars. He wanted to cringe, tell them it was Justin's fault, and yell at Debbie again. If it hadn't been for her, the BMW would still be on the road and they'd be heading to Stinson.

"Thomas." Linda pulled up in her cruiser, shaking her head. "I thought I told you to stay out of West Marin."

"I was driving," Justin said.

"Bunk." Linda smelled his breath. "And smoking pot too, a misdemeanor or a felony, depending on how much I find in your dad's car."

"Officer Kettleman," Thomas said, "don't listen to Justin. I was the one driving my dad's car."

"They were smoking pot, but I wouldn't have any," Debbie piped up, and Thomas, for a moment, thought of kicking her over the side. He walked away from the car, despondent. His new girlfriend was a birdbrain, his best friend was still going to Harvard, and he was going back to jail.

Two weeks later Thomas found himself biking on his dad's old three-speed down Cascade Canyon. He was on his way back from school, he wasn't in jail, he no longer had a girlfriend, and he was happy. He felt the wind in his face. Biking, after all, wasn't so bad, once you got used to the hills, and he could go anywhere as long as he was home by three.

From the Sheriff's Calls Section in the *Point Reyes Light*,
April 12, 2012

BOLINAS: At 11:52 a.m. a resident asked deputies for help freeing a truck that was stuck in the mud saying that they had helped in the past.

Protect and Serve

"You helped me last time, officer." Ardys stamped her feet. "There's no way I can pull it out myself."

"We're not a tow-truck company, Ardys," Linda said, leaning out the window of her cruiser.

"Protect and serve? It says so right on your door." Ardys clucked her tongue. She was a taxpayer, goddammit. She put up with the dirt roads and potholes on the Mesa. Her money had to go for something. And her truck, her dad's old blue Ford F-350, the big one, was deep in the mud. She'd been spinning the wheels for hours, 'til mud was splattered all over the body. "What am I supposed to do, then?"

"Call Triple A."

"I'm not a member." Ardys brushed dirt off her long paisley skirt, the one she'd made out of an Indian bedspread from Cost Plus.

"Then call Cheda's," Linda suggested.

"I don't have their number."

Feeling somewhat out of sorts and remembering when Ardys had drugged her, Linda barked out her next command. "You called me, didn't you? Call Cheda's, call four-one-one for the number if you don't have it. Do something by yourself. I've got to go." She pulled away.

It would be just her luck that goddamn Ardys would call Walter and complain. Ardys called for anything, anytime, and Linda was not amused.

The road, Route One, which wound beside pastures and rolling hills toward Olema, usually made her happy. Even in rain it was beautiful but today nothing made her crack a smile. It was time for her twelve-month review, and she was in for a tough day.

"Car Twenty-Six, Bolinas, and hurry," dispatch crackled into her ear. Linda took a hard U-turn across the double yellow line and headed back to Bolinas. Sometimes being a cop had its advantages.

Driving up the Mesa beside the six-foot-tall grass and shipping containers people used for storage, Linda wondered why anyone would want to live there. Two right turns and one left, and she was back where she had started. An elderly couple stood out on the road, one holding a cell phone, the other gesturing toward a big Ford pickup.

A hand waved from under the truck. It was Ardys, stuck in the mud between the wheels. Not far away a ladder lay on the ground.

"You all right, Ardys?" Linda asked.

"I tried to use the ladder, like I read on the Internet, but it didn't work out so well. I wish they'd explain things a little better."

"We turned off the engine," the elderly man said. "It was the least we could do. But with me and my arthritis, and Ethel in her condition ... "

"I called the cops!" Ethel said brightly, knotting and re-knotting the belt on her blue chenille robe.

"Got a shovel?" Linda asked. As she bent over to examine the soft earth under the truck a mangy yellow collie nosed her behind. She heard a creak as the truck shifted. She backed away, the dog barked, and she called Cheda's.

Thirty minutes later, the bright yellow tow truck arrived with another cruiser. Jerry studied the situation, set his truck in position, and slowly pulled the truck out of the mud.

Linda and Bernard, the other deputy, helped pull Ardys from the thick mud.

"You're lucky to be alive, Ardys." Linda assessed her vitals. She was shaken and filthy, but otherwise all right.

"Four tons on top of me! Four tons! I survived a truck. It fell on top of me. I'm a hero."

"Ardys," Linda sighed. Ardys was one of Bolinas' best. "We've talked about this before. You take too many risks. Think safety." Linda reached for her clipboard and filled out an incident report. Her radio crackled with a new call. She had to go.

"Protect and serve," Ardys giggled.

"Get some gravel. Fill this hole," Linda ordered.

"Oh, they won't let us make any improvements to the roads or driveways," chirped Ethel.

"Who won't let you do what?"

"The County. County rules. No improvements," the man stated.

Linda was about to ask for an explanation when she heard Ardys pipe up.

"Oh dear, Officer, please, oh please," Ardys giggled. "Can you give me a ride?" She batted her eyes. "I'm too nervous to drive and I'm due at the doctor's in ten minutes."

Reluctantly, Linda let Ardys in the back, onto the plastic seat. Some days she just hated her job. She wanted to cuff her, but it really wasn't allowed. Ardys had committed no crime she could think of. She headed out of Bolinas, back up Route One, and was deep in the eucalyptus grove making tight turns, when Ardys spoke up again.

"Protect and serve, right, deputy?" Ardys bounced around on the back seat. "I like it, I like it. Now, on your way back to Point Reyes, can you drop me off in Petaluma? That's where the doctor is and I don't want to be late."

Power Play

"Say again, ma'am?" Linda tapped her pencil on her desk at the police station. She heard a sigh. "Ma'am?"

"I'm calling from next door. My phone's out. I can't operate the TV. The dishwasher's broken. Nothing works and I'm at my wit's end," the caller sobbed. "Someone is shutting off my circuit breakers … and …"

"Start at the beginning, please," Linda asked patiently and wondered if she was ever going to get her supper, which was in the microwave, growing cold. "Ma'am?"

"Would you stop that incessant grinding, Harold?" the woman cried into the phone.

"Someone there with you?" Linda asked.

"Just my husband. Harold! Be quiet!" the caller shouted; then there was silence.

Linda was about to put down the receiver when she heard a whisper.

"Can you help me?"

"And your name is?" Linda asked, her pencil poised over an incident report.

"Pat. My name's Pat. Harold, stop that. I'm on the phone."

"Is your husband abusing you?" Linda perked up her ears. She hadn't been to an abuse case yet.

"Nothing more than normal," Pat said.

"Ma'am, do you need police assistance?"

"It's not Harold, if that's what you were thinking. It's our neighbor, Dan," Pat whispered. "He's stealing my power. Harold is all upset. I told him to wait for you."

"Location, ma'am?"

"Fifty-six Tern Court. Now, Harold, put that down. I've just called the sheriff."

Twenty minutes later Linda pulled up behind a three-quarter-ton pickup blocking a driveway. She brushed crumbs off her uniform. The place was dark. She heard a scuffle from behind thick drapes.

"Harold, don't!"

Linda knocked loudly, and hearing nothing more, broke a pane of glass in the front door with the heel of her gun, turned the lock and entered.

"Pat? Pat?" She held one hand on her Taser, the other on her two-way radio. From inside a dark living room, she saw a soft glow in the kitchen.

A young woman, in her twenties, was looking out the rear window, her feet tucked under her lacy dress. A candle flickered flame.

"Pat?"

"I told my husband not to go out there." Pat tapped on the glass. "I tried to hold him back. Like I told you, it's our neighbor, Dan. Harold's going to kill him."

A sound of crashing came from the back. Linda looked out the window and saw two men in an adjacent yard yelling at each other from either side of a fountain. An orange power cord led from the wall outside Pat's kitchen window across the garden, up over a low fence, and toward the fountain.

"Pat was right," a man said. "You *are* stealing our power."

"My husband, Harold," Pat whispered.

Linda charged into the yard, jumped the fence and faced the men. "What's this about stealing power?"

"She's crazy," a heavy-set man said. He danced around his side of the fountain. Water poured happily over three tiers, making a tinkling, rushing sound.

"So how do you explain the cord, Dan?" Harold closed in on his neighbor.

Dan pulled up a steel lawn chair and held it, poised, over his shoulder.

"What's going on here?" Linda demanded.

Dan, holding the chair, dropped it into the fountain. "You call the cops, Harold?"

"I should have called the cops on you years ago, asshole," Harold spat. He stepped closer to Dan and held up his fists.

"Gentlemen, please! Cease and desist or I'll take both of you to jail."

"You're not taking me anywhere," Dan snarled. "I was just testing my fountain, until he came by and started yelling. You want your cord? Take your goddamn cord." He grabbed the cord that was draped in the water and pulled hard. There was a pop, a blue flash, and he fell to the ground, twitching.

"Pull the cord out, Pat!" Harold yelled.

Dan's eyes rolled inside his head while his fingers kept a death grip on the extension cord, which flipped and snapped around his head.

Pat screamed.

"Do it *now*, Pat!"

With her baton, Linda edged the cord away from his hand and called dispatch. "What is it with you people? Are you all mad?"

With two hands Pat yanked the cord from the wall so hard she broke the cover.

Linda bent over Dan and felt a pulse, a faint one. "You just about killed him, Harold. What were you thinking?"

"Me? *Kill* him? Are you insane? He electrocuted himself!" Harold stuttered.

Dan looked ghastly. Linda knew rudimentary CPR and kept at it until the EMTs arrived, the sound of their sirens a comfort to her heart.

"What's his status?" an EMT asked, taking over.

"He was fine a minute ago," Linda shook her head. "Then he reached for the cord ...."

"Dan, his name's Dan," Harold said, standing over him. "He's going to be all right, isn't he?"

Another EMT wheeled in a gurney, raised Dan onto it, and hustled him away into a red van.

Linda followed Pat and Harold back into their house. They sat on a couch, together, their hands folded in their laps.

"Have you had disputes with Dan before?"

Pat and Harold leaned forward and nodded their heads.

"How long has this been going on?" Linda took notes.

"All my life," Harold muttered. "Our mother always wanted us to get along, but we didn't ever try, did we, Pat?"

"Your mother?" Linda sputtered.

"They're brothers," Pat explained. "Officer, please tell us Dan is going to be all right."

"We won't know for a while," Linda said.

"You don't understand. We've got to see him," Harold pleaded. "We're worried sick. We've always loved Dan."

FROM THE SHERIFF'S CALLS SECTION IN THE *POINT REYES LIGHT*,
APRIL 12, 2012

HICKS VALLEY: At 6:46 p.m. a woman
suspected that a deputy who had pulled her
over a week earlier had stolen her wallet and
food stamps.

Hicks Valley

"Why would I steal anyone's wallet, Walter?" Linda positioned herself in front of his fan. It was an unusually hot day in Point Reyes. "Doesn't make any sense."

Walter drummed his fingers on the table. "You pulled her over, right? You admit pulling her over?"

"Of course." Linda dug a copy of the incident report out of the front placket pocket of her uniform. "Justina Williams, 28, of Nicasio. Driving 75 in a 55. She was belligerent when I stopped her. I almost cuffed her and brought her in."

"Ah." Walter sighed.

"Ah, what?"

"You've got a bit of an attitude."

"Attitude? I don't have an attitude problem."

"Well, we've had quite a few reports about you."

"Reports? What reports?" She thought her time on the force had been pristine. Four arrests a month, perps behind walls, and a reduction in overall crime.

"Justina. She was quite adamant."

"She's crazy." Linda remembered only too well being on welfare. All of that was behind her, now that she'd joined the force.

"We should go out and see her." Walter picked up the phone.

"But boss, we have a lot of paperwork to do."

"Community relations, Linda. It's about time you added that to your skill set – unless it's too much trouble?"

"Not at all, sir." Linda stuffed her cinnamon roll and fresh cup of coffee into the bottom drawer of her desk. She wouldn't see either of those until the morning, if she remembered to look. Damn and double damn.

On her way to the parking lot, she passed Bernard who snickered while she walked by. For what? Her getting chewed on by the boss? Linda stood up straight, squared her shoulders, and hustled after Walter. He had a long stride and no sense of humor. At this point, she wished she were anywhere but with him.

The evening sky was turning rose as they took the Petaluma-Point Reyes Road, passed the Cheese Factory, and headed west on Hicks Valley Road. Even though the highway was straight in places, it was no place to speed; bicyclists were all over the road in their matching spandex outfits, crazy drivers texted while driving, and lost tourists were going 25.

A full milk truck passed on the other side of the two-lane road, sucking the cruiser into the double yellow line. When the driver of the truck let out a blast on his klaxon horn, Linda jumped out of her seat. She was glad she was wearing a seat belt.

For a half-hour, Walter didn't say anything, making it hard for Linda to know what to say. She smoothed the creases on her uniform pants and polished her shoes, one behind the other, with her regulation socks, black, cotton, ankle high. She felt like clicking her heels to make him disappear and was on her way to talking about a movie when he drove his car into a farmyard and up to a young woman holding a baby.

"Ms. Turnbull?" Walter asked. "Ms. Justina Turnbull?"

Justina was wearing day-glow pink platform heels and skinny black jeans. Half my size, Linda thought, and twice the trouble.

"You sure this was the officer?" Walter asked.

Justina slipped the baby onto her other hip. "There's sure as hell no way I'm talking to her. She took my wallet and food stamps. Now, how am I supposed to get enough to eat for me and my baby?"

A wail erupted from inside the mobile home.

"My other babies." She fixed her eye on Linda.

"Ma'am." Walter and Linda followed Justina to her front door.

"No way, no how, you coming in here," Justina waved them off. "You'll scare my children with your uniforms and guns. I'll be right back."

"Whatever you say, ma'am." Walter leaned against a door jamb, while Linda placed her hands on her hips.

"Relax," Walter murmured. "Anyone would be scared the way you're standing. You're supposed to make her feel you're a trusted friend."

"Right, sir." Linda cooled herself against the aluminum siding on the mobile home. She wanted the woman to be scared. Food stamps? Jesus. What kind of scam was this woman trying to pull? And what kind of cop did Walter think she was? Her salary went a long way toward covering all the expenses of the little rental she shared with Mom in Forest Knolls.

They waited a moment until the door burst open. "It's my blood pressure, you know. These kids are going to be the death of me yet," Justina declared.

"So." Walter rocked on his heels. "You said that Officer Kettleman stole your wallet and food stamps. Is that correct, Ms. Turnbull?"

"The food stamps were in my wallet." Justina stuck out her hip and threw back her blond hair.

"These are serious charges, ma'am," Walter said.

"I'm not telling you anything while she's here." Justina jerked a thumb toward Linda.

"The accused party – my officer – needs to hear what you have to say," he offered.

"Good for you, Walter," Linda whispered under her breath.

"Tell us what happened, please." Walter pulled out a notebook and pen.

"The goddamn sirens scared me to death. Made my children cry," Justina sniffed.

"You were speeding, ma'am," Linda said.

"Speedometer's broken."

"I see. It says here in the incident report that you have an expired registration." Walter examined the documents with half-lidded eyes. "Is that correct?"

"Husband hasn't gotten around to it, with all these children," Justina turned and yelled back into the house. "Hey! Be quiet. I'm doing business out here."

"There's no reason I'd want your wallet, ma'am," Linda said.

"You reached for my wallet when I was pulling out my license, and you never gave it back," Justina spat.

"Was that before or after I asked you for your registration, ma'am?"

"She's giving me the third degree, Officer," Justina said. "I'm not on trial here. She is."

"No one's on trial here," Walter stated. "Now, we will need to search your car."

"You don't have to do nothing to my car," Justina shot back. The front door of the mobile home banged open and a half-naked blond boy ran to her. Justina scooped him up. "You're scaring the children. Some other time, then, officers."

"Your car," Walter requested.

"Oh, for Chrissakes," Justina groaned. "Go get my keys, Hayden."

She led them to her 1967 mustard-yellow Camaro. "It was a present from my dad." She scooped Hayden up and tossed the keys to Walter. "Ain't no wallet in that car." A moment later, she yelped and threw Hayden down. "I'm not nursing you anymore, Hayden. Leave offa me." The three-year-old, giggling, ran back inside the trailer.

Linda pulled on her purple gloves and opened the door to the car carefully. She sifted through empty Pepsi cans, hamburger wrappers, Jolly Roger candy wrappers, and stale French fries. She took everything out, examined each item, and placed the items on a pile in the driveway. She closed her hand around something round, green, and in a Ziploc bag.

"And what about this?" She came over to Walter and Justina who were talking on opposite sides of a broken-down dishwasher.

"Parsley." Justina made a grab for it.

Linda pulled it away. She had half a mind to cuff the stupid girl. If she lost this job her dad would be vindicated and she wasn't going to lose her job over a goddamn hippie. "Shall I have the chief verify it?" She handed the bag to Walter. "Or maybe we should take it back to the lab?"

She gauged Walter's look. He was too cool to raise an eye, but both of them knew there was no lab at the station.

"So." Walter pivoted on his heels and tossed the bag back to Linda. "Book the evidence."

Linda caught it and pulled out her clipboard.

"My husband, he'll be here in a minute. He – I – we can throw you off our property."

"You're the one who called us, ma'am," Walter said in his even, still, slow voice.

"But she ... she ..." Justina sputtered.

"Drop the charges against my deputy and we'll forgive possession," Walter offered, his eyes going cold and his hand, somehow, making its way toward his sidearm.

"Deal?" Linda asked.

"Leave me the hell alone." Justina walked to the front door of the mobile home. "Oh for heaven's sake, children – stop that, stop that now." She looked back at the cops. "Deal," she said and went inside.

"That's it then." Walter climbed behind the wheel of the cruiser. Linda followed and they drove away, leaving a cloud of dust behind them.

"Thanks, boss," Linda said, holding the bag of pot in her lap.

"Thanks, nothing, Linda. You were lucky. You're still on probation." He slowed for cows crossing the road.

"For how long?" Linda asked. "It's been almost a year."

"Longer probation for you." Walter geared down for a bunch of bicyclists. "You could do better, you know."

Linda loved the land, the people, the other guys in the station. Police work seemed to fit just as snug as her new underwear from Enchanted Things, a shop in Mill Valley. She stared out the window. "I didn't take her food stamps."

"Of course not. And we didn't take her pot. Toss that shit out the window," he said while passing the pond by the Cheese Factory.

"But it's evidence." Linda pried open the bag.

"It's parsley, deputy. Now buckle up. I see someone speeding down the road."

FROM THE SHERIFF'S CALLS SECTION IN THE *POINT REYES LIGHT*, APRIL 19, 2012

OLEMA: At 11:56 p.m. someone reported a bonfire in the road across from Bear Valley Visitor Center. Deputies found a group of French exchange students who had mistaken the picnic area for the Olema campground. "This is the first time they had ever camped," deputies wrote. "And it shows."

The Campers

Linda put down her pen. She was proud of her entry. Walter always said keep it short, keep it sweet, and keep your emotions out of it. She thought she got this one just about right.

It had been a quiet Saturday night at the station and she'd been playing Angry Birds on her computer, which she knew wasn't allowed, but she was watch captain for the night and nothing was going on. That is, until she got the call.

Ten minutes later she drove into Bear Valley and put on her flashers. That's when she saw it, a bonfire as big as tomorrow, right in the middle of the road. A few people were sitting around the bonfire, on fold-up chairs, while others were barbecuing and having a ball.

Linda stepped closer. Tent pegs, stakes and poles lay in a jumble on the grass nearby. A bundle of nylon ruffled in a breeze.

"What's going on here?" she asked. A few people looked up and grinned.

"*Bonsoir*," one woman said.

Linda tried to remember any of her high school Spanish – it was a romance language wasn't it? but her "*Hola*" fell on deaf ears. She launched right in. "Anyone speak English? You can't camp here. Not allowed."

Two people looked at each other, shrugged their shoulders, and sipped their wine.

"Sirs, madams. This is not a campground. You can't camp here," she said to the group.

"*La feu, c'est bon, n'est-ce pas?*" a tall man asked, gesturing to the fire. He pushed his hat back on his head, stuck out his hand. "*Bonsoir. Avez-vous faim?*"

"It's the law." She cut her hand across her neck and gestured to the fire. "Not okay."

"*Ça va bien?*" The man waved to a woman, who was carrying glasses of wine.

"No, thank you," Linda said. "You can't make a fire in the road, and you can't camp here."

"*Non?*" The man crinkled his forehead. He conferred with the others. He indicated a picnic table decorated with a red-and-white-checked cloth and covered with food. "*Pas de feu?*" The bonfire crackled as it licked at bark. "*No pique-nique?*"

"My name is Officer Kettleman. Would you like me to call for backup?" Linda gestured to her radio.

The guy with the hat shook his head. "*Tant pis. Jacques, vite,*" he said, and a teenage boy came forward.

"How may we help you, ma'am?" Jacques asked.

Linda, relieved that they at least had a translator, told him in no uncertain terms that this was not a campsite and bonfires were not allowed. Seeing their faces drop, she added that they weren't far from a real campground.

"*Qu'est-ce que c'est?*" asked the man with the hat. He turned to Linda. "*Nous somme très fatigués.*"

"This is my father, Philippe, and we are very tired," said Jacques. Philippe nodded hello.

"No need to translate." Linda saw their tired eyes. "How 'bout we put out the fire, pack your things, and," she paused. "Philippe, I have an idea."

"*Une idée?*" Philippe asked.

"At the campground, not far, I'll set up your tents, agreed?"

Jacques translated again. Everyone sighed, put their hands over their hearts and stared at the sky.

"Religious order out of Reims," Jacques explained. "We lead a rather sheltered life. First time in the States. *Pays magnifique? D'accord?*" he said to the crowd. "Say hello to Officer Kettleman."

They laughed and said her name.

Twenty minutes later, Linda helped them unpack their tents at the Olema campground less than a mile away. Philippe had started a small fire in an old rusty wheel. Linda noted his disappointment over the size of the fire, but nodded approval as it grew.

She set up four tents in succession, and was about to start on a fifth, when Jacques brought her a glass of wine. Someone else set up the last tent, while she clinked glasses with Philippe.

An hour and two glasses later, she thought that maybe it was time to head back to the station.

Back inside the office, she stared at the computer game she'd been playing earlier. Nothing in the computer would ever compare with her new French friends. She rubbed her eyes and reached for a cold cup of coffee.

An hour later, Walter found her with wine-stained fingers, unkempt hair, her head on her desk, muttering in French. He was gravely disappointed.

"All this is impossible to believe," he said when she tried to explain. "Too many French mystery novels, Linda. I told you not to bring them to work." He tossed her latest Paris mystery into the trash.

"But it's true." Linda straightened her uniform and smoothed her hair. "Come to the campground. I'll introduce you to Philippe and Jacques. They had a little French flag and everything. I did my job correctly, sir."

"Bunk."

Ten minutes later, when they arrived at the Olema campground all signs of the French party were gone. Walter looked at Linda with dismay. She was losing it already and not even a year on the job. He should never have hired her. She looked like the last 5150 they had picked up in Bolinas.

He was about to turn around when she insisted they check the road in front of the visitor's center. By this time, at least a hundred cars had been in and out of the parking lot and there was no sign of a bonfire or ash.

"Just wait, Walter. Please." Linda stopped traffic and scuffed her way up and down the middle of the road, kicking at dirt. No ash at all. She was despondent.

Back at the station, filling out an incident report, she looked at Walter and sighed. "They were lovely people."

"Give it a rest, Linda. You'll be back at the desk if you keep this up."

"It's the first time they'd ever gone camping." Linda said, hoping her "incident" wouldn't cost her her job. "They were very brave."

"Oh please." And she'd had such promise, too. He pulled out an internal-affairs report form.

Dispatch crackled over the speakers. "There's a bunch of French people at the Station House. And they're trying to give their children wine."

Linda beamed.

"Get the hell out of here," Walter said and sat down in front of the computer. He heard the door slam and swore under his breath. The young deputies were the only ones who ever had any fun. Not for long. He headed for the door.

From the Sheriff's Calls Section in the *Point Reyes Light*,
April 26, 2012

INVERNESS PARK: At 1:30 p.m. two people agreed to leave each other alone for the day.

Alone For the Day

Mildred was delighted. Now Fred couldn't bother her. She checked her chores: ironing done, kitchen clean; that left the garden.

On her way outside, she picked up her gardening bag – clippers, shears, trowel, snips, and green tape. All set. She eyed Fred in his hammock. My, oh my, he was getting bigger. The bottom of the hammock was two inches off the ground.

She'd been after him for years about his weight, but did he listen? Never. She lifted her twenty-pound bag of tulips from Jackson Perkins, thought for a minute of asking him for help, but remembered. He was off-limits today. She set her trowel and tulips on the dirt and crouched down ever so slowly. It seemed that every year the ground grew farther and farther away.

She'd called the sheriff for good reason. That doggone Fred had been pestering her to go out for supper more and said some ugly things about her cooking. Having just seen a BBC mystery where an older woman skewered her husband with a carving knife – and feeling she could do the same thing herself – she'd called the cops and told them her plan. They'd agreed. She dug into the soft earth with her trowel.

Fred, in his hammock, looked over at his wife with dismay. What was with her? All these years together and now he wasn't allowed to talk to his sweetie? He'd only suggested a little respite from her cooking. Yesterday, she'd barely cooked their chicken and the lettuce was all wilted and brown. Then she'd yelled at him, and threatened to pull out a knife. Last night he'd slept on the sofa. Safer, that. He watched her bend over her little bulbs and talk to them as if they were people. Every year it seemed she became more and more of a nut.

So what if he'd put artichoke leaves down the disposal? His father had put broken glass down his, and his disposal had worked fine.

Fred went back to his racing form. It was time he made a fortune on the horses. If he won, he could go the hell to Idaho, hunt and fish and put anything he wanted down the sink. He popped another beer.

Mildred couldn't remember how deep to plant the bulbs. Was it two inches or two feet? The dirt was soft under her hands and she liked the feel of it packing her nails. Tulips reminded her of her mother. She dug deep with the trowel and, pulling up dirt, felt something wiggle on her hand.

"Aaacckk!" She threw it off. The bug was three inches long, had horrible antennas and claws on all its joints, and looked like a miniature lobster. "Fred! Fred! It's the most disgusting thing I have ever seen. Get over here!"

"I'm not talking to you, Mildred. Not today, not any day." He went back to his racing form. Should he bet on Lucy's Wild Child or Candy for Doris? Their stats looked good, fillies all. He couldn't choose.

"Fred! Do something!" Mildred fell over and scrabbled back to her feet in terror. Her little knee-highs had crumpled over her brown oxfords and her dress was covered with dirt.

"You're the one who threatened to pull a knife on me, then called the cops." He grinned. "You said, 'Make sure my husband leaves me alone for the day.' So, here we are. This is your problem, dear."

"There are two of them now! Where'd you put the shovel?" She waited, in vain, for a response. "You mean you won't tell me where you put the shovel?" She stood over a mound of dirt. Her bulbs were scattered over the ground. Those awful bugs were as big as her hands. They were staring at her. She ran toward the hammock.

"Stop! No! Go away!" Fred cautiously rolled one foot over the side, so as to not upset his racing form or beer.

"Off the ground! I've got to get off the ground!" she shouted and leapt. It was too much for the hammock, which tore at the seams and dropped them both on the ground.

"Ow! Jesus, Mildred! First you call the cops, then you jump on me and destroy my hammock? Get off of me." Fred flicked twigs from his hair.

"They were horrible bugs, as big as taxis." She held him around the neck, grateful for his bulk. "Please?"

"All right, all right. I'll go check." She was such a bitty little thing.

"Thanks."

He stood up, thinking. "Under one condition. Promise you won't call the cops on me, again. Ever?"

"But you were being obnoxious." She sat up and brushed off her hands.

"Suit yourself." He headed toward the house.

"I didn't mean it."

"Mildred, what didn't you mean? You want me to go after the bugs or not?"

"Oh, yes, please." She placed a hand on his arm. "Oh please, protect me."

"Then you'll leave me alone?"

"For what? Beer, baseball, or girls?"

"If I had any girlfriends, you'd be the first to know. Now," he squinted, "what about that apology?"

"No more calls to the sheriff then, Fred." She pecked him on the cheek. "Now, please, the bugs."

"And?"

"Sorry about threatening you with a knife."

Fred knew she wasn't sorry in the least. He found two potato bugs crawling in the hole. He helped them into the neighbor's yard. "You're planting a little deep, darling."

"You think so?"

"You want me to finish this?" He held up a trowel and a few of the bulbs.

"Yes, if you would." She eased back onto her patio chair. "Thanks, dear." Another chore avoided. Even though it hadn't gone quite as planned, the outcome had been worth it.

From the Sheriff's Calls Section in the *Point Reyes Light*, April 26, 2012

STINSON BEACH: At 1:54 p.m. someone saw two men pee in the street, change their clothes, and then run off when the caller yelled at them.

My New Outfit

"I wasn't doing anything." Henry bit into his croissant at the Bovine. "Sure I was there, but that wasn't 'til later, and besides …"

Fred looked at his older brother with dismay. He had cigarette burns on his sweater, something white on his shoulder – either bird poop or dog slobber and god knows what on his trousers.

Henry took off his pork pie hat and rested his head in his hands. "Look, it wasn't me. I haven't peed in the street since we were kids. Mom said …"

"When we were six, yeah, sure, aim at a tree, but Henry, you're a grown man now."

"Eighty-six my next birthday."

"And?"

"And nothing," Henry said.

"Why is your sweater on inside out?" Fred smoothed his hand on his brother's arm. "What happened when I went to get ice cream?"

Henry stirred his coffee with a straw. The goddamn stir sticks at the Bovine were too short for his extra large mocha. "What's it to you?"

"Embarrassing, for one thing," Fred murmured. "Unsanitary for another. Mother would not approve."

"She wouldn't approve of half the shit you've done, Fred Rhinehart, and you know it as well as I do. Anyway, who cares? She's been dead for twenty-five years."

Four bicyclists came into the Bovine, jingling the doorbell. Fred shifted his weight on the stool – damn thing was just too small. Henry fit. Henry fit on everything, except in his own mind. Up there, everything was out of whack. "Why did you take off your clothes?"

"Why would I do that? It was raining. I could have gotten a cold." Henry took a long drink of his coffee, being very careful to keep the straw out of his eye. "You won't tell Mildred any of this, will you? She'll have my hide."

"She's with Doris for the next hour, then we need to go over the hill." Across the street, Fred watched people line up for coffee at Toby's. Fancy coffees had never been his thing. "Henry, you really can't be doing that in public. You could be arrested. People will call you crazy."

"They already do. You said so yourself, only last week." Henry drained his coffee.

"We – I mean Mildred and I – don't like you living up on Drake's View Drive. Not all alone, not anymore." This was the big question for Fred, the one that kept him up nights. If Henry went into a home, he and Mildred would be next. "Was it fun?"

"What was fun? Peeing in the street?" Henry twisted his napkin. "Or changing my clothes at the foot of Calle Del Sierra?"

"Exactly." Motorcycles rumbled up the street.

"I had to go bad, Fred. I couldn't wait. Fun had no part of it. Couldn't wait …"

Fred felt like that too, at times, but he didn't want to think about it. Their grandson Owen peed like a horse, but for him and Henry, well, things just took more time these days. "And your clothes?"

"Not so clean, you know, after …"

"Henry!"

"Wasn't my fault. There was no one there at all. It was quiet, everyone was at the beach. How was I supposed to know someone was watching?"

"Do you know who?" Fred asked. Henry had paranoid delusions, among other things.

"It was that goddamn Mrs. Willis," Henry said, "the old bat."

The front door of the bakery opened with a bang.

"Boys! Hello boys!" Mildred trilled.

To Fred, her hair had a slight tinge of blue. "Hi sweetheart." He gave her a kiss on her cheek. Her skin was still soft, but smooth? Not hardly. As crinkly as a piece of paper.

"Good afternoon Henry," she clucked, showing off her manicure. "Hot pink. What do you think?"

To Fred, she looked like a cartoon, pink nails, blue hair and a bright red dress.

"New outfit. New do. New day, eh, boys?" They weren't pay any attention. "Henry, you look like you swallowed a parakeet."

"Not me," Henry said. "I didn't do anything."

Mildred waved to the counter girl. "My usual, Betsy!" She turned around, then frowned at what she saw.

Three bicyclists were sitting on the wooden bench just inside the door. They were dressed in spandex from the tops of their heads to the socks covering their shoes.

"Hi kids!" Mildred swung her patent-leather purse and hit one of them on the shoulder. "Oh! Sorry. So sorry," she twittered. They cleared out in a hurry. She took a seat in the middle of the bench, placed her bag on one side and her hat on the other. "So what's up, guys?"

Henry and Fred, no fools they, exchanged glances across the crowded tiny shop.

"Nothing." Henry drummed his fingers on the counter. "Just a lot of nothing."

"I wasn't talking to *you*." Mildred turned to her husband. "Thick as thieves, you two."

Fred brightened. It had taken him a few minutes to come up with a story and this was a doozy. "We were talking about Frances Ann, and her birthday party."

"Uh … hunh …" Mildred opened and closed the clasp on her purse. "Go on."

"She was a beauty," Fred said.

"She was a floozy," Mildred blurted. "She had no manners."

"You can't talk about my wife like that," Henry spat.

"You and Frances Ann were never ..." Fred started to say, then thought better of it. "Never mind."

'When she was really little, she used to take off all her clothes ..." Mildred giggled.

"All the little kids do that at one time or another." Fred stood up. "Time to go, dear."

"And big ones too," Henry added, lost in the moment. He glanced at his younger brother, and his sister-in-law, who held her mouth half-open. "Whoops," he said. "Whoops."

FROM THE SHERIFF'S CALLS SECTION IN THE *POINT REYES LIGHT*,
APRIL 26, 2012

TOMALES: At 1:03 p.m. a 16-year-old girl
passed out in a hall at the high school.

Alice's Bad Day

"Alice?" principal Hartman asked. "Alice, you all right?"

Alice wasn't sure if she wanted to open her eyes or not. It was nice on the floor, nice and cool. She'd just been so hot, and the other girls had been teasing her about her nosebleeds, and she couldn't explain. They had called her a freak, and she hadn't known what to do. Her heart raced, she felt funny all over, and she went down.

"I saw her fall," Betsy said. "She crumpled like a piece of paper."

"Did she hit her head?" principal Hartman asked.

"No, I don't think so."

"Are you sure?"

"The other girls were calling her names." Betsy leaned against a locker, chewing on a thumbnail.

"We'll take it from here, Betsy. Thank you," the principal said. "Now, go on back to class."

"But Mrs. Hartman?" Betsy took a look at Alice. Her face was the color of Elmer's Glue. She wondered how Alice felt, whether or not she felt anything. Betsy shivered. She never wanted to be like that. She headed down the hall.

Alice felt herself being pulled up onto her feet. She felt her nose. Any blood? Was there any blood? "Least I didn't have a bloody nose, Mrs. Hartman," she said, feeling a tiny bit better.

"But you fainted, dear. You could have been hurt. Do you feel okay? Dizzy? Headache? Did you have your lunch today?"

At lunch, of course, she hadn't eaten much. She hadn't found a place on campus yet, except under the bleachers and it was too gloomy for that, where she could eat in peace and not be pestered by the bigger girls. So she had headed to the library, where she hid and snuck a bite or two. But then, in the hall, lost in thought, trying to decide if she should read *Twilight* or *The Hunger Games,* the bigger girls had found her.

Victoria, the tall blond, got to her first. The rest of the girls had made fun of the marshmallow and peanut-butter sandwich Alice was still holding. Thinking all of this over, Alice did not at first hear Mrs. Hartman's words.

"We'll call your parents. Can you walk? Let me carry your backpack. My, that's heavy. I wonder why you girls don't get backpacks with wheels. That's enough school for today. Is your mother home?"

"Uh, no," Alice mumbled. She was glad class was in session so none of the other kids could see her walk down the hall with the principal hovering over her. "I'm okay, though. Really, I'm fine," she said, feeling relieved she did have help.

"Is this your time of the month?" Mrs. Hartman asked.

Alice felt she was being way too personal. "Heck no," she stated, a bit too loudly, even though it was. As if she cared. All she wanted was to be left alone. "I'm missing Latin class, Mrs. Hartman. AP. Can't miss one class. There's a quiz today."

"I'm sure Ms. Latham will give you a make-up test, dear." Mrs. Hartman held the door the nurse's office for her. "Take a seat. Better yet, lie down. I'll be back in a minute."

Alice sipped a cup of water. She could go back to class, but she'd be the center of attention, again. She could stay here, but her mother, a real estate agent, wouldn't be happy in the least to come all the way from Petaluma in the middle of the day and possibly lose a sale. That left one option. Soon Mrs. Hartman would be back with the nurse and Alice would be stuck.

She picked up her backpack and marched out of the admin office, across the basketball court, and off to the bleachers. Soon enough, Mrs. Hartman would discover her gone and they'd have a big search, but for now, she had peace and quiet.

She was rolling a doobie, leaning against one of the posts, when she saw something bright red on the ground. A bag of candy, perhaps? When she walked over, the red thing moved, and she noticed it was a shoe. She walked around a post and found Betsy making out with one of the boys from twelfth grade. Cutting class and making out on school grounds were worse offenses than pot, in Alice's book.

Betsy opened her eyes, looked at her, and grinned.

"You all right?" she asked.

"Better, with this." Alice took a toke and passed over the joint.

"We've had ours." Betsy giggled. "Just a sec, Tim." She sidled over to Alice. "What made you faint?"

"No lunch … uh, I don't know …" Alice mumbled. Wasn't Betsy one of *them?*

"I saw them picking on you." Betsy ran her hand through her auburn hair. "Scary, when they do that, huh? You have to admit you are a little … weird."

"So?"

"Tomorrow, come and have lunch with me," Betsy suggested.

"Really?"

"'Cause I'm a freak like you, Alice Rhinehart." Betsy waved her four-fingered hand, missing her index finger. "Now, if you'll excuse me?" She went back to kissing Tim.

Alice, feeling buoyant, picked up her backpack and walked back to school. If she was early enough, they wouldn't worry about her. And for the first time, the first time ever, she walked in proud. She had a friend.

From the Sheriff's Calls Section in the *Point Reyes Light*, May 17, 2012

POINT REYES STATION: At 7:27 p.m. someone reported that a couple who had just dined at Café Reyes left the restaurant in a Mercedes, taking two glasses of wine with them and heading toward the Dance Palace.

Two Glasses of Wine

"This is not San Francisco, ma'am." Linda stood in front of a black Mercedes on B Street. "We don't allow drinking while driving."

The woman passenger, well-coiffed with strawberry blond hair, held up her glass. "Cheers, officer."

The driver scowled at his wife and hid his own glass under his leg. "Charlotte, what are you doing?"

"License and registration, please." It was the usual Saturday night and the place was full of tourists who thought they owned the town.

Charlotte flashed a two-carat yellow diamond from a hand that dripped with gold chains. "Tell her, Frank."

Frank stayed mum.

"Tell her we're late for the John Korty retrospective. He said wine and cheese would be served. So we brought our own."

"License and registration. Don't make me ask you again." Linda looked in the car. The back seat was filled with wildflowers, monkey flowers, shooting stars, and sad wilted poppies.

Frank groaned. It hadn't been his idea to smuggle out the wine glasses: it had been Charlotte's. It was a short four-block drive and she'd said they wouldn't be caught. Damn. He reached for his wallet, opened the glove box, and handed over the documents, being careful not to dislodge the wine glass under his thigh. He thought he felt something slip.

Linda ran their licenses. The print on the insurance certificate was awfully small – something she'd noticed lately. It was completely unfair! Twenty-six was way too young to need reading glasses. She researched the perp on her in-car computer and they came up clean. Pacific Heights address, Gold Coast. She returned to the driver's door.

"Can you hurry it up, please?" Charlotte asked. "John Korty is waiting for us. We've come all the way from the City for this."

"The wine glasses, please."

"Oh." Charlotte took a sip and handed over her half-full goblet. "Too bad. Nice Merlot."

"So, Mister Feldman." Linda leaned into the window. "What's with the flowers?"

He shrugged. "Pretty, don't you think?"

"Your glass too, sir."

Frank blushed and pulled out an empty glass from under his leg. Now his wingtips and socks were soaked, he had a fat ticket, and he smelled like a wino. "Caught us red-handed, didn't you, officer? It was a sudden impulse. And it's only four blocks from the café to the Dance Palace."

"You're the driver, the responsible party, Mister Feldman. I'm going to give you two tickets." Linda wrote furiously in her book. "One for driving with an open beverage. The other for stealing." She wished there were a place on the ticket for arrogance and stupidity.

Across the street, a steady stream of people entered the Dance Palace's double doors.

"So, where are you staying?" Linda asked.

"Olema Inn." Charlotte swept her lace shawl over her red crepe dress. "C'mon, Frank."

Liar, thought Linda, writing that down too. Olema Inn was closed.

She watched them meander into the bright well-lit lobby and checked the car again. In their hurry, they had parked in front of a fire hydrant. Delighted, she headed back to the cruiser. Walter will be proud, she thought. A misdemeanor, a moving violation, a parking ticket, and a tow. That would teach those out-of-towners not to mess with Point Reyes.

She was just putting in a call to Cheda's when the radio crackled by her ear.

"What are you doing?" Walter barked. "I've been calling and calling. What are you, deaf? There's a break-in at the Palace Market. You're a block away. And you still didn't answer my call? Make up your mind, Officer Kettleman. Do you really want to be a cop or not?"

From the Sheriff's Calls Section in the *Point Reyes Light*, May 17, 2012

POINT REYES STATION: At 9:39 a.m. a 100-year-old woman who could barely talk reported that half of her bed was "looking very gray."

Colors

Hortense Elliott looked back at her bed. There was something wrong with it. She clicked her teeth. Her caretaker Marianne didn't agree with her. But Marianne didn't see the little green men who came out at midnight to play the blues either, so what the heck did Marianne know?

Hortense narrowed her eyes. Her girl had called the cops and now they were over, quizzing Marianne and talking behind her back as if she weren't there.

"It doesn't matter if the bed is gray. I can still sleep in it." Hortense twisted her Hermès scarf, the purple one that hid her thyroid scar. "Nothing's wrong officer. I'm fine."

Officer Kettleman examined Mrs. Elliott's medicines, which were lined up in a tray like soldiers.

"Mind your own business!" Hortense banged on the table with her cane.

"Yes, ma'am. Sorry." Mrs. Elliott reminded Linda of her own grandmother - flinty, hard, opinionated, and tiny. "Call us if you need anything, ma'am," she said and left.

Alone at last, Hortense turned to Marianne. "Why on earth did you call the cops? I'm okay. I'm talking. I'm walking, and on my own feet too. All limbs intact, senses sharper than yours, and you think you need to call the sheriff because I see colors?"

Marianne covered her mouth. "Whatever you say, ma'am." Still. Mrs. Elliott was looking paler than usual.

"You think I should change my hair color?" Hortense checked herself in one of the four mirrors in the living room. She plucked a whisker from her chin. "Doris might have time this afternoon."

Marianne, who'd also noticed that Mrs. Elliott's hair was bluer than usual, didn't say a word. Doris was a little enthusiastic with her colors, if anyone asked her. But since no one asked her anything, she went back to washing yesterday's dishes.

"If I was a little younger," Mrs. Elliott went on, "I'd drive myself to Doris' – and leave you here to finish up. I'm a good driver."

Marianne sighed. At least this time she'd had the good sense to hide the keys in the freezer.

"I saw you! I saw you snicker." Mrs. Elliott turned on the young girl, skin like new apples, mouth like a red rose, and frightened sky-blue eyes.

"I wasn't snickering, ma'am." Marianne blushed. She needed this job.

"Norman wouldn't put up with you."

"So sorry." Marianne set a dish to dry in the rack.

"Now, about that hair appointment? Call Doris. Time's a wasting. I want to be back in time for 'Fashion Week'."

Marianne picked up the rotary phone.

"Don't bother. We'll just drive. Next time don't call the police, Marianne. My house, my rules. You understand?"

"Yes, ma'am." Marianne placed her hand on the door knob. "Ready?"

"You think she should cut it too?" Hortense touched her hair. "Maybe a permanent?"

"You hate the smell of those chemicals, ma'am."

"Maybe a different color?"

Marianne hesitated. She'd almost said darker blue.

"Strawberry Blond? Passion Pink? Lincoln Park Dark Night?"

Marianne giggled. "Those are nail polish colors, ma'am. You want a manicure too?"

"And a pedicure, yes!" Hortense trilled. "Cover me with colors! Sky-blue hair, hot-pink nails, deep-red toenails – and, oh, Marianne."

Marianne held Mrs. E's hat, purse, and keys. "Ready?"

"What are you doing? You know Norman likes my hair just the way it is. Now, if you'll excuse me." She headed to her bedroom.

Marianne followed, disappointed. Poor Mrs. Elliott hadn't made it out of the house in a month.

"Go get me the world, Marianne," Hortense trilled. "Paint it a thousand colors, bring me green for plants, yellow for hair, blue for eyes, hot red for fingernails – and Doris …"

"Yes, ma'am?" Marianne waited. On Mrs. E's bad days, she got everyone mixed up.

"Bring me a cup of tea honey, today's Herald Tribune, a case of Coke, a vase of flowers, and my water-coloring kit. I'm going to paint."

"Very well," Marianne said. It was a tossup – either Mrs. E would wonder where her stuff was or she'd be fast asleep. Problem is, Marianne never knew which way she'd go.

"But no gray paint, no gray sheets, people think it's a pretty color, but I don't. Anything but gray – oh, dear." Mrs. Elliott hesitated by her bed. "I want to be young again, Marianne."

"So do we all." Marianne helped Mrs. Elliott dissolve into a chair. "Comfortable, then?"

"I'm just so cold. Bring me my blanket." Hortense drew her shawl closer around her. "Oh, and Marianne? Get the door, will you? Someone's knocking. I bet Norman forgot his keys again."

FROM THE SHERIFF'S CALLS SECTION IN THE *POINT REYES LIGHT*, MAY 31, 2012

POINT REYES STATION: At 7:07 a.m. a man wearing an apron but no pants was walking down the road, pushing a shopping cart. The man told deputies he'd made a "makeshift" pair of pants as his other pair was soiled.

Looking Spiffy

"My pants are not soiled in that way, officer." Albert twisted the ends of his mustache and felt offended. "I fell in the mud."

"Are you a long way from home? Need a ride?" Linda took a sip of her fresh coffee and leaned out the window of her cruiser.

"Good thing it's early, hunh?" Albert asked. Among other things, pants being first among them, he needed more mustache wax. He'd been growing his illustrious whiskers since he'd been twenty-five and they were his best feature. Now it was drooping, along with his apron.

"Pardon me, ma'am." He hid behind his shopping cart and adjusted things. It was getting a little breezy.

"Anyplace you can get some pants, bud?" Linda ventured, not sure if she wanted him in her cruiser. Last time, it had taken her more than two hours to get the backseat clean. And that guy was at least wearing pants. "Hop in."

"I'm not leaving my stuff," Albert said, referring to his last smidge of mustache wax, sleeping bag, bags of cans, and shirt, sweater, and jacket.

"Then follow me to the station. I'm sure one of the guys has a spare pair somewhere." As long as she didn't have to touch him. "Okay?"

Albert thought maybe she was going to run him in, take him to Unit B or something. Instead of saying yes, he waved her away. As soon as the deputy drove down Route One, he headed down C Street in the other direction.

He wandered into the Giacomini wetlands, just a bit off into the bushes where he wouldn't be seen. All he needed was water. He looked into the creek. The water wasn't clean enough – but it would have to do for the mud. Otherwise, he'd have to go back into town and find a spigot, and with the tourists arriving any minute, that wasn't a good idea. Slowly and carefully, he sank his mud-covered pants into the creek, and with a stick got most of the mud off. The sun had broken over the hills flooding him with light, but it wasn't quite enough to dry his blue jeans with them on. He spread them out on a rock and, noticing the silence and the birds and all that, lay down against a log, letting his winter-white legs get some vitamin D. That was the new cure-all, wasn't it? He'd read about it online at the library.

Thirty minutes later, he heard footsteps on his little beach. A dog sniffed Albert in the usual dog places, waking him in a hurry. When the beagle went to pee on Albert's pants, Albert jumped up and charged him. A boy entering the clearing screamed.

"Mom Mom Mom! it's a naked man! Mom!" The boy, all of four, took off up the path. Beyond a set of bushes, he reached his mother, still screaming. The dog, hearing all the excitement, ran after him.

Albert covered himself with his apron. He hadn't done anything wrong. People were always talking about going back to nature and he was natural, so what was the problem? He tried to cover himself with his cart again like he'd done in town, but the wheels caught on sand.

The boy's mother peered over the bushes. "Turn around, Sam, and march. That man is exposing himself. My God. Hurry. No, don't look back. I'm calling the cops."

Albert's peace was destroyed. He didn't want to go to jail. He pulled his soaked blue jeans over his warm dry skin and they clung to him, making him shiver. Wishing for a warm cup of coffee and a shower, he pushed on deeper into the bushes, pulling and pushing his cart all the way.

Later that afternoon, Linda found him, a glint of his cart visible through blackberry bushes.

Albert heard the crackle of dried twigs and peered at her.

"I've brought a blanket and a cup of coffee, and the boys gave me some pants," Linda said. "We weren't sure which size you were, so I have twenty-eights, thirty-twos, and thirty-fours. They're old, but they're clean. Shall I turn my back?"

"You're not going to take me in?" Albert asked, sipping coffee that flowed down his throat and soothed his cold, half-naked, skinny body. "A bit down on my luck, I'm afraid. Thank you."

A moment later, he'd downed all his coffee, and was about to throw his empty cup in the bushes. Instead, he eyed her. "How come you're being so nice to me?"

" 'Cause I've been there." Linda patted her equipment belt and wondered how she was going to write up this report. "Tell you what." She clicked off her radio. "We need someone like you at the station."

"A job?" Albert asked, thinking fast. The new pants felt great. But work? He wasn't so sure. He didn't follow directions well.

"We need someone to keep the place clean – outside," Linda said, seeing the relief on his face. "And your name, for my files?"

"Bertrand," Albert said. Lying was his forté. "Bertrand Russell."

"We have a lot of ivy that's out of control, Mr. Russell."

"You're too kind, and I would love to help you. But first, I have one request. One very small request."

"We will provide food for you, if that's what you're worried about, Mr. Russell."

"Food – yes, a good idea. But first, may I trouble you for a small advance? A very small advance?"

"We're not stopping at any bar not under my watch. You're my responsibility now. Don't ruin it."

"Ah, this is not for spirits, fine or otherwise, ma'am. Truth is, I need to buy more mustache wax." Albert bowed his head and held his palms together. "I want to look spiffy my first day on the job."

From the Sheriff's Calls Section in the *Point Reyes Light*, May 31, 2012

MUIR WOODS: At 10:28 a.m. bicyclists were trying to catch a German Shepherd.

The Shepherd

"It wasn't my fault. You're the one who let Daisy go!" Thomas charged down a cul-de-sac following the dog, who looked back at the boys, hesitated a moment, and ran. Justin pulled his bike into a sharp turn, stopped in a cloud of dust, and took off after her.

Behind him, Thomas rode to the right of where Justin had gone and headed into the woods. Until a few minutes ago, they'd been having a great time house-sitting for a friend of his dad's, when Justin had let the damn dog out. Now Thomas was peddling hard into the darkness and silence. His calls for Daisy went unheeded and his bike wheels bogged down on the thick pine-covered path.

Ten minutes later, his calves burning and his throat sore from calling, he descended a gully and heard the sound of a creek. Then something else. Voices. He stopped.

"The way I see it, boss, if we wait until dark," a man said, a cap tucked low around his ears. "We can go in and out. No muss, no fuss. Done."

"Why wait at all?" the other man said. "This is Marin County. I bet all the doors are unlocked."

For a moment, Thomas wanted to catch them in the act and be a hero again. But the two of them were probably street savvy, maybe even armed, and he, at only five-eight, wasn't strong or smart enough. He backtracked up the steep hill, staying behind trees. Bringing his bike around a downed tree, the spokes caught in some twigs and he pulled, making a loud cracking sound.

"Did you hear that?" one of the thieves asked.

Thomas froze.

"Stay quiet," the other man said.

Thomas plastered himself against a downed tree. In the distance, he could hear Justin calling for Daisy.

He heard crackling in the underbrush. The closer it came, the louder it got. Leaving his precious mountain bike behind, Thomas leapt over fallen logs, ducked beneath low branches, and searched for the darkness that was the woods, the darkness that would hide him. He crouched deep behind some redwood trees, panting hard, sure the sound of his breath would give him away.

"These goddamn branches are cutting my legs. Let's get the hell out of here," one of the thieves said.

Thomas heard more crackling, louder now. From his hiding place, he heard heavy breathing.

"Don't you want the bike?" the voice asked. Thomas could see ankles through the trees, a man about to take his bike, which he'd bought with six months of hard work laying pipe for his dad. In the distance, Justin's voice faded away. Thomas felt small and vulnerable, but angry at himself for being such a coward. He lunged through a hole in the bushes and grabbed the man's ankle.

"What the hell?" the thief yelled. They both rolled down the hill. Thomas held onto that ankle as the guy thrashed his leg, trying to get free, trying to stop his fall.

Trees, duff, branches and pine needles scratched Thomas' face, but he wouldn't let go. A minute later, the two of them were at the bottom of a gully, half-in and half-out of a small creek, water dampening the back of Thomas' head, the other man sprawled a bit away, his ankle finally free.

"What the hell you doing, you little punk!" The thief stood over Thomas.

"You were trying to steal my bike, asshole." Thomas crouched and held his puny fists in front of him, feeling he ought to be able take on the world. He felt anything but. This fight was going to hurt.

The thief took a swing. Thomas ducked. His eyes fell on a broken limb and he brought it up and crouched. The thief saw it coming, put out his hand, grabbed it, and Thomas with it. Thomas felt the branch twist and let it go, dropped to the ground, and scrabbled away into the forest. The bigger man was on him. He slapped Thomas across the face. Feeling the sting, Thomas saw another branch, a bigger branch, and dug for it. The thief's hand hit a tree and Thomas clobbered him on the head. He fell.

Shivering from excitement and fear, Thomas felt for the guy's pulse. Alive, thank God. He stood up, brushed crap out of his hair, and tried to remember where his bike was. He backtracked up the hill to his old hiding place and heard the crack of twigs. He froze. The other guy? He didn't think he could handle the other guy. He was about to dive into the bushes when the crackles increased, louder and louder. The footsteps came faster and in a moment, the form was on him, but instead of skin and clothes, Thomas felt fur and scrabbled for the neck, for a collar. He held on. Daisy covered his face with kisses. Thomas heard Justin's call.

"Over here!" He buried his face in Daisy's neck.

Once Justin arrived, and Thomas had someone to hold Daisy, he went and retrieved his bike. They did not pass the thief on their way back, but Thomas knew where he was. As soon as they came to the road, they called the police. At least this time, he wasn't in trouble. He locked Daisy in the house, and thought for a moment of doing the same thing to Justin, but changed his mind and they had beers instead.

POINT REYES STATION: At 4:09 p.m. after trying on several pairs of shoes at the Cabaline, a woman walked out of the store wearing one.

A Pair of Shoes

"But why would a woman walk out of the store wearing only one shoe?" Mildred asked, spreading too much honey on her toast.

"It was one *pair* of shoes, Mildred." Fred closed the pages of the *Point Reyes Light*.

"You think they could have said 'pair,' then?" she asked, dripping honey on her hands. No matter how careful she was, she got honey on the table, her fingers, and in her hair. "What if the woman left her Manolo Blahniks at the store? Wouldn't the owner of the store be pleased about that?" She rushed to the sink.

"People coming to Point Reyes don't wear those kind of shoes." Fred eased into his almond bear claw from Busy Bee Bakery.

"I've seen them! I've seen them! Sometimes they wear those ridiculous shoes. I send them to the beach," Mildred crowed.

"You don't send anyone anywhere." Fred turned on the TV. It was baseball season and he was a happy man.

"I do too, Fred." Mildred cleared the breakfast dishes. "I see them all the time, lost tourists, stopping in the middle of Levee Road, their eyes big like windows, maps and those stupid phones in their hands."

"Not stupid phones, Mildred," Fred snapped. "Smart phones."

"Not too smart if you ask me. Anyway, they're lost. You can tell. And I'm out there, going twenty-five miles an hour, and I see them pull over, so I stop."

"You go twenty-five on Levee Road?"

"If you're going to keep interrupting me, Fred Rhinehart, you tell the story."

Fred groaned. Lincecum wasn't doing so well either.

"I saw a couple. In a Porsche or maybe it was a Tesla, nice wheels, and then ..."

Fred contemplated going in the back yard for a nap but she'd follow him and never stop talking.

"He was bald. She was blond. Half his age. I saw her shoes. Hot pink and high as hell." She giggled. "Anyway, they were looking for a beach, so I sent them to McClure's."

"Honey, that wasn't very nice." Fred watched Lincecum come off the mound. "Timmy, Timmy, what has happened to you?"

"Happened to me? Nothing," Mildred snorted. "Honestly, those women don't have any sense."

"You sent them a half-mile down a rough trail, dear."

"So? The man didn't have any sense either, driving in a sports car, bald, without a hat."

Fred would know. He'd had spots burned off the top of his head and he hadn't liked that one bit. Now he only went into the sun with SPF 65 and a big pork pie hat. "My dad would say you were being unkind."

"Coming to the beach in high heels is just plain silly." She reached for a beauty magazine and flipped to a pair of heels with rhinestones and T-straps. "You think these would look great on me, Fred?"

Fred, deep in thought as to which of the pitchers would next come out of the bullpen, had no thoughts about his wife's shoes. If she would just leave, he could access his hidden stash of beer.

"You're not listening!" She slammed the magazine onto the kitchen table.

Fred jumped. His heart, if only his heart, could take these outbursts. He fell back onto the sofa and reached for his chest. "Mildred, please. *Please* don't startle me like that."

"But you didn't answer my question about the shoes."

"Honey," he reached into his pocket for his wallet, hoping he still had his hundred. He passed it over. He'd kept it for something important. "Take this," he flicked the bill. "Clean. New. Buy yourself a new pair at the Cabaline."

"Like the high heels?"

"Whatever you want," he said, eager to get back to the game.

FROM THE SHERIFF'S CALLS SECTION IN THE *POINT REYES LIGHT*,
JUNE 7, 2012

LAGUNITAS: At 9:49 a.m. a second grader had
a nosebleed.

Playing Cards

"See? See? I'm not the only one," Alice crowed. She looked out the window at Lagunitas Creek. They were staying at Grandma's sister's place in the woods.

"Your nosebleeds started when you were a lot younger than that, child," Mildred snorted, and handed over a pack of cards. "Now, deal."

Alice peeled off the cellophane. "I'm not so different after all, am I, Grandma?" She dealt one card to each of them and waited for Grandma's bet.

"Two cards. Not one," Mildred instructed. "You want to learn Texas hold em? You start by dealing correctly."

"I want to learn enough to win." Alice folded her legs under her. "I don't get nosebleeds when I'm with you, Grandma."

"Of course not." Mildred adjusted her glasses and peeked at her hole cards. That Alice gave too much away. "So, anyone in particular you want to beat? Girls? Boys? Best friends? Did someone hurt you? You want me to call their mothers?"

"Oh Grandma, no," Alice sighed. It would be a good thing, in one way, to have the upper hand once, but using her 80-year-old Grandma in that way seemed like poor form.

"So, who is it?" Mildred didn't like the ways these kids pushed her granddaughter around. She'd give them a piece of her mind. "Alice? Don't you want to bet?"

Alice threw down a quarter. They had a limit of a dollar – and Grandma, who didn't need the money, always won. So Alice kept her bets low.

"The flop, Alice. Three cards, face up."

Alice did what she was told. Seemed a bit odd to her, showing all those cards.

"Grandpa doesn't play, does he?" Alice perused her cards and jiggled her change.

"He's missing out. He misses out on all kinds of things. He loves baseball too much – and that dang recliner of his."

They heard a snore and both laughed.

"So, what is it that's bugging you?" Mildred put down her hole cards, face down, and looked at Alice.

"Girls. Stuff. You know." Alice stared out the window. When she grew up she'd have a house that smelled clean. Grandma's smelled musty and old. White lacy doilies covered everything.

"You're not paying attention, dear."

"It's just that I don't want to tell you exactly who or what is bugging me." Alice suppressed a sniffle. If Grandma kept at it, she'd be done for. Crying was for eight-year-olds, not teens like she was. She dealt another card, face up.

"I won't tell anyone." Mildred eyed her new shoes. Even over swollen ankles, her feet looked beautiful in rhinestones. "Beth Ann? Margaret Sue? A boy?"

"They're not boys anymore, Grandma. They're bigger than you and me." Alice wished she knew what Grandma had for hole cards before betting another quarter.

"Bigger than me? Who cares how big they are? They're babies in my book," Mildred sniffed, calling her bet.

"Which makes me?" Alice asked, worried. Did she really look as young as she felt?

"You're a lovely young woman," Mildred said. "Now deal up the river, the fifth community card." Mildred bet fifty cents, Alice folded, and Mildred scooped the pot. "So, you want to play cards with this Matthew?"

"His name's not Matthew. It's Mark," Alice said, surprised she'd given away her secret. "Mark Adamson." On the last name at least, she lied. "He's cute."

"And for that, you want to beat him at cards?" Mildred adjusted her pearls and watched the clock. She would have to put Fred's supper on and soon. He was always in a bad mood if dinner was late. "Stay cool, and don't give anything away."

"But the other kids get me so upset." Alice gazed at Grandma's pile of money and her own dwindling stack of quarters.

"If you like this Mark guy, let him win. That's how I met your Grandpa."

"You did not."

"Alice, I played cards in high school. Only girls weren't supposed to play, much less bet."

"That's not fair," Alice grumbled.

"Grandpa and the other boys, they played poker behind the school. They smoked cigarettes too." Mildred snickered.

"When was this, 1948?"

"1945. During the war. The boys were all joining up. 'Cept these boys were still in high school. They said the soldiers played poker all the time and they wanted to be ready."

"And Grandpa?" Alice asked. "What about Grandpa?"

"I was the best player in the school. We played every day. Most of the boys were just angry at me, but Grandpa, he wasn't deterred. 'I'll win, you'll see,' he boasted, and we played."

"Girls can do anything these days, you know." Alice stared out the window. Grandma was always going off on her stories and meanwhile, she wasn't getting any better at poker. She dealt the next hand, a hole card for Grandma, one for herself, then another each.

"My dear doubting Alice." Mildred peeked at her cards, then looked over at the man snoring in the next room. "I let him win, but I was better, way better. We married that summer."

"That was quick." Alice was horrified. She wanted a date with Mark, but didn't want to marry him.

"That's the way it was back then," Mildred continued. "We had a few weeks together and he went over. Oh, Alice, I was so happy when he came back. We didn't play cards anymore after that. We got busy having children – your mom came along, and then ..."

"Grandma, you think if I let Mark win, he'll ask me out?" Alice asked suddenly, wanting life to be simple.

"Worth a try. Flatter the guy. Didn't hurt me any, honey."

"And if I get a nosebleed, on my first date?"

"Bring plenty of tissue, dear." Mildred listened to the music her husband made with his snoring. "All these years of marriage, honey, and it all started with poker. Now, deal."

From the Sheriff's Calls Section in the *Point Reyes Light*, June 14, 2012

INVERNESS: At 4:17 p.m. this newspaper reported that a woman who identified herself as a character in a fictional column – loosely inspired by the sheriff's calls – printed the week before had been calling the office, yelling and making threats, such as "You're going to get what's coming to you."

They're Coming After Me

"Oh dear." Mildred pressed her hand to her chest. "My word." She peered into the pot on the stove. She had been canning pickles, her favorite, but it didn't seem like fun anymore.

Fred grunted. The baseball game was about to start and he'd been planning on a quiet afternoon.

"You going to your sister's?" he asked, not that Mildred had mentioned it, but if he could get her to leave the house, it was worth a try.

"I can't go anywhere now." Mildred pulled back the curtains and peered out the window. "They'll see me."

"Who will see you, dear?"

She shuddered. "Last week, I was out for my morning walk with Angel. She was barking like crazy – she gets so excited, you know. I heard this commotion. Pat Grandy – you know her from church – was having a fight with a neighbor and accused him of stealing her power."

Fred nodded his head. He had no idea what his wife was talking about. "Go on."

"Anyway, they were shouting something awful, so I called the police. Next thing I know they arrive, there's a huge bang, and some poor guy's being wheeled into the EMT van. If I hadn't called the cops, Fred, he wouldn't be in the hospital." She paced the small kitchen.

"How do they know it was you, dear?"

"Of course, they know it was me. How many other little old ladies were out on that street with a little dog? Inverness is such a small town."

"I'm sure everything will be all right." If she would just stop talking, he could hear the lineup.

"Oh God, I promise, *promise*, never to call the cops again." She peered out the front window again, then pulled the shades. On second thought, she pulled all the shades in the house.

"Calling the cops is not a sin, sweetheart. You know how people are around here, getting upset about everything. You want some tea?"

"Me? Tea? Not now, Fred. They could be here any minute." She spun on her heels. "You think they put old ladies like me in jail?"

"You're not an old lady, Mildred."

"Wanna bet?" Mildred contemplated telling him how old he was, but it was Father's Day. "Did Janet call?" She thought a moment. "Hattie?" It had been so very long.

"I only wish." Fred pressed mute on the remote. He hated ads. "And your sister?"

"Even if I could go out," she sniffed, "she's not home."

"Ah." Fred was doomed. Chatty Cathy would be with him all afternoon. No beer, no chips, no fun.

"Sometimes I do wonder. You think I'm losing it?" Mildred patted her blue-rinse hair and checked herself in her kitchen mirror, the one over the sink balanced precariously between a can of beans and a bag of marshmallows.

"My sweet girl." Fred peered at his wife through his half-height spectacles. She was looking a little fuzzy, but everything looked kind of fuzzy these days. "Sit next to me then." He patted a place on the sofa that wasn't covered with too much dog fur. "Take a load off."

Mildred paused, not yet ready to settle. It was only a matter of time. She looked out the window at Tomales Bay. The wind was up. "You think I should go out of town for a bit?"

"Sweetheart, sweetheart," Fred cooed. "Lincecum's pitching. Your boyfriend."

"He's a little young for me," she sniffed.

"Maybe he's a little young for baseball." The season was moving along and Timmy hadn't been much of a star. "If it was me," he continued, "I'd just forget about what was in the paper, dear. It's just a newspaper."

"Don't tell the editor that!"

"Honey, people do get confused sometimes, even you," Fred suggested.

"Me? About what? I never get confused."

"Then perhaps you can make us some popcorn?"

"Popcorn? Does it come in a bag or a box or a packet? Then what? Oven, stove, open fire? You remember where you put it?"

"Forget about the popcorn." Fred smiled. "You're my little sweetie-pie, perfect in every way. Now, sit. I've got a spot right here."

Mildred sat, but she was not satisfied. The Giants lost the game.

CHILENO VALLEY: At 7:28 p.m. a man reported
that his 28-year-old ex-girlfriend kept harass-
ing him and his new girlfriend and was refusing to pick up things from his house.

I Like 'Em Hot

"And sir, what would you like us to do about it?" Linda rolled her eyes
toward her boss. It had been a long day.

Walter was watering his ficus plant. Most of his plants had died, but he
was proud of this one. It shadowed his desk and would reach the ceiling in a
year, if he was good with it. "What's the problem, Officer Kettleman?"

She covered the phone with her hand. "Someone is asking me to mediate
a romantic comedy."

"Ma'am?" the caller cleared his throat. "Make her take her stuff out of
my house."

You make her, Linda wanted to say. It was you who let her move there in
the first place. She tried to remember where it said in the Police Handbook
that cops are supposed to take care of unhappy girlfriends.

"I can't move on with my life. She's got her stuff all over – her hairbrush is
in the sink, her pots and pans are in the oven, and she's got a twenty-pound
turkey in the fridge. I can't put that stuff out on the street, if that's what
you're thinking."

"Have you asked her to move out?" Linda was glad she hadn't made the
foolish decision to live with Frank. Now she'd be out on the street instead of
taking care of Mom. Wasn't it time to call it a day? She was beat.

"Of course! I've called her ten times. I've also texted her, sent her emails,
and I talked to her boss. Even Phoebe called her."

"Phoebe? Who's Phoebe?" Sooner or later, this caller would figure out she was playing him and Walter would not be pleased.

"Uh, my new girlfriend."

"Sir." Linda was adamant about this point. Lovers, even jilted lovers, had no place calling anyone's boss. Walter didn't know what she did at night and she certainly wasn't going to tell him.

The caller's voice rose. "Phoebe! Please, no! Don't throw the turkey out the window!"

Linda heard shouting, then silence. She bet this Romeo had a whole circle of girlfriends, changing them as often as pants. Reminded her again of why she didn't date.

"Officer?" The caller was out of breath. "Could you come over? I think she just broke the sink."

Linda grabbed her equipment belt and headed out to Chileno Valley. Yesterday's calls included livestock on the loose, bicyclists blocking the road, someone kicked by a horse, and a dead cow. She decided that today was dumb boyfriends day and switched on her siren.

It wasn't far, about thirty minutes. She pulled up in front of a farmhouse in a cloud of dust. The place was old, with wraparound porches, and it was in the sun. For a moment, Linda wanted to live there, it was so pretty. She walked to the front door, dusted off her regulation shoes, and pressed the bell.

She heard crashing sounds, tested the door knob, called out, and entered. A full coffee cup and saucer came whizzing through the air, missing her head by inches and splattering the wall with coffee.

"What's going on here?" Linda commanded.

"When you asked me to move in, Dylan, you didn't say Jennifer's stuff was still here!" a young woman shouted. "Why the hell didn't you bag it all up? Kick her ass and all her crap out of here? I'll do it if you can't."

"Phoebe, please, calm down," Dylan pleaded.

Linda shouting, "Police! Police!" entered the living room where a large picture window opened up onto a field. Outside cows munched contentedly. Inside, it was a different story.

Phoebe, a blond with dark roots, held an extra-large Hefty bag and was tossing pillows, books, and papers into the bag. Broken bottles were strewn on the floor and chairs were overturned. She was wiping everything off the tables like a bulldozer. Into the bag went a crystal vase; Linda heard it shatter. Another woman sat quietly on the couch, doing her nails, watching TV.

"Hey! Some of those are mine, Phoebe!" Dylan grabbed papers off tables in front of her fast-moving hands.

"Ma'am," Linda commanded.

Phoebe didn't hear her or didn't want to. She moved faster. "We want to make a home here. How can we do that with all her crap in my house?"

"Your house? This is my house." Dylan reached for the bag.

"Dylan, get out of the way." Phoebe grabbed his laptop.

"Officer, please! Do something," he pleaded. "She's out of control."

Linda, knowing she shouldn't touch perpetrators unless she was cuffing them, put her bulk in front of Phoebe's thin frame. Phoebe looked at her with stunned red-rimmed eyes. "Stop ma'am. Stop now. Please."

Phoebe held her hands in front of her, her fingers twitching, and burst into tears.

Dylan put down his books and newspapers. "I'm sorry darling. Jennifer, she just takes her time. She'll leave. Just give her a minute."

The woman sitting on the couch let out a laugh.

Linda thought Dylan looked familiar. She'd seen his picture in the paper. "Heading to Chico in a few months, then?"

"I'm coming with him," Phoebe added, all smiles, the trash bag at her feet. "Gotta go somewhere special. This place is way too provincial for me." She wiped her eyes, held onto Dylan's arm. "We're engaged."

"You bet, darling." Dylan wrapped his arms around Phoebe's waist.

"But there's a small problem." Linda gestured to the other woman.

"Jennifer? Time to go, dear," Dylan said.

"Not until I'm good and ready," Jennifer replied, getting comfortable.

Dylan shrugged his shoulders, then set some chairs right. "She'll leave in a few minutes, no worries. Right, Jen? Good. Everything's back to normal. Thanks, officer."

Linda pulled him aside. Phoebe was filling another bag. "Don't you think she's a little hot-tempered?"

"Phoebe's Italian," he whispered, "I like 'em hot."

"Well, Dylan, date who you like, live like you want, but please, keep the cops out of it, okay?"

"You bet, officer. Thanks for your help."

Linda walked out. She was between the front door and the cruiser when she heard the shot. She ran back inside.

Dylan was lying on the floor, holding his leg which was bleeding all over the rug. "Good thing she missed my heart, hunh?" he asked, grimacing through the pain. Phoebe was holding a pocket pistol, gripping it with all her strength. Her hands shook. She pointed the barrel at Linda, at the picture window, and at Jennifer on the couch. Then she turned and aimed it at Dylan.

"He wouldn't make her move out," she said and fired.

From the Sheriff's Calls Section in the *Point Reyes Light*, June 21, 2012

INVERNESS PARK: At 3:37 a.m. a woman staying at her parents' house reports that the downstairs tenant often played his piano very late at night or very early in the morning, like at 4 a.m.

A Little Night Music

"It's not like I don't like Chopin's 'Nocturnes'," Margaret Philips said over the phone to the deputy. "But at four in the morning, I can't bear it."

"You want someone to come over?" Linda nursed her third cup of coffee. These graveyard shifts were killing her.

"And make more commotion? I think not," Margaret snapped. "Don't bug me, bug him. I've got to get some sleep. Goodnight," she said, and hung up.

Bleary-eyed and shuffling in her bedroom slippers, Margaret, two weeks after her 63rd birthday, slipped back to bed. As soon as she put her head down, she heard the tinkling of Mr. Jacobsen's piano from downstairs. She tried to hear his telephone. Cops didn't call? Why the hell didn't the cops call? Another report to the Sheriff's Department wasn't going to help her any. She needed to take action.

She put on her pink robe, the new one she'd just bought from Saks, and thought a moment. Weaponless, she felt vulnerable. She walked into the kitchen and picked up her cast-iron fry pan. If that doggone Mr. Jacobsen wasn't going to listen to her, at least she could bang some sense into him. Disturbing the peace, indeed.

She crept down the back stairs, waking her cat Hedges who slept in a ball on a patch of blanket by the front door. He liked to sleep outdoors, winter, summer, spring and fall, even in the rain. She wished she had his ability to sleep.

Just outside the door to her parents' rental unit, Margaret fingered a clump of keys and knocked a few times. Now he was doing scales! She almost screamed.

"Mr. Jacobsen? Mr. Jacobsen?" She knocked louder and hearing nothing, opened the door. "It's Margaret from upstairs. Hello? Hello? Are you going to stop that infernal racket?"

David Jacobsen, lead soloist for the San Francisco Symphony, felt that his fingers were on fire. He blazed through the scales – up, down, faster, faster, the notes resonating one on top of the other as he used the pedals. He loved the pedals! At the top of one of the scales, he held the note, and heard something. Something not music. He paused. Nothing. At the bottom of the scales, something again. Oh dear. If he missed another note, he'd never be ready for tomorrow's concert.

Was someone at the door? At this hour? He turned to see his landlady in the living room, wearing pink and holding something dark. What was she doing here? He often practiced without his glasses and his living room was fuzzy. He put them on in a hurry.

"Ah, Ms. Philips," he cooed. "Good evening. You enjoy Chopin? Excellent. Pour yourself a glass of wine. I'm about to start the next piece."

"Music, at this hour?" Margaret was dumbfounded. "What do you think you're doing? I'm trying to get some sleep."

"Chopin makes for great dreams." He played a trill with his right hand. "Or would you prefer something else? A little Mozart, perhaps?"

Thrown off her game, Margaret wasn't sure how to talk to this idiot. "No, no Mozart. No Chopin. No more goddamn piano."

"Ah," David muttered. "I thought it was too late to play the tuba, but if you prefer?"

"No goddamn tuba! No music of any kind!" Margaret raised the cast-iron pan behind her back. Didn't this guy have any sense? "Again, sir, let me explain. We sleep at night. Play piano during the day. You understand?"

"Ah." David tickled high c. "My piano needs a tune, don't you think?" He'd heard every word, but like his mother taught him, an argument wouldn't start if he didn't respond.

"I called the cops, you know. You don't listen. I said …"

"You want a ticket to my next concert, Ms. Philips? I'll buy you dinner at Le Jardinière across the street. They make the best soup."

"Mr. Jacobsen. Let me remind you. This house is a shared building. Think of others for a change. When you make noise, I can't sleep."

"San Francisco Symphony doesn't think my music is noise, ma'am, Michael Tilson Thomas says …"

"I don't bloody care what he says. Please, Mr. Jacobsen, have some consideration."

"Tickets, front row, orchestra, bring your husband."

"I don't have a husband!" She waved her pan. "Not since he ran off with that hippie redhead from Bolinas."

"You hungry?" David asked in his calm, soothing voice. "I make great omelettes."

Margaret was going to kill him over that voice. Reminded her of that goddamn Flores.

"Fresh eggs from Sun Farms. You brought the pan. Good. Sun Farms butter too. Orange juice, fresh squeezed. Blue Bottle coffee?"

"I don't drink coffee."

"Ah, tea, then. Whatever you prefer. What's your favorite music, your favorite tune?" He stifled the word "dear." He could keep practicing if only she'd calm down. He kept messing up this one phrase, three 32nd notes and a long rest.

"Rock and roll," Margaret said suddenly, wanting to insult him.

" 'Rock Me Baby,' 'Rock of Ages,' or 'Singing in the Rain'?" He played the melody.

Oh dear God, thought Margaret. She took a seat on his tiny red-roses-covered sofa. "'Singing in the Rain,'" she said, dreaming of the day when Flores had proposed. It had been pouring, no one was coming to the restaurant, and when he entered, holding roses, he was singing that tune. She put down her fry pan. "If you will, thank you."

"As many times as you like, dear," Mr. Jacobsen said and started to play.

FROM THE SHERIFF'S CALLS SECTION IN THE *POINT REYES LIGHT*,
JUNE 21, 2012

STINSON BEACH: At 11:42 p.m. someone dialed
911 and was heard in the background saying,
"He's not your son."

Dreaming of Penélope Cruz

"Well, he's not." Arlene Berkowitz pulled on her dishwashing gloves.

Calvin, a man in his forties, deep in debt and out of a job, still felt it was important that he continue with his fatherly duties. Arlene's words stung, but ... he picked up a dropped pillow and set it on the couch, at an angle, just the way she liked. "You don't have to be so negative."

Nicky, a fifteen-year-old boy, changed the channel on the TV. Nothing was on. He was too hyped up to go to bed. He hoped Penélope Cruz would come back on Jay Leno; she was one hot number, and he'd never tire of gazing at her. Meanwhile, Mom was still doing dishes. It took her longer and longer to do them, but she wouldn't let him help.

"Nicky?" Arlene put the last dish away. "Did you see my cell phone? Someone called nine-one-one. Did you sit on it?"

Calvin didn't want to say, but it had been him. He felt if he called 911, maybe the cops would come and make Arlene stop arguing. Now it seemed everything was messed up again. "Nicky, it's a school night. Get up to bed."

Nicky put up with Calvin. He was an okay guy but he wasn't his dad. So he was used to the standard directions and ignored them, as he had for years.

"Nicky!" Arlene's voice rose. "Bedtime!" Nicky, hearing the real boss in the family, set down the remote and headed up the stairs. Maybe he'd be lucky and dream about Penélope Cruz again. Just as he reached the door to his bedroom, voices rose from downstairs.

"How's that job search coming, Calvin?" Having inherited money, Arlene didn't need to work, but that didn't matter. She didn't like slackers and Calvin was a slacker. They'd been together five years and that was enough. She dried her hands on a dishtowel and watched him watch TV.

"I love him, you know." Calvin popped through the channels. "He does well with me. He's a good kid."

"That's all well and good Calvin, but he's got a dad."

"In Boston. What good is a dad if he sees him once or twice a year?"

"They spend summers together on the Cape. You know that."

"Summers? Summers are nothing like day to day. Kids need their dads. It's guy stuff. I didn't have a dad around when I was a kid." Calvin looked up the stairs to Nicky's bedroom.

"You told me that before, but that's no excuse ..." Arlene didn't want to be mean, but he'd been out of work two years now.

"I do – I mean, I am trying." Calvin stared into his beer. It was stale and lifeless, like he was. A general contractor, he was used to the feel of a job, the bustling guys, barking orders, all the paperwork. Now, knee deep in the recession, no one was building anything anymore. "I'll make some more calls."

"You've got a month. I have to move on."

"What do you care, Arlene? House is paid for, I do all the yard work, and I'm here for Nicky when you go to your endless meetings about the Bolinas Lagoon. Kind of taken a long time, don't you think?"

"It's not my goddamn fault they keep ordering more reports." Arlene shoved the chairs against the wall making the china rattle.

"It's not my fault we're in the middle of a recession either." Calvin slipped on his boots. "I'll be back in a little while."

"Don't you think you're being a little hasty?"

"Hasty about what? I'm only going to the Sand Dollar for a pop."

"That's what you said the last time and you were gone until two a.m."

Calvin grunted. On this point, she was right. He'd met someone at the bar – and they'd connected. It was dreamlike, wonderful, she loved him and everything he did. His skin tingled at the thought. "You know she moved to Hawaii."

"And tonight? You going to Hawaii too?"

"I'm not like that. I repented, and apologized. What else do you want me to do, Arlene? Bleed? Come with me, then, if it's so important to you."

"But Nicky, he'll be alone."

"He's a big kid now. He can take care of himself." Calvin held the front door open.

"Sometimes you say just the right thing, even if he's not your son." They closed the door behind them.

Upstairs, Nicky watched the taillights disappear down the long driveway. He picked up his iPhone. Celeste was home, she was available, and she did look a little like Penélope Cruz.

NICASIO: At 9:31 a.m. a woman reported that marijuana growers may be tapping into her water source, as they had done in the past.

The Secret Life of Plants

"My water. They're stealing my water," the voice spoke through the receiver.

"And how long has this been going on, ma'am?" Linda asked and watched Walter wipe down his ficus plant. It had grown well over his head and he was standing on a steep stool. She was imagining the entry in the Sheriff's Calls Section of the paper: "Sheriff engulfed by ficus plant, breaks leg."

It had been a long night, but she'd had two cups of coffee and was feeling frisky.

"They've hooked into the ag well at the back corner of my property. Hoses running all over the place and they're not mine."

"Everybody safe, ma'am?" Linda asked, automatically reacting. She'd been so worried about her last call about someone stealing power and the electrocution. Dan was lucky he was all right.

Walter was now leaning back in his chair, reading *The Secret Life of Plants*.

"What's your address?" Linda asked. She took it down, collected fresh batteries for her walkie-talkie, got a pool car, and headed out. Walter was still on her about keeping her radio on; the last time her batteries died he didn't believed her. She rolled the AAAs in her palm, and as soon as she gained Nicasio Valley Road, turned on her siren. Neighbors didn't care for the sound much in town.

She found the place, a ramshackle ranch spread out on a lot of land. Chickens fanned out to greet her. A woman in a faded blue-jean dress waved from a large front window, hopped into her Ford F-350, and headed down a dirt road. Linda followed.

She reviewed her tool kit as she tracked the white truck. Taser ready, sidearm cleaned and polished, hairspray tucked in her purse. Five minutes later, the truck pulled up to an irrigation pond, spun, and stopped. Two white pit bulls jumped down from the cab, followed by the gal in blue.

"Name's Dorothy. It's right here." Dorothy pointed to her irrigation pump, a small manifold, and two white hoses leading into the trees. "I'd never use white hoses, Officer. They don't blend well with the landscape."

"I'll take it from here." Linda figured she'd find an empty camp, a smoldering fire, and an abandoned tent. The growers were a shy bunch and never hung around. They followed the hoses into the forest.

Deep in the redwoods, they heard the sound of barking and eventually entered a clearing where hundreds of six-foot-tall marijuana plants reached for the sky. It was an entire field of green. A million dollars? Maybe two? Linda reached for her radio.

"Don't. Not yet." Dorothy rushed to Linda's side. "It's beautiful. I've never seen such healthy plants."

"It's a weed, ma'am," Linda said, and before Dorothy could laugh at her little joke, she added, "and it's illegal."

"Don't I know it." The two white hoses were connected to irrigation pipes that disappeared into soft brown earth.

Walter will be pleased I found such a large grow, Linda thought. A flash of movement caught her eye. Two bulky guys in overcoats rushed out of the woods.

"It's not what you think," one of them said, carrying a shovel. "Medical marijuana, medicinal use only."

"For you and your buddy?" Linda asked. "Must be a pretty sick bunch." She'd heard of these guys with their endless stories.

"We supply to Aegis Living, you know the old people's home out of San Rafael? The one near the Civic Center?" the burly guy asked. "And other old people, patients suffering from cancer treatments. I have a list. You want to see it?"

"So." Linda grabbed for her notebook. "Your names, please?" She licked the tip of her pencil, a contractor's short one that her dad had given her. If only he were near her now. If she had to, she'd use it for a weapon, in the eyes? How close did she have to get?

"James Watson and Francis Crick," the burly one said. "I'm Watson."

"Right then," Linda answered, "physicists. You guys study at Harvard or Cambridge? Licenses, please."

The thin one rolled his eyes, then tipped his head to the larger guy. "I'm Francis Crick."

"Ah." Linda tapped her radio three times. That was the signal she shared with Walter. "Then, Mr. Crick, your license, please. Don't make me ask again."

She saw Watson sidle up to Dorothy.

"What'd you call her for?" he asked.

"You haven't been giving me my cut."

Dorothy knew these guys? They were upon her before she could unbuckle her weapon.

"I've never liked injections much myself, sister, but I bet you'll like this." The burly guy said, holding up a syringe.

Crick pulled out a gun.

"Wait! Wait!" Linda blurted. "Medicinal marijuana it is," she stuttered. "Let me file a report. I'll make sure to keep ATF away from your land, Dorothy. Seems like a good idea, helping people."

The two men were surprised with her sudden cooperation and let their attention lapse for a moment. Linda spun on her regulation boots, knocked the syringe out of the burly man's hand and kicked the other man in the balls.

She bent to grab the syringe, stuck it in Watson's neck, then ran after Francis who was doubled over and clutching his stomach. She smashed her foot down on his instep, spun him around, grabbed his gun, and cuffed him. She turned, too late, to see Dorothy loose the dogs on her. She aimed the gun toward the dog rushing her. "Call them off or they're dead!" She pulled back the safety and aimed high. Before she squeezed off a second round, Dorothy screamed for the dogs to stop.

Linda cuffed her. Satisfied she had two cuffed prisoners, two dogs chained to their master and a drug dealer out cold. Her jiu-jitsu training had come in handy. Hands trembling, she dialed Walter, but didn't have to. His truck pulled up in a cloud of dust at the edge of the field and he came running.

"Got them all? Jesus Christ, Linda! How'd you do this?"

"Some training at the Academy paid off, don't you think?" she said, feeling better about her job than she had in months. Dad would be proud.

Walter whistled when he saw the crop. "My mom could use some. The local shops closed down and she's desperate for pain meds. I'll just take this little bit." He reached for a plant.

"I'll do it for you, boss." Linda tore the tops off a dozen plants. "Guess there's a lot you can learn from plants," she said, as Walter, stuffing his own pockets, called for backup on his radio.

MOUNT TAM: At 10:36 a.m. rangers reported
one of their kind missing.

One of Our Kind

"One of their kind of what?" Mildred dried her last dish and placed it on
the rack. "I swear to God, Fred, the sheriffs around here are a weird bunch."

"What was that, honey?" Fred, on his hands and knees, was digging under the sink for a wrench. The faucet had sprung a leak and he was trying
to turn off the water. He used to fit under the sink; now, he wasn't so sure.
Looked kinda small in there.

"One of their kind of officers?" Mildred giggled. "One of their kind of
dogs? Why can't they say?"

"Just a minute, dear." Fred tried not to hit himself on the kitchen counter on his way up. The cold-water turn-off valve was stuck and he couldn't
budge it. Mildred's sister was coming over in an hour for Sunday brunch and
without water, it would not be a pretty sight. He stood up with difficulty and
looked down upon his thin, little wife.

"If they only said what they meant." Mildred stuffed the *Light* into the
recycle bin. "I mean, do I call the editor, the sheriff or those Mount Tam
rangers? Their kind, indeed."

"I have to turn off the water at the street and get a new valve," Fred said.

"You're going to leave me high and dry?" Mildred held her hands up to
her frilly apron, the one covered with yellow roses her mother had made
when she'd been ten. "Fill a couple of pots and pans, for God's sake. I still
have to make my pies."

A few minutes later, Fred headed to the hardware store, with his list. In
his early days, he had done some plumbing, spending hours looking for

washers in Uncle Duane's supply shop, but now he felt a little lost. None of the hardware stores had bins of washers anymore. What did people do? Throw out perfectly decent faucets? What a waste. Didn't anyone know anything these days?

He was in kind of a mood by the time he pulled up to Building Supply and squeezed his Buick between two SUVs blocking the road. Town was full of tourists, slowing him down.

"I'm in a hurry here!" he shouted to a middle-aged couple, dressed in plaid, staring into their iPhones. They jumped when he drew up to turn. He nosed up on the curb, knocked over a wheelbarrow, and, satisfied, turned off the engine. It was about time he talked to Doc McClintock, who ran the store, and tell him to keep his junk out of the parking lot.

Once inside, he realized he'd left his list and had to go back to the car. Good thing he forgot to lock it. The keys were still in the ignition. He grabbed both.

"One of those sink valves," he said to the blonde kid behind the counter, the blond kid who, Fred was sure, had never spent an afternoon under a kitchen sink. It didn't help matters when he had to ask twice and the clerk still looked puzzled.

"What are you trying to fix, sir?"

"My sink! I'm trying to fix my sink. I turned off the water. You got one of those valve thingies?"

"Uh. Okay. Let's take a look." The clerk walked Fred to the plumbing section. "Kitchen or bathroom? What kind of sink?"

"Oh, for Heaven's sake I'll know it when I see it."

The clerk, no fool, left Fred to peruse the items on the shelves and went to get Doc. "I asked him what he wanted, boss, but he wouldn't say."

Fred stood in front of a display, totally confused. They had moved everything!

"Good morning, Fred," Doc came over and extended a hand. "What can I do for you?"

Fred jerked his thumb. "*He* didn't know what I wanted."

"I see. Under the sink again, then?"

"Mildred's sister's coming over," Fred sniffed. "And I had to turn off the water."

"Trying to earn a Mr. Popularity prize today?"

"I'd rather stay here all afternoon." Fred sighed. He had always loved tools. "Shut-off valve under the kitchen sink is jammed and I can't turn it."

"Ah." Doc steered him to the valves and faucets. "You've had problems before, as I recall." He gave Jason a wink.

Jason stood by, impatient to call his girlfriend Sophie. If he was lucky, he could get over the hill and see her in twenty minutes.

"Problem is, we're closing early today," Doc said. "Promised the wife I'd take her shopping in Petaluma."

"What if I need something else?" Fred asked, hands full of pipe clamps, plumber's putty, and assorted screws.

"Have Jason fix it for you."

Jason stood up, at attention. Sophie wouldn't be pleased if he was late again.

"Bet he doesn't know a thing about plumbing."

"He bends like a pretzel and loves to get under a sink," Doc said.

"He's too young," Fred said.

"He needs the money, he's dependable, and he's fast." Doc pressed the basket of parts into Jason's hand.

"And if he fails?" Fred asked.

"Here's my cell," Doc grinned. "Give me an excuse not to go shopping."

"Right here, sir," Jason said. "And how about a new faucet? You'll like it. One handle."

"My two faucets have worked well for fifty years," Fred snorted. He'd wanted to show Mildred he still had it. Now what was he going to do?

"Time's are a-changing, and I'm a-closing." Doc led them to the register. "Put it on his account, Jason." He shot a glance at Fred. "He's one of our kind, and don't worry, he'll fix everything." And with that he was off.

A minute later, Jason and Fred walked out of the store into a bright afternoon.

"You sure know how to park this Buick, sir," Jason said with a grin. "I'll direct you out."

"No need." Fred backed up into a set of trash cans.

"Good job," Jason said. "Now perhaps you'll let me? I would love to drive a stick. Sit back and enjoy the ride. Column shift? Great." He shoved it into first. Maybe later, after he fixed the faucet, he could borrow the old car. Sophie would love it.

From the Sheriff's Calls Section in the *Point Reyes Light*,
July 5, 2012

MARSHALL: At 9:30 a.m. someone called to ask if it was legal for a dog to ride in the front passenger seat.

Trixie

"You didn't have to call the cops, Grandma." Alice stared out the window. It was early and the wind was blowing hard, kicking up whitecaps on Tomales Bay. They were staying at Mildred's sister's house on the water, while Mildred's house was being fumigated.

"It doesn't seem safe to me." Mildred clutched her alligator purse close to her chest.

"Grandma, the cops don't care." Alice was trying to decide whether she should call Beth Ann while they were in town for Grandma's hair appointment. Only Beth Ann was always busy. "Are you ready yet?" It had taken hours for her to get this far.

"Put Trixie in the back yard. I don't want her near my feet while I drive."

"Grandma, we discussed this last night. I have my learner's permit. I need to practice. You hold Trixie and I'll drive."

To Mildred, Alice was getting a bit of an attitude – and at such a young age too. "Leave the dog at home."

"But Grandma." Alice scratched Trixie behind the ears. The little cocker arched its back, came closer for more.

"Forget her, Alice, and step on it. Doris doesn't like me to be late."

Alice grabbed the keys and took a look at Trixie, the only thing that made her smile these days. She had planned to take her to the Giacomini wetlands. Now what? She couldn't disappoint those warm brown eyes.

"I'll be just a minute." She disappeared out the back door. With a kind word, she tucked Trixie under her jacket on the floor behind the passenger seat, told her to be quiet, and they were off.

There was a lot of traffic going south on Route One. A bunch of sports cars went by with their tops down, and they were going way too fast. One was passing! Across the double yellow line! Dear God. Alice tightened her grip on the wheel and stepped on the brake as the other car went by.

"Jesus, girl, don't drive like a maniac." Mildred held her hands up to her face. "Easy on that pedal. You're giving me heart palpitations."

"Sorry." Alice answered. Driving was nerve-wracking. A line of cars was growing behind them, and some of them were honking. The road dropped off sharply on the right to the water, while MGs sped by on the opposite lane. She wished she were still at home, sitting in the window seat and petting Trixie. She felt a tickle in her nose and closed her eyes a fraction of a second.

"Eyes on the road!" Mildred barked. "If you are going to sneeze, pull over. Jesus! Didn't your dad teach you anything?"

Alice pulled over as soon as she could, her hands trembling. About twenty cars sped by.

"You've got to keep up with the flow of traffic better than that," Mildred scolded. "You blocked all those people. What if they were on their way to a baseball game or, ... or ..." She looked at her watch. "Heavens to Betsy! My appointment's in ten minutes. Get a move on."

Reluctantly, Alice pulled away from the side of the road, and, checking for traffic, eased out onto Route One.

"I swear to God, Alice, I wish your parents were home. My nerves can't take this." Mildred fluttered her hands as she looked at the yellow line. If she concentrated hard enough, maybe she could control the car from the passenger side.

A minute later, approaching Millerton Point, Alice saw a coyote flit across the road and she slammed on her brakes. A car behind them, going from twenty-five to zero in forty feet, nosed up onto the Buick's rear bumper. The crash woke Trixie, who started barking.

Mildred let out a shriek.

Alice grabbed the wheel and burst into tears. "I hate driving." She killed the engine. She was about to climb out of the driver's seat to assess the damage when the other driver marched up to her window.

"Learn to drive somewhere else, lady. You're a menace to the road!"

Trixie jumped into the front seat, barked, and growled at the intruder.

"I'll take care of this." Mildred unbuckled her seatbelt.

"Not on your life, Grandma." Alice felt frightened and excited at the same time. She fired up the car, slammed down on the accelerator, and sped off, leaving the driver holding onto his hat and disappearing in her rear-view mirror. She sped down Route One and squealed around the corner at Mesa Road, where there were no cars, thank God, and she could slow down, at least a little bit. Trixie looked out the window and barked at cows, while Grandma buckled and re-buckled her seat belt and muttered, "Oh my. Oh my, Alice," until they pulled up in front of Doris' and killed the engine.

"What an adventure!" Mildred marched halfway to Doris' front door, stopped, and spun around.

"Oooh Alice, that was fun! Let's do it again. This time, let's put Trixie in the front seat where she belongs," she said, and climbed back into the car.

FROM THE SHERIFF'S CALLS SECTION IN THE *POINT REYES LIGHT*,
JULY 19, 2012

INVERNESS: At 6:29 a.m. a woman who had purchased a bottle of gin at Costco the day before – and had partaken of it that night – said she realized the seal had been broken and a small amount of liquid taken.

A Bottle of Gin

Linda finished off her bear claw. "Boss, I mean, are you serious? At this time of day? I don't want to go out there. Obviously she's delirious, and I haven't had my espresso yet."

Walter grunted from underneath his ficus tree. It had started to look poorly again and he wasn't sure what to do. "Go on, Linda. Just go. I have a headache. Do your job." As for Walter, he had had more than his share of the juice from the juniper tree the night before, and it was way too early in his book to be up, much less at work. He had to show Linda he was in charge. He waved her off and reached for his bottle of Tylenol.

Linda headed down Levee Road. No need to put on her siren. No one was out, just the occasional hay wagon and milk truck. She waved to the drivers. They were going the speed limit, which gave her comfort. Once they went around the corner, all bets were off. She saw Cindy's lights on in the Busy Bee Bakery; maybe later she'd come back and get her free cup. Cindy gave free drinks to anyone in uniform.

Linda slowed as she entered Inverness proper and headed up the hill. The Crown Vic grunted as she negotiated the sharp switchbacks and arrived at the house, a 1930s cottage, leaning a bit to the left, with a stunning view of Tomales Bay.

She knocked but didn't have to. A middle-aged woman, wearing a blue caftan and blue pushers, swept open the door. Her blond hair was teased into a bouffant. She was holding a cigarette lighter in her hand.

"Thieves! Those goddamn kids from next door. You know, the Nowell boys. I bought this half-gallon bottle of gin from Costco," she hiccupped, "saving it for my bridge party. And next thing I know, wham, bam, they're in here, knocking through my pantry and drinking my gin."

"Miss, Mrs.?" Linda pulled out her spiral notebook and pen.

"Thornton. Mrs. Eleanor Thornton. Executive assistant to Mr. Richard Furthington, the head exec at PG&E. Retired. Never give up your title, I say." She thought a moment. "Can you take shorthand?"

"You called … regarding …" Linda sniffed for alcohol on Mrs. Thornton's breath. "The gin bottle, ma'am?"

Mrs. Thornton raised her arms over her head as if giving incantations to a great Inca spirit and staggered to the kitchen, the fringe of her caftan floating behind her. "It's here, right here." She ducked below the counter, came up with a gin bottle, and with a mighty heave, set it on the counter. "Not enough for my bridge club, as you can see, and I certainly don't have time to go to Costco before one p.m."

Linda glanced at her watch. It wasn't even 7:30 yet, but that wasn't all that was bothering her. It was the gin bottle, half-empty.

"Did you have any of this, ma'am?"

"Do I look like a liar to you?"

"Well, you said, when you called in …"

"I don't drink gin straight, and I don't drink alone." Mrs. Thornton reached for the kettle. "Tea? Coffee? Milk?"

"Uh, no thanks, ma'am." Linda examined doors and windows for obvious signs of a break-in. "You said they came through the front door?"

"Right next to my bedroom. The thought of, those, those hooligans, coming so close to where I sleep and me in my new Chantilly lace."

Linda was about to confront her when they heard a door open. She grabbed the butt of her gun.

"Honey. Is that you?" asked a gruff voice from the hall. "I reached over in bed to find you, but there was no one there." A bear of a man, at least six feet tall, rolled around the corridor wall, wearing only a towel. "I hate waking up alone. Oh hi," he said and noticing Linda, dropped the towel.

"We had a call, sir." Linda had not asked Mrs. Thornton if she lived alone. If Walter heard about that, she'd hear no end of it. She kept her eyes aimed at the ceiling.

"Norman – I'm so sorry," Mrs. Thornton cooed, coming and putting her arms about him.

"You call the cops, Eleanor? Why – were you having a problem? You could have told me first, darling." He slurred his words.

"I would, but you were snoring, sweet nums. I didn't want to wake you."

Linda cleared her throat. "I'm here because Mrs. Thornton said someone broke in and drank her gin. Now, sir, did you drink any?"

"How rude of me, Officer, not to offer you a beverage," he said. "I make a mean martini. It's a little early, but we'll keep that to ourselves, don't you think?"

"Well, we're all wrapped up here," Linda said. They were both loaded. On her way out the door, she shook what felt like cobwebs out of her head.

She was half-way to her car when she heard a shot. She ran back inside.

Norman was lying on the floor, his white towel blossoming red.

"I didn't mean to, but he drank half my gin," Eleanor said and floated back into the hall.

TOMALES: At 7:57 p.m. a Flying Scott appeared in distress.

The Flying Scott

"Fred!" Mildred thumped her cane on the kitchen floor. "There they go again, spoiling my perfectly delightful morning. I wish they would just explain, for Chrissakes."

"Maybe you shouldn't read the *Light*, dear." Fred queued up the baseball game. Lincecum was pitching again and he was a happy man. Not so delighted as to actually go to the game – that was a dream that was never going to come true. He took a sip of his Bud. Mildred had said it was okay, because it was light beer. He winced as the sour-tasting liquid went down. If she left, he could access his secret stash.

"Tell me," Mildred demanded. "Is a Flying Scott a bird? A plane? A dog?" She had always loved dogs. She went back to doing the dishes. The deep farm sink was full: it was going to take a week.

"Nope, not a dog, honey. Flying Scott's no dog." Fred wished Buster Posey would steal second. The guy was just so slow.

"Cormorant? Pelican? Bi-wing aircraft?" Mildred pulled back the curtains and stared at the fog coming in. Almost all of Tomales Bay was obscured; in another few minutes she wouldn't be able to see a thing. "How can they fly in this soup?" She scrubbed her copper pan with a Brillo pad. She was going to get the goddamn thing to shine no matter what.

"Planes? They have radar." Fred slipped one of his hidden beers from the pocket of his recliner. All he had to do was spill it and it would all be over. It was tight in there; he heard the can crumple.

"Birds don't have radar, Fred. You're not listening." She gave up on the copper pan and lifted up a jelly jar. They'd been using them as drinking glasses for years. It was time she bought another case from Building Supply.

"So what *is* a Flying Scott? And what does it look like when it's in distress, Fred?" Inadvertently, she dropped her jelly jar into the enamel sink. It didn't break, thank heavens. She extracted it with soapy hands, set it on a rack to dry, and sat next to Fred.

"Game's boring." She grabbed the remote and set the channel to "The View." She'd always loved that Rosie O'Donnell.

"Hey, wait a sec." Fred was stuck in the fully reclined position on his chair and couldn't reach the handle. "Damn! Would you please, sweetheart?"

"This is way more interesting than baseball." Mildred sat up in a hard-back chair and reached for her knitting. "I've always been interested in lesbian mothers. Who would have ever thought?"

"Please," Fred said. "Honey."

"Hush Fred. It's true confessions time," she trilled and clapped her hands.

"I'm stuck here, Mildred!" he shouted, twisting and turning and feeling the chair start to rock.

She sat up, primly, and jerked the handle. "I told you to exercise, and now, look at you."

He shot up in the chair with a bang. "The remote, please." He hoped he hadn't sloshed his beer.

"Fred, you should be ashamed. A potato, a half-drunk potato, drunk on baseball and beer. It's a silly pastime," she clucked, and moved her chair out of his reach. She pivoted the TV cart, so he couldn't see much more than a corner.

"Honey. Sweetheart. Don't you have dishes to do? Don't you need to see your sister?"

"Bunk. Just another one of your ruses to get me to give over the remote. No deal, buster. Calm your liver and watch. We're going to find out who her lover really is right after the next commercial."

"Maybe I'm the Flying Scott in distress, Mildred, ever thought of that?" Fred stood over his skinny little wife, all six-two and 275 pounds of him. "Mildred, please. The game."

"You're not Scottish." She increased the volume.

"And you can't fly." He reached for the remote.

"Tut-tut, a little domestic argument." Mildred tucked the remote inside her blouse. He would surely not grab it there.

"It's the last inning, for Chrissakes."

"Here they come. I knew it. Even the pretty girls are lesbians, Fred. It's such a shame."

"You made up that story in the paper just to distract me, wifey-poo." Fred reached for the pocket of his recliner. He was through with her setting the rules of what he could or could not drink. He pulled out a Stella, gulped it down, and gave her a dirty look.

"Do you think the Flying Scott is a guy in baseball, Fred?" Mildred giggled. "Or a player stealing bases? Who would it be?" She traced the buttons of the remote through her blouse.

"I don't bloody care about a goddamn bird!" Fred bellowed. "Please, the game, I need to watch the end of the game."

She stared at him. Poor guy, blood pressure through the roof. "Have your stupid remote." She threw it at him.

"About time." He settled back into the recliner. This time he stayed sitting up. There was no telling what would happen if he leaned back again.

"Suit yourself. Game's over, anyway." She needed to check on her roses. "The Giants lost."

"Jesus, Mildred, you really know how to hurt a guy."

"Oh sweetheart, don't watch if it upsets you so." She stood between him and the TV and gave him a kiss on his bald spot.

He craned his neck to see the screen.

"I'm way more important than baseball, dear."

Fred, knowing better than to argue, put out one pudgy hand for her thin one. "Come, sit on my lap, and we'll watch the post-game show together," he cooed, hoping to get her at least to move.

"My sister says we don't get along." Mildred settled her skinny body next to his big one. He seemed to have more bumps than he had last time. "But that's not true at all."

"Watch Buster. He's in the interview room."

"He looks like a kid. How old is he? Twenty? Nineteen?"

"Twenty-three this year." Fred adjusted himself. "Now, shush."

"But what about the bird?"

"Forget about the bird, Mildred, this is way more important. This is baseball."

Note: Flying Scott is a kind of sailboat.

MUIR WOODS: At 1:18 p.m. neighbors were arguing over the use of a weed eater.

The Weed Eater

"You've had it for hours," Harold said. "It's my weed eater, not yours, Dan. You promised I'd have it back by noon."

Dan, who had all his safety gear on – eye goggles, ear protectors, and thick leather apron didn't hear a thing. He was edging along a bunch of weeds by the sidewalk, and all he had to do was finish this last stubborn patch. He ground the weed eater into dirt.

Harold eyed his brother. Out of the hospital a month now, Dan was back to his own self, his cheeks pink, all rested and ready to go. And as stubborn and selfish as always.

"Dan!" Harold came closer. Dan hadn't thanked him for sitting by his hospital bed the first two days after he'd been shocked. Harold had even hired an electrician to wire up Dan's fountain, but had his brother been grateful? Hell no. Then he'd given his brother the keys to the tool shed. Another stupid mistake. Now he was hogging all his tools and wouldn't return the key. Calling a locksmith was a hundred dollars Harold didn't want to spend. He tapped Dan on the shoulder.

Dan swung around with the weed eater, which went after Harold's white hairy legs with determination. "Don't you see I'm working?"

Harold raised the rake and Dan, no fool, kicked off the weed eater and dropped it. It sputtered and died.

Harold tried to start the weed eater. "No gas. Well, that's par for the course, given how you usually leave things. Dan, you gummed up the works with your goddamn palm fronds and now it's broken. Three hundred bucks, brother. Pay up."

Dan, hot and sweaty in the uncharacteristic warm afternoon, walked away. He needed quiet, not this incessant buzzing in his ears. He heard Harold panting and grunting behind him and turned around to see his brother with his fists up.

Harold wasn't a fighting man, but it was high time Dan learned his lesson.

"Go ahead, hit me if you want. Honestly, Harold, this is not the way adults behave. It's only a stupid garden tool. Chill."

"Stay still, you puny little rat." Harold tried to focus on the figure dancing around in front of him.

"Go ahead, make yourself proud." Dan ducked his brother's too-slow blow. What a wuss. He'd taken boxing classes in high school and had never forgotten how to move.

"Mom always loved me best." Dan held his hands loose at his sides. He watched his brother's face sour and his lips grow thin. "She told me. At bedtime."

"I was there all the time. Bunk beds, remember?"

"But you were away at camp when she told me everything. It was great. You were an unwanted surprise, she said. Six months into their marriage. Maybe your dad was the mailman, instead, eh? People have always said we don't look alike."

"You little …" Harold spat, doing his best not to take the bait. He'd heard this kind of bullshit for years, but it still hurt. He raised his arm, made a fist, and heard a crash. He looked at Dan, but his brother's attention was focused below, on the valley floor, where a Toyota had hit the back of a small truck. People gathered around. A woman, in the Toyota, was screaming. Harold ran to his shed and extracted a crow bar and a hammer. Then he dug his cell phone out of his pocket, and punched 911.

When they got to the car, Dan started talking to the lady, who was stuck behind the wheel. She kept screaming about her baby. As he worked on the wheel with the crowbar, Harold checked the back seat. The baby was crying but wasn't hurt. Gently and carefully, he extracted the baby and cooed to the little boy dressed in blue.

In front, Dan broke off the wheel, but before he could continue helping the mother, fire trucks pulled up, sirens blaring and lights flashing. Paramedics checked her vitals and placed her gently onto a gurney.

She sobbed. "Thank you. Thank you ever so much. You boys are so sweet."

"Our pleasure," the brothers answered together.

"My name's Harold," Harold said and set his tools on the ground, "and this is Dan, my little brother."

"Your mother should be right proud of her fine set of boys," the woman said. The paramedics wheeled her to the EMT van.

"I'll call on you in the hospital!" Dan stood next to the gurney. She was so pretty. "What's your name?"

"Betsy, Betsy Rowland," she muttered.

"Hey, Miss Rowland, what's your number?" She whispered something to Dan. He hastily wrote the number on his palm.

"Hey, I saw her first," Harold grabbed for his brother's hand. "Besides, you're married."

"So are you, little brother," Dan said, and shoved his hands into his pockets.

HICKS VALLEY: At 2:45 p.m. Cheese Factory employees reported that a rude customer had threatened to throw cheese at them.

Save Some for School

"That's no way to behave." Mildred popped a blackberry in her mouth. It was mid-summer and she and Alice had been picking blackberries all afternoon in the Giacomini wetlands.

"Was it stinky cheese, Grandma?" Alice picked one for herself. It was perfect.

A day with Grandma was better than any day with Mom and Dad. They were making blackberry pies at Grandma's house in Inverness Park. Later, she might let her drive to Petaluma. More practice! Soon she'd have her own driver's license. Alice couldn't wait.

"I don't know what those people were thinking, dear," Mildred sniffed. "When I was younger, no one threatened to throw cheese. I mean, really."

Alice thought a minute. There were kids at school – she could throw cheese at them, no problem. That stinky Melissa, for instance.

"Did you put sugar in the blackberries?" Mildred asked, smoothing the pie crust into a glass pan.

"Of course." Alice wished Grandma would change the radio station. Those old 1940's tunes were grating on her. She went to turn the dial.

"Don't you dare!"

"I'll get my book then." Alice dug into her backpack.

"I used to dance to Tommy Dorsey with Grandpa. My, oh my, he could cut a rug."

"Grandpa could dance?" Alice asked, incredulous.

"What's next?" Mildred adjusted her glasses.

Alice looked at a dog-eared 3" x 5" recipe card. "Sugar and cornstarch. What's cornstarch?"

"Didn't your mother ever teach you anything?" The doggone dough kept sticking to her rolling pin. She'd never get all the pieces together, assemble the pie, and bake it before 5 p.m. It used to be so easy.

"So, what do you think made the customers so angry?" Alice searched through Grandma's dusty pantry. Some of the bottles looked really old. "What am I looking for, exactly?"

"Yellow box and hurry. This is about to break apart." Mildred wiped her nose with a floury hand and got a smudge of butter on her glasses. Things were not going well. If she took off her glasses, she couldn't see, and she was in no mood to wash her hands and start over. They were already greasy from all the butter in the crust. And that girl was taking too long. "Alice, did you find it?"

"Already done and in the mix," Alice replied, earbuds dangling around her neck. She went back to reading *The Hunger Games*.

"What makes people think they can get away with being so rude?" tssked Mildred.

"I dunno." Alice held the blackberry mixture above the lumpy and broken pie crust. "Isn't the crust supposed to cover the whole pan or something?"

"I've been making pies since long before you were born, girl. Pour. I don't have time to waste. Chop, chop." Mildred examined her granddaughter's book. "What the heck is this? Why aren't you reading the ones I gave you?"

"In those books, girls don't do anything, Grandma. This one's about a girl named Katniss. She shoots a bow and arrow. She's tough."

"Sounds like trash to me." Mildred placed the pie in the oven. "It's not ladylike."

"Ladylike?" Alice croaked. "She's strong and powerful and fights back. She's cool."

"You can't find a husband when you try to rule the world. Think of your future," Mildred argued. "If you listened to me ..."

Alice wasn't thinking of her future, she was thinking of buying a bow and arrow. Would Mom object? Probably. "I'm fifteen now, Grandma." She stood up and took aim at a boat out on Tomales Bay. "If you could buy one, I could learn to shoot." And Melissa wouldn't push her around anymore.

"Ever seen such a great pie?" Mildred crowed. She still had it.

"But in your day," Alice settled onto a kitchen stool, "girls couldn't do things like they do now."

"What things? We didn't have to shoot guns or arrows or throw cheese to get our way. We were polite. What are you saying? You think your Grandma is a wimp?"

"What? Uh, no." Alice suddenly felt very small. Grandma was just a skinny little thing, hunched over, with crab-like knobby knuckles and white hair tucked up into a bun.

"Who do you think pushes me around?" Mildred held up her spatula and narrowed her eyes. "Grandpa? Cops? Your mother? You?"

"Uh oh ... No, sorry. I didn't mean anything, Grandma," Alice stuttered.

"I should think not. Let's go and get some fresh air while the pie cools."

Alice, eager for more driving practice, trotted along behind Grandma. The fog was lifting off Tomales Bay and they could see sailboats dancing out on the water. Someday, somehow, she'd be strong and the girls in school would stop pushing her around.

"Let's go over to the Cheese Factory, dear."

"And throw cheese?" giggled Alice, taking the keys.

"If that's what you want." Mildred fluffed her hair. "But don't you want to save some for school?"

From the Sheriff's Calls Section in the *Point Reyes Light*, August 9, 2012

OLEMA: At 10:20 p.m. a cow was on a blind curve.

The Blind Cow

"Were the cows out driving?" Alice giggled and closed the paper and folded it carefully. Grandma liked things neat.

"Honestly, Alice, you and your imagination," Mildred clucked. "The cows were loose. They get out all the time." She was pulling down her dirty gingham curtains. Perched on a kitchen stool, she didn't feel at all safe. The damn rod was stuck. She backed down carefully and slowly. "Last day of summer vacation, Alice. Make yourself useful. Take down the rest."

Alice, watching dark clouds pile up along Inverness Ridge, chewed on a fingernail. Junior year loomed starting Monday and she wasn't nearly ready. She climbed the rickety stool and, holding onto a cabinet door, reached for the curtain rod. The door wobbled under her weight.

"You trying to kill me, Grandma?" She pulled on the curtain rod so hard she slipped a bit and the bracket broke.

"It's just curtains, Alice, honestly."

Alice jumped back down onto the kitchen floor, grateful to be on solid ground again. "You're going to hurt yourself with all this wobbly stuff. Why can't Grandpa do it?"

"He's sleeping. You want to wake him? Go ahead. But I wouldn't if I were you." Mildred stuffed the gingham curtains into a hamper with other grayed, threadbare linens.

"Can I go back to my book now?" Alice was supposed to be reading a boring book for school, but she was nearing the end of *The Hunger Games* and didn't want to put it down. She was just settling back onto the couch when she heard a yell.

She found Grandma lying on the concrete floor of the laundry room, her basket of linens and curtains spread all around her, one brown oxford shoe caught on a ledge.

"Grandma!"

"I've told Fred to fix that ledge a thousand times, and now look what he did. Put my dress down, girl, right this second. Avert your eyes."

Alice, embarrassed, saw Grandma's athletic-type stockings rolled down to just above her knees. White puffy skin spread out above, freckled and wrinkled. Alice fixed her dress.

"Fred! Fred!" Mildred struggled to sit up. The pressure and coldness of the concrete floor seemed to suck all the energy out of her.

"Should I call nine-one-one, Grandma?"

"Get your grandfather!" Mildred hollered and lay back down on the hard concrete.

Fred was awake and distraught by the time the paramedics arrived. They loaded Mildred onto a stretcher. Alice watched them, examined the ledge on the concrete floor, and looked at him.

"I was asleep, for Goodness sake's, I didn't make her fall," Fred cried, desperate for absolution.

"Mrs. Rhinehart will be fine, sir. If you'll just give us a little space, please," the paramedics asked.

Mildred pursed her mouth. "I can get up. Don't push me down, young man. What do you know about little old ladies? Ever been one?"

"No ma'am, but I do know – "

"Nothing." Mildred put a stop to the paramedic's nonsense in a hurry.

"Does she really need to go to the hospital?" Fred asked. Who was going to make his dinner? All Alice knew was how to make grilled-cheese sandwiches and he wasn't supposed to eat cheese.

"Fred." Mildred kept an eye on her husband as the team walked her down the rickety back stairs. She glanced at Alice. "You're in charge. And for God's sake, put the laundry in."

The paramedics lifted her up one impossibly steep step.

"Hey, watch it! Who's heading this outfit? You? Why, you're no older than my granddaughter, Alice. And she's a helluva lot smarter than you. Keep an eye out. They say there's a blind cow on the road." Mildred kept chatting as they closed the doors of the EMT van and sped away.

Fred leaned his bulk on the back stair balustrade, and wept. "Alice, where are they taking her? Oh God, I forgot to ask."

"Give me a sec," Alice answered, and pulled out her iPhone.

While she punched in the sheriff's number she watched Grandpa stare down the road, his shoulders slumping, his body caving in on itself, one hand reaching for the railing, and the other for his wife.

FROM THE SHERIFF'S CALLS SECTION IN THE *POINT REYES LIGHT*,
AUGUST 2, 2012

INVERNESS PARK: At 6:03 p.m. a woman
found cash blowing down the street.

Nothing Ever Happens in Inverness Park

"Holy Moly, it's raining money!" Henry watched bills fly through the air.
Despite his arthritis he could move pretty fast, but some of the bills escaped
just as his heavy hands drew near. He ran after them as other people came
streaming out of Busy Bee Bakery and Perry's Deli. Henry, having more
sense than to run faster than his heart allowed, stamped on bills and stuffed
them in his pockets.

A gray Nissan Sentra peeled away up the road, cash flying out
the window.

In a few minutes, the street was quiet again. Three people were standing
around, hunting for more. The goat farmers from across the bakery came
out to look at the commotion, and found a few bills in their fence. Three
or more flew into the yard, and the farmers ran into the pen, disturbing the
goats closing in on what they thought was food.

"Just like Christmas." Henry kept his eye out for traffic and strolled back
into Busy Bee Bakery. This time he could have a sticky bun and a cup of coffee. His Social Security check never went far enough.

"Was it a drug dealer?" asked a woman who was standing by the coffee
urn and peering out the picture window. "They usually have more money
than God."

Henry ignored her. Hiding his stash behind the wall of the booth, he
pulled piles of crumpled bills from his pockets. He flattened the stack with
the palm of his hand and counted. Twenty dollars. His to spend. Delightful.

The door to the bakery opened, making the doorbell chime.

"Anyone seen my money?" a tall man asked. He was dressed in blue, about six feet tall, with a pony tail half-way down his back. "My whole day's take out the window. It flew down the road right in front of this place. God will know if any of you are lying."

Henry looked at the table in front of him. He palmed his bills, slipped them into his lap, and into his pocket.

"You saw my money, old man?" the man asked.

"What a shame. Too bad I didn't see anything, too busy reading Sheriff's Calls in the *Light*." Henry moaned and rubbed his leg. "Arthritis, it's a killer."

The guy noticed the woman at the window. "See anything, sister?"

Eleanor Reynolds snorted. As if she would tell him anything. "The people across the street – at the goat farm – they're sweeping their fence, isn't that peculiar?" She'd hidden her stash deep inside her Prada purse.

"I swear it was right out there," the guy pointed to the street. "Anyone? Anything?"

Emily Ann Tonkin-Lewis, the clerk at the bakery, slipped her hand under the counter and pushed 9-1-1. "Cup of coffee, then, sir? On the house. Sounds like you're having a bad day."

"I had a bad day in '47," Henry piped up, glad to be changing the subject. "That's the day my father died. He went to war," Henry stared out the window at the goat farmers, "and he came home whole – my mother was so pleased. Next thing I know, bam, he dies of a heart attack."

"Old man, I don't give a shit about your dad," the man in blue spun on his heels, "I care about my money. Now, where is it?"

"We'll be glad to help. Name's Henry," Henry said, standing up, offering a hand. He'd seen Emily Ann use the phone and felt safe. He hoped the bump in his rear pocket was not visible. "And you, sir, what's yours?"

"I got three people in this shop, two decent people and one liar, or maybe three liars. Which is it, folks?" the man asked. Outside his Nissan Sentra rumbled in the parking lot. "Pressed the wrong goddamn button and the rear window went down."

"Were you talking on your cell while you were driving, perhaps?" Eleanor examined her reflection in the window. With the extra cash, maybe she could get highlights. "It's illegal, you know."

"What's it to you, sister? You got my money?"

"I'd check everywhere you've been today, sir, I mean, if it was me who'd lost all that cash," Eleanor trilled. Well past middle-age, she hadn't had so much fun since her birthday when they'd had oysters for breakfast.

A sheriff's cruiser pulled up in front.

"Oh shit," the man said. "Goddamn uniforms. None of you ever saw me." He ran out the back door.

Linda came in, bored and tired. She was going on in an hour, and had been up all night with Mom who had the flu. She needed a double espresso like right now. As soon as she walked in, she noticed a silence. Henry Rhinehart was staring into his coffee. A woman by the window looked at her with eager eyes, and flinty Emily Ann, behind the counter, caught her breath.

One by one they pointed their fingers toward the back door.

"And what am I supposed to be looking for?" Linda asked and noticed the Nissan with the engine running.

Henry followed her out, eager to be a hero. "That guy - he's around here somewhere."

"Mr. Rhinehart," Linda asked, "what guy?"

"It was the guy with all the cash," Henry went on. "He also stole my car. I drove my Caddy here, and now it's gone."

"Mr. Rhinehart, perhaps you'd like to sit down? Should I call your brother?"

Henry would follow directions but there was a thief on the loose. "Big black car, you've seen it, I've been driving Black Beauty for over forty years now." He dropped his face into his hands.

"Let's start at the beginning." Linda pulled out her pen and steno notebook. "What exactly happened here today?"

Henry nodded, eager. But too eager. Something was wrong. Oh God. Ever since he'd seventy. "Give me a minute, will you," he said, and hurried around the building to the outhouse.

He was about to open the door when it swung open. The thief stared at Henry.

"She gone?"

"What did you do with my Caddy?" Henry demanded. "I drove it here. It's a '67 black convertible, with whitewall tires. I spent all day polishing it."

"I don't have your car, old man," the thief said and bent down to wash his hands at the spigot. The sound of running water did not help Henry in the least.

An old bike rack was leaning against the wall of the building. It didn't look too heavy. Henry picked it up and hit the man over the head with it and the man fell.

"You shouldn't go around stealing cars," Henry snorted. Feeling young again, he walked around the store, eager to show the officer his handiwork.

"Mr. Rhinehart, what is it?" Linda asked and followed him around to the back where the thief was on the gravel, holding his head and moaning.

"He stole my Caddy," Henry said, "my beautiful car."

"Mr. Rhinehart, you can't go around hitting people like this. We'll have to bring you in, sir." Linda checked the downed man's pulse. "Honestly."

Emily Ann joined them to check what was going on. "By the outhouse, of course," she muttered, "nothing around this place surprises me anymore." She clapped her flour covered hands and headed back inside.

"Mr. Rhinehart." Linda pulled out her handcuffs. Her radio crackled by her ear. "Yes, I see. Palace Market. Spewing cash all along Levee Road. At gun point. Good God. Yes, I have him." She cuffed the thief to the water pipe.

"We could deputize you, Mr. Rhinehart," she joked. "Now, about the money?"

"It was all gone by the time I got out there." Henry stuffed his hands into his pockets. "I didn't see anything."

"Mr. Rhinehart," Linda repeated, "there's more to this story, and I'm waiting."

"Officer, no need to wait." Henry rocked back on his heels. "As you know, nothing interesting ever happens in Inverness Park."

FROM THE SHERIFF'S CALLS SECTION IN THE *POINT REYES LIGHT*, JULY 30, 2012

POINT REYES STATION: At 2:02 p.m. a resident asked to talk with deputies about a "disturbing rumor that is going through the community."

The Rumor

"Heavens to Betsy." Mildred flipped through the stained and flour-covered pages of her Fannie Farmer cookbook. "Fred, call the Sheriff's Office, and tell them I'm just fine. Somebody is spreading a rumor that I succumbed."

"Everyone around here knows you're very much alive, dear." Fred adjusted the volume on his new remote. The doggone cable company had sent him an adapter, and he couldn't make it function properly. His beloved Giants were going on and a black box kept filling the screen.

"The community thinks I'm a goner, Fred. All I did was spend two nights in the hospital with a swollen ankle."

Fred would know very well when his wife passed, the whole world would crack open and no one would know what to do, especially him. "I'm so glad you're fine, sweetheart."

"Did you have a nice time with Alice?" Mildred chased a curl. Ever since Doris went on vacation, the other hairdresser had been hopeless. Now her hair seemed kind of limp and lifeless.

"Alice and I watched baseball while you were gone, she's becoming great with stats," Fred said, pleased the TV was clear again.

"Can you take me to town? I need to see Doris."

"Give me twenty minutes tops." Posey was up.

Mildred undid the ace bandage on her ankle. It didn't look very pretty. "Ready now?"

"Ah, come on. I fixed the curtains, the fountain, the steps. Can't you wait a sec?"

"No."

"All right, yes, of course." Fred had learned long ago what marriage was. While she was getting her hair done at Doris' he could be at the Western, having a pop, and watching the game.

Mildred gathered her *In Style* magazines. She wished there was a magazine for the senior set but no one but AARP wrote for her group and she hated AARP. A bunch of old farts if anyone asked her. "But what about the rumor in the paper, you know, about that gal that got hurt?" She put on her straw hat and secured it with a hat pin. She would be safe enough with that four inch hat pin if any murderers came near her. The big pink flower was looking a little sad. "Fred?" She followed him to the car.

"What gal in the paper?" Fred held open the door.

"Someone's keeping secrets around here." Mildred pursed her lips. "I go away for two days and wham. Everything around here goes to shit."

"Mildred, no one has been killed. No one died. Forget about it." Fred pulled out onto the main road. If he could just get to the game.

"Then what is the rumor that no one is talking about?"

"Honey, sweetheart, please, just be quiet," Fred said, a little too loudly. He eased out onto the road at twenty miles an hour. "You're ruining my concentration." He held his hands at ten and two o'clock, just like his dad had taught him. A long line of cars grew behind the car.

"Find out who did it; find out who's keeping secrets." Mildred caressed his shoulder. "Do it for me, sweetheart."

A two year old and a mother holding a cell phone stepped off the island in front of the Saltwater restaurant. Fred screeched to a stop not ten feet away. "No, no, no, Jesus, Mildred, be quiet. Please."

"You don't have to shout. I'm the one who just got out of the hospital," she sniffed.

"Yes dear," Fred said, "I know. That's the rumor that's going around, people are delighted," he added with a smirk, "and surprised you're home, and doing so well, actually."

Mildred swatted him with her purse. "So that's the rumor, then, Fred, that I'm still alive?"

NICASIO: At 12:10 a.m. a beige van drove into a tree.

The Sound of Sirens

"This time it wasn't me!" Thomas cradled his iPhone by his ear. He'd pulled over when he'd seen the beige van weave down the road and hit the tree.

Justin, beside him, was loaded, but Thomas was not. He'd been paying attention to what Officer Kettleman had been saying to him over the last few months. Now she was on the other end of the phone and didn't believe him.

"It's unfair, officer, I'm fine. No, I have not been drinking. I am the driver. But the people in the van?" Steam was rising out of the hood. Was it going to burst into flames?

He left Justin in the leather passenger seat of his father's BMW, and, palming the keys, walked slowly up to the van. A door flew open and a man staggered out.

"Are you okay, sir?" Thomas asked. The man scowled and turned on him. He was wearing a plaid jacket and carrying a small brown paper bag. Except for the ribbon of blood dribbling down his cheek, he looked all right.

"Anyone else in the car?" Thomas asked.

"No one except for her, and she's dead." The man tried to steady himself. "It wasn't my fault, boy, and don't you forget it."

Thomas didn't like the look of him. Where was the sheriff? They were miles from anywhere and it was the middle of the night. He looked back at the BMW. Justin was no use; he was passed out cold. Thomas circled around the driver, keeping his distance. "So, where'd you pick her up?"

The headlamp of a car swept over a distant hill, and Thomas felt comforted for a moment, until the car slowed, saw the accident, and took off up a hill, radio blaring.

The man wiped one meaty forearm across his face, leaving a smear of blood. "She was hitchhiking. Pretty little thing. Too bad."

"Let's take a look anyway," Thomas suggested. Maybe she was still alive and he could do something. He took a step closer.

"You little twerp. I bet you already wrote down my license number. Going to call the cops, you shithead?"

"But she could be hurt or something, sir."

"You bet she's hurt, bud. Blood all over the place." The man squinted. "That's close enough. She's gone, like I told you."

Thomas heard what could have been a moan but it was hard to tell. There was a slight wind and it was so damn dark. The van lights were still on.

"You idiot. Go on home. Get the hell out of here." The man took a swig out of a brown paper bag.

Thomas ran to the passenger side of the van. There, her dress in tatters, was a girl from school. Judy! Her head was to the side, against her shoulder, lolling there, awkwardly, and there was a splat of blood the size of a dinner plate on the broken windshield.

"Oh dear God, it's Judy." Was she breathing? For Chrissakes, where was the sheriff? If he could only do something. He reached inside, took hold of one thin wrist, felt for a pulse.

"She's dead, like I told you, you insolent little shit." The man growled at Thomas' shoulder and raised his fists. Thomas wheeled around, blood on his hands. He ducked. The man lunged for Judy, and Thomas grabbed him, trying to pull him back, trying to get him off of her.

Thomas grabbed the guy's legs, his pants, the odor of drunken sweat filling his nose. That was Judy, Judy sitting there, and the man's hands were enormous and Thomas kept hitting him and hitting him, while all he could get was the bastard's back side.

"What's going on here?" Officer Kettleman's voice broke behind them.

"Don't go after me – it's Judy, she's in there," Thomas yelled. "He keeps saying she's dead, but she can't be dead. She's only seventeen."

Someone grabbed the driver. The paramedics closed in on Judy. Thomas had been so slow, so goddamn slow. She looked so gray. "Don't cover her! She's my best friend's sister!"

The EMTs unfolded a gurney and placed her on it. Thomas ran after the EMT van as it disappeared in a blaze of flashing lights and the sound of sirens.

Officer Kettleman stood next to Thomas and asked for details.

"He was reaching for her, he kept saying she was dead, but why would he reach for her if she was dead? I was too late." Thomas paced in the dirt.

"Twice your size and drunk to boot. You're one brave kid, Thomas." Officer Kettleman barked orders into her radio. "All clear on Nicasio Valley Road."

"She's alive? She's dead? Tell me!"

"We won't know until morning," Officer Kettleman said. "But if it wasn't for you, Thomas…"

"I didn't do anything. I couldn't even save her, oh God," he sobbed. "I never even got close." Disconsolate, he looked at Officer Kettleman, into the ink black night, the flashing red lights on the cop car.

Officer Kettleman's radio crackled and a voice broke into the silence.

"She's got a pulse," Officer Kettleman said.

"Oh God, thank you," Thomas cried and hugged her.

From the Sheriff's Calls Section in the *Point Reyes Light*,
August 14, 2012

BOLINAS: At 11:30 a.m. someone found a newborn calf on the side of Horseshoe Hill Road and an upset mother cow on the hill above it. The animals' owner said the calf must have tumbled down the hill as it slid into the world.

The Calf

"I don't know about you, Beth Ann," Alice finger combed her hair, "but that calf's slide into the world, pretty cool, don't you think? But that's not what my Mom said about me when I was born."

Beth Ann Ferguson, all of fifteen, sighed. Alice was, well, a little weird. Their mothers were best friends and since Alice's mom was forever going out of town Alice stayed with Beth Ann, whether she liked it or not. She chewed on a fingernail. "My Mom said my delivery was fast as lightning."

Alice groaned. Mom said hers had taken days and she'd never let her forget it.

"Mom said I was perfect," Beth Ann crowed. She wondered if she could pull out her cigarettes. Would Alice tell? Probably. She stuffed her hands back into her pockets.

As for Alice, she couldn't say the same thing about her own mother. And as for her being perfect, Mom had never said anything of the kind. Most days she just pointed out Alice's faults. She kicked at a clod of dirt. "Shall we go see the calf?"

"Nah, I got a better idea." Beth Ann put away her cell phone. Reception was always kind of crappy out here and she was bored silly. "My brother's practicing downtown with his band. Come on. We'll hitch."

"I don't know. Mom said…."

"Your Mom said what? That you shouldn't hitchhike out here?" Beth Ann laughed. "Who do you expect drives around here, axe murderers and maniacs? The only people who live out here are hippies, goofballs, and farmers." She tapped her feet. She was going to have to talk to Mom and change their arrangement. "Alice, don't be such a wuss."

Alice wasn't sure. She had a chemistry quiz coming up. She could stay and be a nobody, and the other kids would whisper about her like they always did, or she could just go. And be one of *them*. "Sure," she said, feeling uneasy. She'd never hitchhiked before.

The girls marched down the dusty driveway, Beth Ann taller in her three inch platform shoes, leggings that looked like jeans and Alice feeling awkward in her Grandpa's Giants T-shirt, her favorite old jeans, and beat up old tennis shoes. Alice longed to be as cool, as developed, and as beautiful as Beth Ann. Her hair was scraggly and thin, and she was going to be flat forever. She scuffed her worn out shoes in the dirt.

Twenty minutes later a farm truck - a beat up old Ford F-150 - came flying down the road, and Alice thought that he would go right by them, he was going so fast, but the driver slammed on his brakes half-way down the hill, ground the car into reverse and backed up.

"Howdy." He tipped his hat.

Beth Ann opened the door and hopped in. Alice hesitated.

"No reason to be afraid, little lady, I'm a local," the driver said to Alice. "I deliver hay for Toby's."

Alice knew everyone in town but she couldn't quite place him.

"Come on, what are you waiting for?" Beth Ann tucked her purse beside her on the seat.

Alice didn't want to say. She never went to the feed part of the store; she only went to Toby's to buy birthday cards with Grandma.

"Name's Michael." He put out his hand. "I can't wait all day, you in or out?"

"Alice, come on," Beth Ann whispered.

"You heard about that calf?" Alice asked the driver. "The one who rolled down the hill as soon as it was born?"

Beth Ann rolled her eyes.

Michael laughed. "Stony View Farm. I'm going there myself. Hop on in. You love animals, then? Just like me."

Alice stepped in.

Michael let out the clutch, turned up the radio, and rolled down the hill. "You girls from around here?"

"You bet," Beth Ann trilled.

Alice didn't want to say. She watched rain dribble down the window. She pressed on her legs to keep them from trembling and hoped she wouldn't get a nosebleed.

Cranking his way up Horseshoe Hill Road, Michael slowed down for a lost tourist in a BMW. "Hey girls, rain's disappeared. It's a great day, how 'bout a ride to Stinson? You surf? Yes? No?" He passed the tourist on a straightaway. "My brother Tommy taught me to surf and if it weren't for Hester here," he slapped the metal dash of the truck, "I'd go all over the place, but she does cough and sputter some, and a few times left me high and dry – just like my last girlfriend." He sped up.

Alice grabbed the seat. They were on the narrow part of the road deep in the eucalyptus forest where the turns were really tight and trees packed in tight.

"Could you slow down a little bit?" Beth Ann asked, feeling a little sick.

"If you drive this road all the time like I do," Michael crowed, "you can go any speed you want." He leaned on the horn and crossed the double yellow line around a horse trailer. "I just love driving in the country, don't you?"

Beth Ann grasped Alice's leg. "Make. Him. Stop." She held her hand over her mouth.

Alice wasn't sure what to do. Beth Ann grasped her tighter, digging in with those sharp nails of hers. Michael turned up the radio. The truck went around a particularly tight turn way too fast, going up on two wheels. Both girls screamed.

"Weenie-butts!" Michael laughed and sped on as the truck bounced back onto four wheels with a clunk. Beth Ann's face went white.

"When he hits the stop sign," Alice whispered into Beth Ann's ear, "jump."

Michael saw the stop sign before the girls did and he was prepared to blow past it, but there might be a black and white on the side road, just waiting for people like him, so he slammed on his brakes, downshifting just so, with the revs high, the car in first, and he was ready to pop the clutch, like right now, when he heard a door open. Funny, he thought he'd locked them all. He stepped on it, but the girls were faster than he was, and tumbled out of the truck followed by his wrench, hammer and a pound of two penny nails.

The girls fell in a patch of bushes. They were not hurt, just startled. Beth Ann and Alice still had their purses, and shoes, mostly, 'cept Beth Ann had lost hers. Alice was surprised she felt a thrill.

"You okay, Beth Ann?"

Beth Ann was crying and Alice felt bad for her. "Anything hurt, broken?" Alice was not thinking about the tiny thorns that penetrated her Grandpa's Giants T-shirt and stuck into her back. She was way luckier than Beth Ann, who cried so hard mascara ran down her cheeks. She helped Beth Ann out of the bushes as a cop car pulled up. It was Officer Kettleman, her Grandmother's friend.

"I'd put you in the back seat, girls, but I already have company." Linda thumbed toward the back seat. Michael glared at the girls from behind barred Plexiglas windows.

"Oh honey." Alice pulled thorns out of Beth Ann's leggings. "You sure fell into the prickles." She sounded just like her Grandma Mildred.

"Thanks." Beth Ann hiccupped through tears.

"Kind of like that little calf." Alice said. "We popped right on out, didn't we?"

"You girls know better than to hitchhike," Linda lectured. "You could have been killed. And whose idea was it to jump out at the stop sign?"

Alice looked down at her shoes. "Mine."

"Smart girl," Linda said, "you were both lucky."

"And I'm the one who said we should hitchhike," confessed Beth Ann. She rubbed her cheeks with the back of her hand. "My best friend was right," she sniffed, "we should never have gotten into that truck."

FROM THE SHERIFF'S CALLS SECTION IN THE *POINT REYES LIGHT*,
AUGUST 23, 2012

POINT REYES STATION: At 7:11 p.m. a woman
said she had lost her husband's wallet.

Invincible

"What do you mean you lost my wallet?" Hank James, 65, of Inverness, California, yelled at his wife inside the Palace Market.

"I was just holding it a moment," mumbled Alexandra James, 32. She adjusted jangling bracelets that were forever digging into her wrists and tried to ignore her husband.

Officer Kettleman pulled out her pen and steno notebook. This was a mismatched couple if ever she'd seen one. It wasn't just their age differences that bothered her, it was something else. Hank was bald and round and had a patrician air and this miss in her designer shoes. "I didn't get your full name, Miss?"

"Alexandra James," Alexandra said. Hank was going to kill her when they got home. For the moment she felt safe with the officer present.

"I see." Linda flipped through the pages of her steno notebook. "And where were you when the accident occurred?"

"It was no accident. I was in the middle of the market, pulling out cash for our cousin's Bar Mitzvah, then, boom, someone's hand came down from out of nowhere, and the wallet was gone." She feigned tears. That's at least what she thought happened, wasn't it? All she knew was that she'd had his wallet in her hand in the dairy section and next thing, by check out, the wallet was gone. "And no, I didn't put it on the conveyor belt, if that's what you're asking, I'm not that stupid."

Hank sure thought she was. Lately, she'd been kind of a klutz. He should have known better than to lend her his wallet. "Damn it, Alexandra, think and think hard. It's Labor Day weekend, and we're already late. Trace everywhere you've gone today."

Alexandra looked around at the sea of people whirling around her. Bicyclists were clunking their shoes while they walked, campers were itching mosquito bites and tourists were checking out the wine selection. Outside a barbecue was in full swing, with ribs and corn and oysters on the grill. God, she was hungry. If only she could extract herself from Hank's grip tightening on her arm.

"Darling, you're hurting me," she whispered under the gaze of the officer. About Sarah's age though a bit heavier. When she got home, maybe she'd give her stepdaughter a bit of motherly advice, though Sarah didn't seem to listen well. Another item on her to-do list. Her wrist tingled. "Hank!" He dropped her arm.

"My wallet," he hissed. "Where the hell did you put my wallet?"

"I can't remember." Alexandra remembered where hers was – in her red leather handbag, in the car. Top down? Not with the top down! She charged out of the shop. Hank had told her he'd stay in the car. Why had she trusted him? The sidewalks were full of tourists blocking her way and staring into their iPhones. She couldn't remember where they'd parked. She ran down 'B' street, looking for Hank's little red Viper, but there were just BMWs, Porsches and farm trucks.

Hank hadn't followed her. She was glad for that. She went down C Street, and saw the car. She ran the half-block in her impossibly tall red shoes, her spike heels striking the pavement like machine gun fire. A few boys were standing around the car. They were about to steal her stuff. Where was Hank when she needed him?

She caught up with the car, out of breath. If she accused them of stealing right off the bat, that would not be so good. "Nice car, eh, boys?" she said and strolled over to the passenger side. There, on the floor, was her red purse. Damn. With two big hunks just about to lean on the car. Hank had forgotten to turn on the alarm.

"Not as nice as my dad's Porsche." One of the kids lit a cigarette.

"My father says his Tesla's coming next week," said another, looking deep into the car.

"You're so full of shit, Paul." The taller boy ran his hand through a shock of dark brown curls.

"Screw you, Mike."

"Your dad works for the sanitary district," Mike giggled. "Shit and shoes, that's his game."

"Leave my dad out of it." Paul raised his right arm.

Alexandra wouldn't care about the fight but they were close enough to the car to hurt it. Mike leaned back. When Paul's swing went wide Mike fell backwards into the car.

"Guys, guys," Alexandra exclaimed. She could kick one with her foot but all three? "If you don't mind, gents, take your fight elsewhere, I need my car."

"This yours?" Mike crawled out and practically fell out on the street. "Nice."

Paul stepped forward, his fists up.

"Not in front of the lady, son," Alexandra said, wanting to feel tough but mostly being terrified. At least she hadn't said the word "boy."

Mike lifted her purse from the floor of the car and held it like it was a disease. "Is this what you're looking for?"

Alexandra gasped.

"Nothing in there but tampons and condoms," she blurted. "Important to me – but to you guys, maybe so – you want the condoms?"

Mike dropped her purse on the ground. Alexandra picked it up, rummaged through it, and closed her hand on her own wallet.

"How many you need?" she asked. The boys fled.

Sweat tickling her temples, Alexandra grabbed tight to her purse and heard footsteps coming down the sidewalk. She didn't think she had it in her to say anything that would make them go away a second time.

She turned to see. It was Hank with a reddened face and a worried look. Worse than the boys any day. She dashed to the passenger seat, reached into her purse for her lipstick and comb. Pulled down the mirror and heard him open the driver's door.

"Oh hi, sweetheart," she said and put her things away. On the way into the recesses of her giant red purse, her fingers felt something different. Had one of the boys left something in there? She closed her fingers around some wide weave cloth, something small, something the size of her palm.

"Last time I take you anywhere," Hank grunted.

"Last time I borrow your wallet." Alexandra handed it over. She wanted to throw it at him. With a sigh she checked the mirror again. Her face felt flush and her pulse was racing. Close call with those boys. She looked over at Hank who was jamming the key into the ignition.

"You like adventures, honey? I can think of something else we can do," she asked. It had been so very long. She'd fended them off, those boys.

"No. We're going home. You're not to be trusted." Hank shoved the car into gear.

But Alexandra knew better. As soon as they got home she'd go out. She was invincible.

From the Sheriff's Calls Section in the *Point Reyes Light*, August 23, 2012

LAGUNITAS: At 7:16 p.m. a concerned citizen captured an injured skunk.

The Skunk

"There's something wrong with him, I can't just leave him; he's hurt, Beth Ann." Alice watched the animal's chest rise and fall, rise and fall. He was lying on his side, not running away or anything. "He's just a baby."

"Don't ask me to come any closer." Beth Ann stood back. "He's still a skunk."

"He's not going to spray you." Alice crouched down and examined the poor little thing. "I could take him to Wild Care."

"Not in my dad's car." Beth Ann frowned. Alice was crazy.

"But what if it was you, injured on the side of the road? You wouldn't like it one bit if I left you there." Alice wondered what else she could do. At least wrap the little kit in something. He stared at her with wide, frightened eyes.

"Call the sheriff, then." Beth Ann brushed dust off her mother's new black and white shirt. She'd snitched it while Mom had been out. Now, wearing it around Alice and her little skunk didn't seem like a very good idea. "Alice, come on."

"I could take it to the vet."

"You'll never get the smell out of your Grandmother's car."

"I'll walk. Honestly, Beth Ann, you are heartless."

Beth Ann had already caught on. She knew she sounded like an awful person, but she wasn't. She took in strays herself, strays like Alice.

"I helped you out last week, Beth Ann. Get a grip."

Beth Ann held back tears. It had been Alice who had made them jump out of the crazy man's truck. Ever since, whenever any of the kids at school said anything mean about her, Beth Ann told them to shut up. "Give me a minute." She went to her house and got a towel.

"He doesn't look so good," Alice said when Beth Ann came back. Alice floated the towel over the skunk. The animal cocked its tail.

"Oh God, oh God, he's going to spray." Beth Ann ran away across the lawn.

"It's going to be okay," Alice cooed to the skunk. The little animal dropped its tail. "Some friend you are, Beth Ann. Scared of a little bitty critter."

"It's a skunk. Alice, have you lost your mind? Spend all day with your new friend; I'm heading to the barn."

"I'll tell all the kids about you," Alice said. The little skunk was panting. "You don't care about anyone but yourself." It wasn't quite Alice's way to be so bullish, but she didn't care.

"You wouldn't," Beth Ann pleaded. "Take it back. Don't tell anyone anything."

"Then just take the other end of the towel and quit being a wimp. The little guy doesn't need any more loud noises, unless, of course, you want it to spray?"

"No, of course not." If it weren't for Alice, Beth Ann would be on a cold hard slab in San Francisco. "You've always had some common sense, Alice."

"Some?" Alice snapped. She concentrated while they cradled the skunk. It would have been easier if he wasn't wiggling around trying to get out.

They set the skunk down outside the front door to the vet's while Alice kept the towel closed. Beth Ann rang the bell.

"May I help you?" Dr. Carter asked, her white coat billowing out behind her.

Beth Ann didn't say anything. She didn't want the vet to think she was stupid enough to bring a skunk to her office.

"This little skunk's hurt," Alice said. She followed Dr. Carter into the coolness of the building, all the way into an examination room.

Dr. Carter turned down the lights, held out a fresh clean towel. "You might want to step into the hallway for a minute, dear."

Alice, backing up, bumped into something soft and jumped a little. "Oh hi, Beth Ann."

Beth Ann wondered why they were out in the hallway. Was the vet going to put him down? She pushed by Alice.

"No, don't," Alice said, "she's expressing."

"Oh." Beth Ann grew quiet.

In a minute, Dr Carter gestured for the girls to come back. She raised her eyes at Beth Ann, the much bigger girl. "Well, your friend here, we had a discussion..."

"Still smells in here." Beth Ann held her nose.

"And it will for a bit," Dr. Carter said. "Now, let's examine the little guy."

Alice leaned forward and placed one hand on the examining table.

"The little skunk is malnourished, but feisty, as you can see." Dr. Carter waved one triple gloved hand over the skunk's smooth little face. "Mom must've been killed. Now, skunks make great pets if you remove their scent gland." Dr. Carter bundled the skunk up and set it in a crate. "We'll give it some milk, some kitty kibble, keep it safe. Now, which of you girls want to keep him?"

"I found it, I rescued it," Alice said. "I saw him first."

"I did!" Beth Ann raised her hand.

"Beth Ann, that's not true!" Alice said. "You were the one who..."

"Oh Alice, Dr. Carter," Beth Ann said. "Please. I've got to be able to keep that skunk – he has the most beautiful coat. Don't you think it would be cool? We could dress alike, black and white, cute as buttons, while we glide down the street."

OLEMA: At 4:55 p.m. an innkeeper reported that a man carrying a bag over his shoulder had come in, asking for beer, wine or a job.

Beer, Wine or a Job

Jeffrey Cooper, manager of the Farmhouse, leaned on the oak bar. "What is it that you want again? A drink? What kind?"

"Wine and beer, like I said," the customer mumbled.

"Both?" Jeffrey wiped the counter. It was closing in on Friday evening and the regulars would show up soon.

"Exactly."

"They don't mix well," Jeffrey said.

"I didn't ask for a mixed drink, sir." The customer eased himself onto a bar stool. It had been a long day. He'd walked something like twenty miles from Bolinas. No one would give him a ride. His feet hurt, his legs hurt, and he was nowhere closer to seeing his baby, Hannah Bea, who lived in Petaluma. If only he could have something to drink. The ice cream bar he'd had at noon had left a sticky residue on his teeth.

"All right, then." Jeffrey returned with a glass of house chardonnay and a pint of Bud Light. Everyone seemed to like Bud Light except for him. "Seven dollars, please."

The customer took a sip of his beer, felt it soothe the inside of his ragged throat. The wine he'd have later. As for the seven dollars, that would present a problem. He only had four.

"Uh, man," he muttered to the bartender with the thin mustache and the wide suspenders. He took another sip of his beer. God, it tasted good going down.

Jeffrey studied his customer. "Yes?"

"Name's Bill." Bill put out his hand. His name was really Beauregard, but in these parts, being a traveling man, he didn't want to say.

Jeffrey leaned on the bar. He'd seen them all, rich or poor, tourists and locals, come into his place. This guy looked more tired than most.

He heard the tinkle of chimes. A mother came into the bar, pushing two whining children. Mac and cheese and milk, and a mess, no drinks, and no profit for his struggling bar. Jeffrey shrugged his shoulders, focused on Bill. "So, what can I do for you?"

"You asked for seven." Bill downed his beer. "I have only four. Hard times, man, hard times."

Jeffrey pulled back the glass of chardonnay. "Sampled this, bud?" He knew better. Once the drink was poured, there was no taking it back. But he didn't have to give it away, did he? He hid it behind the counter.

"Anything I can do around here?" Bill wiped his face with a bar napkin and stared out the window with tired, sad eyes. "I haven't had anything to eat today and I walked all day. From frickin' Bolinas, man."

Jeffrey looked outside; not much action in the parking lot. If it kept up like this, Jesus, he wouldn't even make payroll.

"My feet are killing me." Bill made himself at home at the bar. He placed a colorful cloth bag on the stool beside him, dug out a tired empty wallet, and showed it to the bartender. "Please, it's all I have."

"Sorry." Jeffrey adjusted his suspenders. "We don't have anything for you."

"I'm not inclined to take advantage of you, kind sir," Bill said. "It's just that I'm having temporary difficulties."

Jeffrey could call the cops and this guy would never know. He held his finger over the red panic button under the counter.

"My daughter lives in Petaluma," Bill continued. "I was just trying to get up there and see her. She's a beaut. Her name is Hannah Bea. Such a cutie. Expecting to see her old man. You going to break my daughter's heart, mister bartender?"

Jeffrey paused. Gabriel was short handed in the kitchen. The dishwashers hadn't shown up yet, but they'd be pissed if someone took their jobs. "Tell you what," Jeffrey whistled under his breath. "Yard work, can you do yard work?"

Despite his sore feet Bill wanted to jump out of his chair and hug him. Instead he acted cool.

Ten minutes later he hid his cloth bag in the bushes and was in the parking lot with a broom, cleaning up. Cars sped in and out for hours, full of tourists, teenagers on a tear, police cars on patrol, crying children, tired families, and still he swept. He trimmed hedges; raked trash out of the bushes near the creek, and noted some guy's gear tucked under some trees. He made a note of that. If he had to, he'd sleep there too.

Not a stick, a twig or a leaf was out of place by the time he was done five hours later when Jeffrey came out and called him in.

Back inside, Jeffrey placed a plate of brisket, creamed corn, mashed potatoes, and the glass of wine in front of Bill. "Sorry, it's all we have left," he said.

It looked like heaven to Bill. He ate hungrily. His shoulders and arms ached. His feet had gone beyond pain, swollen in their two small shoes, his little toes crushed. He would lose the nails for sure. Jeffrey gave him two twenties. Bill slid one back to pay the seven dollars for the drinks he'd had earlier. Jeffrey refused it, flipped the lights in the bar off one by one, and escorted Bill to the door.

"Tomorrow, then?" Bill asked, blinking back fatigue.

"Tomorrow will work fine – we'll put you in the scullery. All right – that work for you?" Jeffrey locked up the bar, saw Bill take off down the road and headed to his own car. It was time he told the boss they had a new hire.

Around two in the morning Bill was back. He'd been careful to memorize the security code when Jeffrey had locked up. He'd seen the stack of cash in the open pouch under the register. He was in and out in a jiffy, five hundred dollars in his pocket. Back in the woods again he tucked himself under the lean-to he'd made, buried his money under a rock, and kept an eye on the parking lot until the first truck pulled in a little before ten.

He brushed himself off and knocked at the bar's front door. Inside people were running around and making frantic phone calls. A cruiser pulled up in the parking lot.

"I wasn't sure we were going to see you again." Jeffrey looked surprised as Bill came in. "We got robbed."

"What a shitty thing to do," Bill said and shook his head.

A cop burst through the doors. "We'll have to frisk him," the cop said, tipping her head toward Bill.

Bill raised his arms and stepped wide. Five years in jail; he knew the drill. "Good morning, ma'am."

Officer Kettleman contemplated taking him in, but he only had a twenty in his wallet and Jeffrey vouched for him. She headed back to her cruiser.

"It's such a small community...I don't know what I am going to tell the owner," Jeffrey muttered, wiping the smaller tables down. "It's going to take months to make up the loss."

"What a damn shame," Bill said. "Anything I can do?"

"One of the boys quit," Jeffrey offered. "If you're interested."

"You bet, boss," Bill muttered. He headed downstairs, through the kitchen and into the scullery beyond. It would be a good place to spend the winter. As for Hannah Bea, he'd call her in a few days. They had a long and interesting relationship, and she knew he'd get there eventually.

FROM THE SHERIFF'S CALLS SECTION IN THE *POINT REYES LIGHT*,
SEPTEMBER 20, 2012

POINT REYES STATION: At 5:43 p.m. a man
told deputies he was not living in the storage
container in question.

The Container

"No, of course not, I would never live in a container." Jacob Whitney III
settled himself against a tree near the Palace Market. "How could you say
such a thing?"

"Sir, there was a complaint." Officer Kettleman shifted the weight of her
equipment belt. It was getting on toward evening, and she was looking forward to going off shift. Her mother hadn't been so well lately and if her supper was late, there'd be hell to pay.

"Complaint about what?" Jacob banged the side of the steel storage container that – until an hour ago – had held his things; sleeping bag, cook
stove, battered and beat up backpack. Luckily, he'd just had a shave, so he
looked and felt fit and trim.

"Sir, would you mind opening the container?" In her year with the West
Marin Sheriff's department, Linda had seen them all. Mostly arrogant tourists and people who couldn't drive. She wished the perpetrator would move
to Bolinas where he belonged.

Jacob shrugged his shoulders, produced a key, and with a squeak of hinges, opened the door. It wasn't his fault he was down and out. A few gum
wrappers were on the floor along with a couple of scrunched up balls of
paper. Place smelled clean; he was proud about that. "It's been in my family
for years," Jacob said, "I'm not bothering anyone. I use it for storage."

"Thank you, you may close it now." Linda tried to remember exactly who
had called the sheriff's department. One of the little old ladies from the sa-

lon? Or a snotty kid out for a good time? "You'll have to move it, sir, containers don't belong in town." She passed over Cheda's card. "They tow just about everything. Twenty four hours, then I'll be back," she said, and drove away.

Jacob nodded and smiled. Shit, he had the perfect spot. He could watch everything in town, and after nine p.m. when everything closed up, he could climb into his container, get under his down sleeping bag, lie on top of his extra thick pad, and, by the light from his flashlight, make his way through a dog-eared copy of *Walden*. Now, what the hell, he didn't have money to find a new place or enough money for a tow. Crap.

He walked down the street, away from the tourists and restaurants, and was soon opposite the propane tanks at the entrance to town, where there was open, brushy land, and he could hide and stash his gear. Wasn't going to do his hygiene and fresh clean trousers any good to sleep in the bushes. And if he looked messy, what then? No one would hire him. Damn that cop. She was new. There was no going into the public service building and looking for Max. Not now.

He walked with a limp. A gift from two tours in Iraq. After eight years, his knees still bothered him some, especially after a rain and in the spot, just above, where the shrapnel hit and they couldn't get it out. Once, a long time ago, back when he was flush, and was somebody in the military, the security people in the airport would salute him when he'd saunter through. Now security systems, airports, civilization - it was all too much. He walked deeper into the woods.

It was quiet. He heard the birds chirping and crows cackling and the blackberries were ripe and that was good, and there was a patch of sun, still bright, on that bit of grass there, and he lay down a bit, and wanted to fall asleep, but he couldn't get comfortable.

A half hour later Jacob gathered his things and headed back to town, straw in his hair. Ten years service to his country and now this, homeless, but not helpless. His VA benefits were all messed up, and without a phone, he couldn't stand going to the VA for hours and fill out forms. Last time he'd gone in, after a wait of two hours, they'd said sure, where do we send a check and Jacob, open mouthed, hadn't been able to answer. Now if it hadn't been for the people at the Palace Market slipping him day old food, he would be hungry too. He shoved the last chunk of his morning's blueberry muffin into his mouth and slipped behind the playground.

His container was still there at least. Home. Home at least for one more day. The corrugated walls hung in the air in front of him. He pulled out a key, but the lock was gone, the door open a little. Had the cop broken in? Light broke through the crack in the door, spilling onto the sidewalk. Was she inside?

Jacob peered in. This was his place, his home. Instead of the officer he saw a much smaller woman, crouching by the wall, crying, a Bible opened beside her, a scarf around her neck, a beat up backpack by her feet.

Jacob opened the door wide, making the hinges creak, and she jumped up, wide-eyed.

"I didn't, I don't have to, oh please, please, sir, please don't hurt me. I saw this place…" She held her backpack and stood against the wall.

"You surprised me," Jacob said and put down his things. He was tired, and she was sitting in his favorite spot. "Please, go sit over there in the other corner."

"I have no right to be here, you see, my husband, he drinks, I had to leave," she said, drawing her scarf down to hide her face, moving over, and dropping the flashlight so that the light went wild. It illuminated a cold corner of the container.

Jacob hadn't had a girl, a real girl, address him in a long time. Most of the time people pretended they didn't see him at all. He was taller and stronger than she was, that is, unless she was carrying a shiv? "You armed?" he asked, sounding like a fool. Feeling bad he wondered if he could share his container with her. He was a Christian man; cruelty was not in his DNA.

"Armed? What, me?" She held up her bible. "The good Lord, he says, not to hurt a thing. Mister, I'm recently homeless, we have shelter, and I am a decent person. Have you read Matthew?"

"Not all of it," Jacob lied. "Last night for the container in Point Reyes. Miss, what is your name? Cops were here today."

"Don't let that bother you." She opened up her shawl and let out her long gray hair. "I'm one of God's treasured souls."

"If that works for you, honey," Jacob said, "but the cops – they don't read the same verses."

"From what I know they don't read any verses at all. My name's Meghan. My parents made a mistake, there's no Meghan in the Bible – you think they meant Ruth, and screwed up?"

"Maybe, maybe not," Jacob stated. "I'm Jacob, from the Old Testament."

"And I'm from the new." Meghan put out her hand.

"The new, new." Jacob shook her hand and eased out his sleeping bag. He longed for her warmth, her humanness. "I promise I won't bother you."

"Looks like home to me." Meghan pulled out her blanket, lit her candle and rested her back against the wall. "Thanks."

"They want me to have it towed away," Jacob said. The candle light danced in the dark and made him sleepy.

"I don't know how they can." Meghan dusted off her pant legs. "Your container. My land. They don't have a chance."

Twenty minutes later Officer Kettleman pulled up in her cruiser on her way home. Light was showing under the door. That doggone bum, he should've been long gone by now.

She opened the door, ready to bring him in. She saw him tucked into a sleeping bag and cradling a woman beside him, a candle casting wild shadows on the wall. The woman was reading aloud softly as he listened, his head against her shoulder. Linda hadn't the heart. A long time ago she'd been homeless too. Tomorrow she'd talk to Walter and see what they could do.

FROM THE SHERIFF'S CALLS SECTION IN THE *POINT REYES LIGHT*,
SEPTEMBER 20, 2012

DILLON BEACH: At 2:05 p.m. someone reported that a woman was dancing on a roof. Deputies found and questioned her. She said she was enjoying life.

Nope, I'm Cool

Jessica peered over the edge of the roof at the cruiser. "What do you want?"

"Miss." Linda held her hand over her eyes to block the late afternoon sun. "It's not safe for you to be up there."

"Says who?" Jessica lay down on the asphalt roof and placed her chin in her hands. "What's it to you? I like it up here." She had been dancing in her home-sewn Greek dress and felt like Isadora Duncan, that is, without the scarf. Mom had said no accessories, but a pearl necklace didn't count, did it?

The teenager had no business being on the roof of a two story building. "Miss, do it for me, then, please. Just come on down."

"I thought you were Ashton Kutcher or something, calling up to me. A modern day Romeo and Juliet, eh? And what do I find, a cop, a lady cop? Man, what a disappointment." Jessica made a pirouette. She was so good at them, she made another.

"Miss, please, you could get hurt." Linda didn't want to use the word "fall". That made people want to jump, Walter had said.

"I'll be in trouble if you stay up there, Miss," Linda offered. What the hell, it was worth a try.

Jessica stopped, mid turn. "You? I thought I was the only one who ever got in trouble." She chewed on a fingernail and turned up the volume on her iPhone. She loved music, especially Nine Inch Nails. "Lights In The

Sky" was her absolute favorite. She had been at one of their concerts once, close enough to kiss Trent if they'd let her. After rushing the stage she'd been escorted back to her seat, where she'd stood and screamed his name throughout the whole second set. "Hey officer, you like Nine Inch Nails?"

"You might slip up there. Miss, need a ladder?"

No response from above. Had the girl disappeared?

"I don't need a ladder, I have a window, but you know, it's like, closed."

"Then how'd you get through?"

"What a silly question. I closed it after I came out here. Security first, isn't that what they always say? So," Jessica paced the roof, "perhaps you can come up?" She was flying high now. She eyed a tree branch close to the roof.

Linda paced below. Every call was different, and every call was potentially detrimental to someone. Isn't that what Walter always said? None of the perpetrators ever listened to her worth a damn. Now she was surprised to see the girl back off from the edge.

"I'm coming, don't you worry." Linda shifted her equipment belt. Better yet, she took it off and put it in the cruiser. Walter would never know. If she hurried with this last call, she could still head back to the town for Mom's hair appointment. The back door to the house was unlocked and she ran inside.

She swept the dark living room with eat-in kitchen and knotty pine paneling and cocked her head? Music? Hadn't there been music a moment before?

"Hello?" Feeling a little vulnerable without her equipment, Linda ran upstairs and checked every room until she found the one that overlooked the driveway. The blond girl was saying something from the other side of a window.

"Hold on, honey! I'm coming." Linda pulled up on the double hung. It stuck. Bracing herself with all her strength, it flew up with a bang. But the girl had disappeared.

Linda stepped out on the roof. She felt gravel slip under her rubber soles. "Miss? Hello?"

"If the squirrels can do it, so can I." Jessica waved and jumped into a tree.

Linda ran down the stairs as fast as she could, expecting to have to call the EMTs or the coroner. Jesus.

"Hello there, Officer!" Jessica waved from a branch ten feet off the ground. The bark had been rougher than she expected, but that flying feeling, that was cool. She jumped into a pile of leaves.

"Miss? You okay?" Linda came over to check. Another 5150? The town was full of them.

"Never better, watch and I'll do it again," Jessica said, and ran back inside.

FROM THE SHERIFF'S CALLS SECTION IN THE *POINT REYES LIGHT*,
SEPTEMBER 27, 2012

TOMALES: At 7:01 p.m. a man reported that his mom was trying to kick him out for no reason; she had punched him in the arm and he had called her his favorite four-letter word.

Her Favorite Word

"At least it wasn't *the* five-letter word." Jason shrugged his shoulders and leaned against a door jamb and stared at the officer. "Anyway, what do I care? She started it."

"Jason, get back in here." A small flinty woman peered out from a darkened room. She didn't want the cops around. Why did he have to go and call them?

"Ma'am, Sir." Linda had to be careful; domestic disputes were the worst. "We've had complaints. Your names, please?"

"Barbara Lee Benton, and don't you forget it." The mother stepped forward. "Jason, tell the officer we don't need her type here."

"But Mom, you hit me."

"Officer, let me explain," Barbara Lee Benton went on. "My son Jason is both lazy and a bum. He won't keep his junk out of the living room. With his stuff all over the house, how the hell am I supposed to get the place clean?"

Linda scratched her arm. She'd been out chasing a loose dog and got into some poison oak. "Do you want to press charges, ma'am?"

"Officer, she's always at the William Tell," Jason whined. "Who's going to mind the baby if I get a job?"

"You have a baby?" Linda asked.

"Don't worry, ma'am, Julie's fine, give me a minute," Jason said and disappeared into the house.

Barbara Lee Benton gave Linda a look out of narrowed, deep blue eyes. "Wasn't my idea that he went out and got her pregnant."

Jason came back outside holding a bundle. Inside the blankets a baby sucked on a pacifier and blinked in the light. "Isn't she just the cutest thing?"

"So, Ms.. Benton, what would you like us to do?" Linda asked.

"Take a look at my son, officer. Jason's an able bodied young man, unemployed, and back home again." Barbara Lee Benton patted Linda's arm.

Linda stepped back. She didn't like anyone touching her uniform.

"Where the hell am I supposed to go, Mom?" Jason spat. "And me with Julie? You keep trying to kick me out. It's heartless."

"I trip over your crap and the baby's toys all the time." Barbara Lee turned her attention to the officer. Maybe Jason calling the cops hadn't been such a good idea. "We could try and get along better, I guess." She didn't want to go back to jail. What would they do with her? Two offenses, and now, a third?

"I could've called you by a nicer, sweeter name, ma," Jason cooed, still pissed. "You know, like love?"

Linda tried her best to hold her temper. Jason looked all of 24, if that, or maybe 19, with his peach fuzz. Probably never shaved, and the baby, what, six weeks, less? "Where's the mother?"

"Way the hell and gone to Idaho," Barbara Lee Benton said with a snort.

"She had the baby, came by for a visit, and left." Jason cooed to Julie. She rooted around in the blankets.

To Linda, the baby looked comfortable enough, and as for Jason, there was no crime in being unemployed. As for Ms. Benton, she hadn't broken any laws either.

"Gotta go, soup's burning," Ms. Benton said and dashed inside.

Linda and Jason both heard the sound of a dead bolt striking home.

"Now, what?" Jason asked, facing the locked door. The baby began to cry. "Ma?" He banged on the door. "Ma, come on, let me in, quit joking."

Linda listened at the door.

"I'll go around the back, I have a key." Jason placed Julie, in her blankets, into Linda's arms. "I'll only be gone a minute."

Linda, surprised and not at all sure what to do, held the warm baby away from her uniform. Little Julie smelled of soap and sunlight. She was beautiful, a little curl on her broad, clear forehead, and a tiny rosebud mouth. Having had no younger sisters or brothers to care for, Linda felt like she might drop her. Her equipment belt and a gun dug into her hip just inches from the baby's feet. But none of this felt as bizarre as she did, outside a locked house, at eight in the evening, holding a baby and no dad or grandma in sight.

Five minutes later Jason had not returned. Linda went around the back and called and knocked but there was no answer. She checked again at the front door.

She was about to use her walkie-talkie when little Julie put out her hand and reached for her glasses. Linda pulled back and at the same time heard a ruckus from deep inside the house. She had to go in. She couldn't exactly put Julie on the front seat of the cruiser and leave her there while she broke down the front door. She called dispatch.

Walter, back at the office, was not pleased when Linda called in. What was the matter with her? It was a simple domestic dispute, mother and son, but the baby – that presented a new twist. Spraying his ficus plant with another shot of Miracle Gro, he called Child Protective Services, grabbed his gun, and headed out the door.

In Tomales, Linda was feeling a little desperate. It was getting cooler, and from the dampness on her arms, the baby was wet and so was her uniform. One half hour had passed, and despite her knocking, yelling and going around the house, no one had answered the door. She headed back to her cruiser, made a nest on the front seat with her jacket, lay the baby down, and tucked the wool blanket she always kept in the trunk around her. Linda closed the windows and watched the baby kick her legs and swing her arms, open and close her fragile fingers and coo. When she began to cry, Linda turned on the radio, and the sound of the dispatcher making calls lulled Julie to sleep. Linda snuggled her and kissed her and looked out at the front door from time to time. No one came in and out.

Twenty minutes later in a flash of lights and sirens, Walter pulled up in his cruiser followed by another car containing a social worker and Protective Services staff. All the commotion made poor little Julie cry, and the social worker came over, and Linda held the baby a little too long, smelling her, feeling her warmth and her uniform got soaked again, and with a sigh, gave up the baby.

Standing there, in the late dusk, with the trees weaving in the wind, and the fog crawling over distant hills, she felt suddenly bereft, as if a part of her heart had been stolen. With the baby gone, the wetness spread, and Linda felt cold while she and Walter surrounded the house. With a shout, they were in, and found both Barbara Lee and Jason sprawled on a trash covered couch, both drunk, watching the baseball game, with the volume so loud it hurt Linda's ears. Jason looked up at the cops and smiled.

"Coming for the last inning?" He gestured to a worn spot on the sofa that was not covered with newspapers, beer cans and empty pizza boxes.

Linda had expected something more, something better for Julie.

"Mom says later, after the game, that I should clean up, and I will – but ma, oh no, they struck him out. Pull the umpire, you idiots."

Barbara Lee, quiet now, dozed in a stained recliner.

"Don't bother her, she's sleeping," he stated.

Linda wanted to ask him didn't he care about the baby, but stayed silent. Little Julie deserved better.

"Officers, please, you must understand. I stopped calling her names, and she's out cold, so no problems, right?" Jason asked. The blue-green light of the TV flickered across his face. He glanced at Linda with a frown. "What did you do with my baby?"

"We have some paperwork to do," Linda said. There was a way, wasn't there, for her to talk to Protective Services? She could manage with Julie, couldn't she?

"Where's my little girl?" Jason closed in on Linda.

She stepped aside. The other deputies cuffed him. Barbara Lee Benton woke up with a snort.

"She made me do it, you know, drink too much, I didn't mean to," Jason bellowed. "She started the fight; she punched me in the arm first. But it's okay, I love her; she's just a little old lady, officer. We all have bad days, sometimes. Hey, quit pushing me around." Another officer cuffed Barbara Lee.

"Child endangerment," the officer said.

"Jason's no child, he's over twenty-one," Barbara Lee laughed as they took her away.

Silence descended, making Linda feel all alone in the quiet.. She heard Julie's wail from the other car and instinctively reached out for her. The other cars drove away, leaving Linda disconsolate. She headed back to her cruiser and touched the seat beside her. It was still warm.

From the Sheriff's Calls Section in the *Point Reyes Light*, October 4, 2012

BOLINAS: At 2:48 p.m. a passerby reported a thin, young man, dressed in Capris and a distinctive hat, standing on the side of the road, holding a guitar and rocking back and forth with a bloody nose.

The Thin, Young Man

"See Grandma, even grown men have bloody noses." Alice peered at the newspaper and felt satisfied.

Mildred was making chocolate-chip cookies and had her hands deep in the batter. "Fetch me a cookie sheet, would you dear?"

Alice rattled through a drawer full of baking things.

Mildred hadn't minded too much when Alice had been little and she'd set her up in the kitchen with a wooden spoon and all her pots and pans. All that rattling around was now giving her a headache. Maybe she'd had a little too much whiskey.

"I don't just let my nose run like that, not when I'm in public," Alice said. "And I certainly wouldn't be out in front of a store, playing guitar and bleeding."

"I should certainly hope not," Mildred sniffed. She tried to remember how she was supposed to wash her hands. If she just ran them under the tap, everything would be greasy, and soap wouldn't help at all.

"I'll do the rest, Grandma." Alice peeled cookie dough off Grandma's fingers and placed dollops onto a cookie sheet. They were making cookies for a fundraiser for a new library for her school. Alice figured one hundred big cookies at two dollars apiece would get her a prize for the most sales. Being with Grandma made her happy.

"Where's Grandpa?" Alice noticed the empty recliner. Her heart felt empty and a little hesitant. Why hadn't she noticed earlier?

"Oh *him*," Mildred sniffed. "He's at the Western. Baseball. You would think someone would have something else to do."

"During post season?" Alice asked, checking the score on her iPhone. There wasn't anything more important than baseball when the Giants were in the playoffs.

"How have your bloody noses been, dear?"

"Not so bad – I didn't have any on my date."

"Told you so," Mildred clucked. "Was he a gentleman?"

Alice didn't want to say. This was a sore spot. Her date had been a disaster. Why had she mentioned it?

Mildred noticed that her granddaughter's face was clouded. "Did he make you uncomfortable, honey?"

How could Alice lie? She was a terrible liar. It's just that she was so ashamed. She wouldn't put out, that's what he was going to tell all the boys at school. "It was awful."

"Awful?" Mildred stood up tall in her Oxfords. "What did he do to you?"

To Alice, Grandma seemed to loom over her.

"He hurt you, honey?" Grandma repeated. "He try and take advantage of you? What was his name?"

"At least he took me home on time," Alice said, hoping that would keep Grandma from asking any more questions.

"Right after? Right after what? Did he try to entice you? With drugs, alcohol, sweet talk? I know how boys are."

"At least I didn't get a nosebleed," Alice crowed. "Maybe I should've. And cover his bright white shirt with spots of blood. He was squishing me, Grandma. Like a man."

"Boy," Mildred sniffed. "At fifteen he's just a boy."

"I don't care what you call him," Alice argued. "He seemed like a man to me."

"I bet."

"He tried to kiss me. I turned, oh Grandma." Alice buried her face with her sleeve. "The kids think I'm weird already – if he tells, I'm dead."

"Things weren't that hard in my day." Mildred pulled out one batch of cookies and set another in the oven. This was going way too slow; she was going to have to double up.

"I hate dating, I'm never growing up." Alice dug for her iPhone. She listened to the game a moment.

"You're only a teen, honey, you have lots of time."

"I have no time. I'm going to end up like that guy in front of the store, begging for quarters, playing on a pathetic guitar, and having nosebleeds."

"Oh honey." Mildred held her youngest granddaughter. All the rest of them seemed to have no troubles at all, but this one, this Alice, she was special. "Maybe – if you want, we could take out the next batch, turn off the oven and head to town. And watch the baseball game."

"I can't go to the Western," Alice sniffed. "I'm a minor."

"So? The owner will never know once I dress you up."

"I look fourteen, twelve sometimes."

"You want to watch the game, dear?" Mildred grabbed a hat out of the closet. It had a broad brim, and a feather. "Then don't complain."

"You're crazy, Grandma."

"Oh, don't you start." Mildred applied lipstick and rouge to Alice's clear white skin.

She missed a few spots. Alice examined herself in the front hall mirror. She hoped no one from school would recognize her.

"You look a lot like a grown-up, Alice." Mildred dabbed her own cheeks with rouge.

Alice giggled. Mom and Dad never had time for dress up.

Mildred wrapped her best tiger silk scarf around Alice's white oxford cloth shirt. "You look like Mata Hari, my dear."

"Mata-what?"

"Never mind." Mildred kissed her on the forehead. "We have to hurry, it's the seventh inning."

Alice, feeling silly and having trouble negotiating the front steps in her Grandma's old pumps, concentrated on getting to the car in one piece.

"Just look at you, girl." Mildred pulled over on the corner in front of the Western.

"Momwould kill us if she sees me like this." Alice tried not to giggle. She still smelled faintly of chocolate chip cookies and wondered if anyone would notice.

The Western was packed. They snuck in the back and sat down, not bothering to look for Fred. He found them a little later on his way to the restroom.

"You didn't tell me your sister was coming," he said and sat down beside them at a tiny table. A roar went up from the crowd as Buster Posey hit a grand slam.

Excited, Alice grinned at Grandpa, who noticed her at last.

"It's a great day, girl, a great day." He patted her on the back, while Alice, choking a bit on a piece of ice, hoped she wouldn't get another nosebleed.

From Sheriff's Calls Section in the *Point Reyes Light*, March 28, 2013

WOODACRE: At 8:49 a.m. a man reported that his wife had left him with only a few bottles of nuts.

Nuts

"What kind of nuts?" Mildred asked Fred over breakfast at the Station House.

It was his birthday, and he was having scrambled eggs, sausage and a glass of whole milk, his favorite. Tina, the waitress, was making eyes at him and he was delighted. 82 today. He felt like 40. "What did you say, dear?"

"Nuts. What kind of nuts, Brazil, cashew, in a bottle, not a jar? How 'bout steel nuts, hexes, or bolts?"

"Oh sweetheart." Fred moved his chair closer. She'd been getting upset about all kinds of things lately; he hadn't been able to soothe her quite enough. Baths helped, soft candles at bedtime helped, but more often than not he found her in the middle of the night, in her pink nightie, wandering around, calling for their daughter Hattie and their son, Peter.

"Maybe the wife had been having a bad day, and became confused. But why leave nuts?" he asked.

"I'm not having this breakfast." Mildred shoved her plate aside, rose from her chair and walked out to the patio. It was foggy, and a cool wind blew through the fence, making the heat lamps wobble. From inside Fred watched her for a bit, and eventually went to get her.

"I miss her, Fred, I really do," Mildred said, taking a seat under a fruit tree. "We used to sit here when she was a baby, and she'd giggle so, and splash her brother at the fountain."

"Angel." Fred sat down next to her. He wiped a bit of egg from the corner of her mouth. "Cold out here. Come on inside. Want some toast?"

"Wheat Berry, sourdough, gluten free?" Mildred stood up and rattled her cane against metal tables. "There are too many choices these days." She marched back into the dining room. "Nuts, indeed." She sat down in a huff.

Fred eyed Tina, tasted his eggs. Cold. She'd fill his coffee, but re-heat his eggs, never.

Mildred dunked a corner of her toast into her coffee. "Mmm." She tried another, swallowed it, and studied her husband. "So, if I left you, I'd take the nuts."

"Excuse me?" Fred sputtered into his tea. "You have some idea of leaving me? Now?" They'd been married for years; her lively conversations were as natural to him as breathing.

"Nope, I wouldn't leave you with a thing."

"Ah." He had no idea what she was talking about. Nothing new there. "What about those Giants, hunh?" he asked, hoping to bring her back to reality.

"All finished?" She stood up to go.

"Wait. Now Mildred, sit a spell. It's my birthday. Rest." He eased out her chair, patted the seat. "What would you like for your birthday, dear?"

"Roses." She twirled her finger on her water glass, making it hum. "A bouquet of flowers. Oysters. Dinner at Nick's Cove – and of course," she sighed, "dancing with you at Toby's." She thought a spell. "I'd give it all up," she sniffed and looked out the window, "if, Fred, if Hattie came home. It's been years."

Peter was gone, Fred knew that, it had been a while, but Hattie, Hattie was right there, living in Menlo Park, being difficult. She could call them on the phone. Make his birthday happy and mend her mother's sad little heart.

"I would never leave you," Fred said, taking her hand. "Not anymore."

"And when did you change your mind?" she snorted.

"I didn't mean to say that. I…" he stuttered, losing his footing. Tina was probably a lot more even tempered than Mildred. She probably didn't talk to trees, but he loved his little wife, was used to her footfall, her interesting take on just about everything.

"I suppose I would leave more than nuts…" Mildred went on. "I'd leave pots and pans, and household cleaners…"

"Gee, thanks…"

"And everything…but the photos. Never the photos."

"Mildred, please, what is making you go on so? You seem upset. Over some entry in the paper? Come, have some more coffee then, or tea. Want the paper? Anything? Honey?"

But Mildred didn't say anything. She grabbed his hand, dug her nails into the soft skin on his arm, and pointed her finger out the window. "It's …it's her…" she sputtered.

Fred squinted through the windows, looked around other diners, and saw a forty something year old woman milling about out on the sidewalk. A tourist. He looked back into his milk. If he ignored Mildred, she'd stop fussing eventually.

The door bells chimed as people came inside. One figure waded deep into the dining room, marched past the hostess asking if she needed help, strode toward the windows at the back of the restaurant, and dropped her heavy bag on the carpet in front of Mildred and Fred.

"Happy birthday, Dad," she said and Mildred burst into tears.

FROM THE SHERIFF'S CALLS SECTION IN THE *POINT REYES LIGHT*, OCTOBER 11, 2012

POINT REYES STATION: At 10:14 p.m. a woman reported losing a purse at the "bakery next to the clothing store that sells dancing shoes."

Dancing Shoes

"Dancing shoes, Fred?" Mildred hummed and stared out the window. It had been a beautiful autumn day, no fog, no mist, and now it was getting cooler. She loved fall. Something was rustling in the yard. Was it those doggone raccoons again?

Fred, despondent that the Giants had lost their third game of the National League Championship, was trying to tie his shoes. Oh, he remembered how to do it - but his gut got in the way and he wasn't as flexible as he used to be. Getting old sucked.

"Dumb tourists." Mildred ankled her feet in their Oxfords. She hated her shoes. She still had pretty ankles; she could show off her feet if the goddamn doctor hadn't made her wear those awful orthopedics. She heard Fred huffing and puffing. "You want some help, darling?"

"I'm fine!"

"Ah," Mildred muttered. Lost his hearing aids again. She thought she had a spare pair somewhere. "Bet there's no place in Point Reyes that sells dancing shoes."

Fred, frustrated it had taken him ten minutes to tie his shoes, eyed his wife over his reading glasses. "Damsels? In town? Really? Since when?" He figured Mildred had gone around the bend. Most of the time he ignored her.

"Shoes, Fred, pay attention, I was talking about shoes."

"Are you making fun of me?"

"Oh for heaven's sake, calm your liver." Mildred grabbed her knitting.

Fred cleared his throat. "I bet if there were dancing girls in Point Reyes you wouldn't let me see 'em." She'd promised him, years ago, that she'd take him to see some dancing girls, and had never delivered.

"My dear husband. Don't you remember?"

"Dancing girls? I would remember dancing girls." He wiped his forehead with his sleeve. Seemed kind of hot in the house. "Did you turn up the heat?"

"No." She closed her sweater and buttoned it tight. She liked it warm. "Not my fault."

"What's not your fault, the dancing girls or the heat?"

"You're driving me crazy!" She marched off into the back of the house. He didn't listen. What was the use? Seemed like she had to spell everything out for him these days.

The canopy over their bed fluttered from the hot air coming off the furnace vents. She kind of liked it; it felt like they were living like Bedouins. For all his faults, Fred did have his amusing side. She found his extra pair of hearing aids in the medicine chest, hidden behind some four year old aspirin. She didn't understand what all that fuss was over outdated medicines – in her age aspirin lasted. As for her, she checked herself in the full length bathroom mirror, she still had her figure, even though gravity and eighty years had done their work.

She held out her arms in fifth position like she used to do years ago in Mrs. Brooks' ballet class when she'd been in Bluebirds, and eyed her head and shoulders at an angle in the mirror – yes, there, a hint of Margot Fonteyn. Heck, if Fonteyn could dance at sixty, she could do it at eighty. She rushed back into the living room.

"Fred, dearest Fred," she cooed into his ears and brushed his white hair back from his forehead. There wasn't much but it was silky smooth. She caressed his hands and he snuffled awake. "Care to dance?" She turned an ankle so he could admire her.

Fred, without his glasses, couldn't see much and she was a bit of a blur, but he could feel her all right, light as a bird, and wiggling soft on his belly. He nudged over to make room.

She dropped his hearing aids into his palm. "They're not going into your brain, just push. Care to dance, my love?"

"Mildred, I'm old and cranky and I can't touch my toes anymore."

"As if you ever could," she snorted.

"My point exactly." Her voice was perky and happy. Perky had left him a long time ago and happy had taken the bus. "So what is it that you want? Money? I don't have any. Shoes? You got your rhinestone shoes? The TV remote?" He handed it over with a sigh. "Season's over as far as I'm concerned."

"I'll put on Perry Como," she suggested.

"Oh, aren't we the hip set? Sixty year old tunes."

Mildred turned on the hi-fi, pulled a record out of a sleeve, set it on the turntable, and scratched the hell out of it with the needle.

"For God's sake, girl, easy, easy, you'll break the thing." Fred jumped out of his chair to fix it, like he did with everything Mildred touched.

"What's your problem? I didn't break the boom box, you did." She stood by the volume knob waiting to turn it up full blast.

"And I suppose you'll blame me for breaking the cassette recorder, too?" He lifted the needle and set it on automatic. The turntable arm lifted slowly and clicked into place.

"It wasn't my fault you dropped it in the river." She listened to the first few notes and imagined she was twenty again.

"The Pelican case was supposed to be waterproof." Fred went back to the couch.

"Fred." Mildred put out one gnarled hand, "dance with me."

Her skin was soft and buttery.

"You remember the waltz?" she asked, "one two three, one two three?"

"The foxtrot is my favorite," Fred counted, "one two three four."

"You never could count to three." She placed one hand on his shoulder. It seemed so far away.

"Now dip," he said, leading her into a turn.

"So you can dance," she said, wanting to add 'despite your bulk'. He smelled like pine trees in the rain.

As for Fred, holding his wife in his arms was as close to heaven as he'd come in a while.

"Not so bad for an old fart." He took her for a stroll across the hard linoleum floor.

"So, you still can cut a rug," she laughed, "but something doesn't seem quite right." She stopped and let go.

Losing his balance, Fred flew into the piney wood paneled wall. "Jesus! What are you doing?"

"These shoes are no good. They don't slide. You think that store will have my size? Pink, yes, of course, with garnets and ribbons, and a soft sole. Fred? You listening? What are you doing?"

"Sleeping." Fred climbed back into his recliner. "You're wearing me out."

Mildred, disappointed, reached over to raise him again. But he didn't seem to hear, even though he was right there, his eyes closed. She stood up to think. On the coffee table she saw a glass of water and two pink things inside it. His hearing aids. His soft snores filled the air. Resigned, she took off for her bedroom again. Tomorrow, no matter what, she'd buy a pair of dancing shoes. Pink, not black, this time.

STINSON BEACH: At 9:42 p.m. someone heard a woman yelling "Help!" and "Boy!"

My Name is Hannah Bea

"Boy?" Linda asked. "What do they mean, boy?"

Walter angled his head around his ficus plant that blocked his view of both Linda and the rest of the office. His plant was doing well which pleased him no end. It helped him imagine he had a private office. "What is it?" He wanted to add "now"and be difficult but that usually helped no one but him. There were just all these incessant calls.

"Boss." Linda had heard the irritation in his voice. "People are yelling 'help' on the beach. I got that, but 'boy'? What is that supposed to mean?"

"Linda." Walter wished it were a quiet night. He wanted to get home and finish up the final season of "Lost". "The 'help' is of some concern, deputy, concentrate on that."

Linda fumed. It was closing in on midnight, the end of her shift, and if people were stupid enough to go swimming in the dark, it was their own fault if they had problems. Didn't they have any sense?

The look on his face was unmistakable.

"I'll go check it out," she said, rising and clanking through the office as she put on her equipment belt.

"Just make your presence known, deputy. No funny stuff. And this time…" Walter thought a moment. "On second thought, you want me to come?"

"Not on your life." He was still at it, trying to protect her. Damn. "I got it – could be nothing. I'll call, I'll call in." She headed out of the public safety building into the cool night and headed down the coast.

The Stinson beach parking lot was dark by the time she wheeled through the entrance and parked near the restrooms, a concrete building that was the only structure on the beach. She went inside.

She waved her mag light into each stall, and finding nothing, went outside and walked up and down the beach, noticing the usual, beer cans, trash, and ashes, still warm. She wrapped her jacket tighter around her middle and was heading back to her cruiser when she heard a small cry, a sound that was definitely human. She headed back inside.

"Who's there?" She splashed her beam on the concrete walls. Another cry. It came from the far corner of the ladies' room, somewhere near the janitor's closet.

She opened the door, her hand on her weapon.

"I know what it looks like, ma'am," said a small woman. "I needed a place to sleep and now, this. Damn."

Linda turned on the overhead light. The girl was sitting on the floor next to the janitor's mop and bucket.

"I was trying to be so quiet. They said it was going to be easy, but they lied."

"Who said what, Miss?" Linda asked, finger over her call back button. The girl didn't look so good, in her twenties, maybe. She got down on the floor.

"Boyd...took off," the girl sniffed. "Couldn't stand the sight of me."

"You all right? What are you doing down there?" The girl was wearing a long skirt, Uggs, a military type jacket, and held bundles of cloth in her hands. "What do you have there, honey?"

"Don't call me honey. You sound like a goddamn waitress."

"Right," Linda agreed. "Then what's your name?"

"My dad named me Hannah Bea and there's nothing right about it."

"Now, Ms. Bea." Linda took out her notebook. She would call Walter if she needed to.

"First name's Hannah Bea, last name is never mind!" The girl gave out a sharp cry.

"You hurt? Bleeding? Cut? You fell?"

"If that's what you call it."

"Then come out from behind the slop sink, Hannah, so I can help you."
Was this girl on drugs? PCP? Something else?

"Eat shit and die."

"All right. I'll stay here. You said you were bleeding?"

"Bleeding? You think so? You are an idiot." Hannah Bea caught her
breath. "My dad's going to kill me."

"Seems a strange place to spend the night, Hannah. Kind of cold back
in there."

"You think?" Hannah Bea spat. "Natural, they said. Easy. It's cold everywhere for me. Don't come any closer."

"What a place to have a baby, Hannah Bea." For the love of God, the
poor girl.

"I couldn't make it to my car! I threw up. Stopped here. Go away. Leave
me alone."

Linda called the paramedics, called Walter, and turned back to see Hannah Bea, crouched over, breathing hard. Between screams and sobs, Linda
managed to give her her jacket and gently pried the bunch of fabric out of
her hands.

"Baby clothes," Hannah Bea moaned between contractions. "Whatever
you do, keep them clean."

Linda wondered what part of the bathroom would be clean enough. She
set the clothes on a bench on top of stacks of paper towels and grabbed another bunch for Hannah Bea.

"They say God moves in mysterious ways," Hannah Bea gasped. "But I
don't believe in God, do you?" She grasped Linda's arm tightly and pulled
her down. "Tell me, then, what kind of God's plan is this?"

The floor felt slippery under Linda's knees. Hannah Bea smelled of sweat
and blood.

"Jesus, it's so hard," Hannah Bea moaned. "Boy, I'm going to kill that...
oh!"

Linda wanted to get her more paper towels and leaned forward to get up.
"Don't move!"

Linda had been trained in emergency births, but training was nothing like this. The walls of the bathroom were yellow, hard and cold. An omnipresent smell of pee seemed to emanate from the concrete floor, and it was all wet under Hannah Bea. Where the hell were the paramedics?

She adjusted Hannah Bea's clothes and examined her. Hannah Bea closed her eyes and pushed, her face changing to bright red as she banged on the floor. "Oh my God, Jesus, help me!"

On the paper towels, under her clothes, Linda saw something new, something pink, a very small head. "Easy now, dear, just puff and don't push. Easy now."

The rest of the baby came out in a swoosh, and Hannah Bea opened her eyes, and locked them on Linda's. Linda had taken off her uniform shirt, her equipment belt, and wrapped the baby in her shirt. "You've got a girl, Hannah Bea, you brave thing. A baby girl."

Hannah Bea collapsed back on the floor. "Wrap her in those clothes please, and take her away."

"Oh Hannah Bea." Linda tucked the baby in the blankets that she'd set on the bench. Linda held the baby close to her chest, blankets around them as the paramedics came in with their first aid kits and efficient ways. They placed Hannah Bea on a gurney, and were about to give her her baby when she let out a cry.

"Don't. I can't keep her, I'm a bum. I don't deserve a baby." She turned her face away.

"You'll feel better later, once you get some rest," Linda said and reluctantly handed the baby to the paramedics. She had felt so warm.

"We'll take it from here," the paramedics said. Linda watched them leave the cold, despairing place. Left alone with her thoughts she suddenly felt panicky and ran up to the van. "She doesn't have a friend in the world," she said, and went to climb in with Hannah Bea and her baby.

"There's no room, officer," a paramedic said, "unless you're next of kin."

"She's my sister," Linda said and stepped inside.

OLEMA: At 8:15 p.m. a woman reported that her boyfriend disappeared during their camping trip, leaving a goodbye note on her tent.

Going to Olema

"So, what kind of jerk would do that, Fred?" Mildred asked. He was mowing the lawn which pleased her no end.

"What was that again?" Fred jammed the mower into a tall section of Bermuda grass.

"This guy – he went home and left his girlfriend in the campground." She climbed out of her recliner and thunked him on the arm with the paper. "Don't you read Sheriff's Calls?"

He stopped, turned off the mower. "So?"

"So, nothing. This is way bigger than just taking a stroll. They were camping. He took off in the middle of the night. And the poor thing, she wakes up in the cold morning and he's gone, no sleeping bag, no duffle bag, no car, no nothing. I bet he even took her purse."

"Did the paper really say that?" Fred wiped his forehead with his sleeve. "I can't see what a guy would want with a gal's purse, unless he's that type, you know, and then why would he go camping with her?" He was puzzled. Ever since the 50s, his world had taken a turn to the left and he'd never been able to keep up.

"It doesn't say anything about the guy being gay." Mildred adjusted her skirt. Damn thing kept migrating around her hips. "That's a terrible thing to do."

Fred thought for a moment. He could imagine having an afternoon off. It would be quiet and he could watch all the baseball he wanted. "How 'bout those Giants?"

"That's abandonment, Fred."

"So, what happened after that, dear?" He wondered if it was too early to work on his hidden stash of beer. Since last Thursday she hadn't yet found his second case of Negro Modelo hidden behind the stacks of empty paint cans in the garage.

"How am I supposed to know?" Mildred worked on the buttons of her cotton sweater. She'd miss-buttoned them, again? She paced the small concrete-covered patio. "Let's go see her," she said, abandoning her project.

"Maybe she was arguing with him and he headed to the Farmhouse for a beer. Maybe he was frustrated. Maybe he wanted some peace and quiet." Fred wanted to turn on the mower and drown out his wife's voice.

"There's a gal in distress and you're going to ignore her?"

"Hey." Fred was the one in distress. "Look, I'm having a perfectly happy Sunday morning doing chores like you asked. The baseball game starts in an hour. You want to search through the campground, of, say, thirty or forty people, and ask if any of them saw a gal alone in a tent?"

"If I was in distress, I would certainly want your help," Mildred sniffed.

"You've never been in distress since the day I married you." Perhaps he'd made a mistake by spoiling her so much. "They'll think we're crazy and call the cops."

"Poor thing. She's probably crying at the Farmhouse."

"She's probably crying into her beer." Fred grinned. "All those guys there and a pretty girl to boot. She'll be fine."

"Not if she's not pretty, not if she's old and unattractive like me."

"Now, wait a minute." Fred felt like he had lost his footing. "I am not going to the campground on a fool's errand. You want to go, go, you know where the keys are." The thought of all that beer made him feel bold. If she left now...

"So," she took down sheets from the laundry line, "I should go to the campground, a woman of 82, with my bad leg and cane and rattle everyone's nerves? Alone, Fred? What if someone comes after me? How am I supposed to defend myself? With a clothes pin?"

Fred was lost in thought over Sergio Romo's pitching. He liked his style and he liked his beard even more. Neat and tidy, not like that hairy pitcher, Wilson. He headed for the storage shed, and saw, at the last minute, his wife heading for the car. He heard a low rumble and the crash of metal garbage cans. He found his wife in the Buick, car sputtering in neutral, her shouting at him from behind the wheel.

He held his hands on the window, gestured for her to open it and kill the engine. Instead she revved it up.

"Sweetheart." He pressed his palms on the glass. "Dear."

"Oh me?" She took her time rolling down the window. "I told you a thousand times to move the garbage cans, yet you still leave them in the middle of the driveway. Now push them out of the way."

"You're on the lawn, dear."

"Lie all you want, you big oaf, Fred Rhinehart. You make me a prisoner in my own home. You won't let me drive. You won't let me help that poor woman. You're cruel and heartless, Fred."

"Hand me the keys."

She raced the engine, backed up and shot forward. He barely got his toes out of the way. The car stalled and died.

"Emergency brake, darling, let me help you." He opened the driver's door and asked her to move down the bench seat.

"Now, where to?" he asked.

"Town," she muttered, as he eased them down the driveway. "Stop. I forgot something." She threw her sweater on the floor, ran into the house, and returned a second later, a determined look on her face and a box under her arm.

"You want to go to the market? See Doris?" he asked, eyeing the box. "What do you have there?" He dialed in the baseball game. There was still time, wasn't there, to catch the fourth inning?

"Bullets," she said, pulling the sweater off the floor. "Guns aren't any good unless they're loaded, Fred."

"Who are you going to shoot this time?" he laughed. "Last time it was the cops, the trash cans, raccoons, and bears."

"This time it's you," she said, aiming the gun at him. "I told you I wanted to go to Olema."

From the Sheriff's Calls Section in the Point Reyes Light, November 1, 2012

STINSON BEACH: At 9:09 a.m. a frizzy-haired man dressed only in jeans was found locked in the library at Audubon Canyon Ranch.

Dressed Only In Jeans

"I couldn't help it, the door locked behind me." Anson Baker ran one hand through his frizzy hair. "And no, I wasn't stealing, if that's what you're thinking. Heck, if I was going to rob something, I'd go to a bar." Well, he would if he could break in; the Sanctuary had been much easier. He rocked back on his heels. Damn. He'd be lucky if the officer believed any of it.

Linda eyed the perpetrator. "You were in the library, after dark. What were you doing there?"

"Reading up on birds, ma'am," Anson said. That much was true; he had been bored to tears. "Ma'am, I'm a student at Dominican, we're studying water birds. I was doing original research." How was he supposed to know they wouldn't have any cash? "Some of them are endangered, ma'am."

"Tell it to the judge, sir." Linda sized him up. He looked like hell, scraggly hair, three day old beard, torn and tattered trousers. "And your shoes?" she asked, noticing his bare feet.

"Have you ever been in the Bolinas Lagoon? If I wore shoes, I'd lose them in the muck." Anson gazed out the open door. If only he'd never come inside. Jesus, how could he have been so stupid?

Linda held her pencil to her lips. "Your name, sir – and don't give me a bad time, I've heard them all." She needed to get home and fill out all those adoption papers for Hannah Bea's baby. "License, please."

"Anson Baker." Anson held out a weatherworn wallet. "I don't drive officer, and therefore have no license." He hadn't driven legally in over five years; he just got confused with all the other cars on the road.

He was heading for the door. "Mr. Baker, you can't just take off during an interview."

"But William H. Macy did it in Fargo. And he got away."

"Mr. Baker! Stop. It's too early in the day. Don't annoy me. Is that clear?"

"Yes, ma'am," Anson said, feeling put upon. He held still.

"Your address then, Mr. Baker?"

"Fifteen Mayberry Lane." Anson wondered if that was a movie or a real place. He lived in the bushes, but he sure wasn't going to tell her that. "San Rafael."

"Very well." Linda wrote it down. "How'd you get here?"

"I got a ride," he answered. "Can I go home now, ma'am? I spent the night in the library, I have to use the bathroom, and I'm freezing."

Linda looked at the pathetic little man with the impossible hair. "Let me ask if they want to press charges. Don't move."

Anson eyed the hills nearby; they were so close.

"Or I'll cuff you. You want me to do that?"

Anson, who was desperately afraid of small spaces and bridges, couldn't stand the idea of being chained. No movie hero he knew liked it either. He stood at attention like De Niro, hands at his sides. "Ma'am, I will stay right here."

He hung around the office door, whistling, looking out at the birds settling in the mud in the Bolinas Lagoon and wishing he could run. A long time ago, the Lagoon had been full of water. When he'd been a kid he could sail there in his little Sunfish. Now it was a mud hole and it stank all the time. Back then no one told him what to do. Back then everything was beautiful. He was a kid, eight, maybe, digging for clams, tummy over the belly of his sunfish, gazing into the water, and Mom had been around.

"Mr. Baker?" Linda jolted him out of his reverie.

"Yes?" he replied, wishing like anything he was eight again. At least then he knew where he belonged in the world.

"You're free to go, sir."

Anson wasn't sure what to do next.

"Mr. Baker," Linda ordered. "Stay away from Audubon Canyon Ranch. Confine your bird watching to the Giacomini wetlands, and for God's sake, wear your shoes." She snapped her notebook shut and headed to the cruiser. The place should've brought charges – Anson had been burglarizing the place. That much was true, but he hadn't anything on him, and they were kind, too kind. She sped off, sirens on, for there was another call from dispatch.

Anson watched her drive off. It was a nice day, clearing up and all, and the mist was rising off of Inverness Ridge. He could wander back into the marsh again, and see the blue herons and egrets feeding, but he was too hungry for that. Or he could hitch into town, bum a meal, but there were too many people there. Still, the thought of eggs and bacon and sausage and sourdough bread made him crazy.

He put on his shoes, stepped out onto the road, and stuck out his thumb. At this hour, there wouldn't be much traffic. From up the road he saw a flash of lights and dove into the bushes.

"Mr. Baker."

He heard the officer's voice.

"I know you're here. I bet you're hungry. Get in." Linda got out and opened the door for him. The wind had come up and he looked cold. "I'm heading to Stinson and not to the station if you're worried." The agency had called and had wanted to know what kind of person she was.

"You sure you're not taking me to prison, ma'am?" Anson studied the barred windows and hard plastic rear seat. De Niro would never step inside.

"Mr. Baker, I'm talking about breakfast." Everyone, in her book, deserved to eat. "It's on me."

"You bet." Anson grinned and crawled inside. De Niro would understand.

FROM THE SHERIFF'S CALLS SECTION IN THE POINT REYES LIGHT,
NOVEMBER 15, 2012

POINT REYES STATION: At 5:19 p.m. someone reported seeing two or more kids and one adult trying to herd sheep in the road – a "hazardous" situation.

Mister Humphries

"Hazardous for whom, Grandma?" Alice asked, chasing one of the sheep. There were so many of them bleating out on the road, they made her laugh. "Grandma? Can you hear me?"

Mildred was on the other side of the rail fence, horrified. If one of those big galoots came close to her they'd knock her down. "Shoo, shoo."

Two neighborhood boys, Kenny and Bruce, were standing in the road, calling "Here little sheep, here little sheep," but the sheep weren't paying them any mind. They had seen a patch of new grass and they were heading toward it, right toward Mildred's open gate.

"Get them away! Get them away!" She banged her cane against the fence.

Philip, a neighbor, had been listening to Dave Brubeck's "Take Five" when he heard the ruckus and came outside. He still had his painter's palette in one hand and a paintbrush in the other. "What the hell?"

"It's the end of the world!" Mildred shouted. "The animals are taking over."

"Grandma, I'll fix it," Alice said, not laughing now but wanting to. She closed Grandma's gate. There were about ten sheep running from one side of the road to another, their bells going off in a shuffle of snorting and huffing and bleating. "Heavens, you big dope," she said, grabbing one behind the neck.

"Be careful, they bite!" Grandma shouted.

"They're just big and bulky, come on, big guy." Alice grabbed wool and tried to corral the now stubborn animal leaning on her and trying to step on her toes.

"Oh for God's sake." The artist put down his brushes and waded into the mix. "I'm in the middle of a commissioned work – watch it, buddy." He shoved one of the larger sheep aside, and moved toward Alice. "Where do you want them, honey?"

"Away from me – oof – and away from Grandma," Alice answered, bristling with the word honey. No one but Grandma was allowed to call her that.

The boys, Kenny and Bruce, had closed all the gates at the end of the dirt driveway cul-de-sac. That left the road behind them as an escape. A Pomeranian, a block away, was barking, running all around and charging at the herd.

"Enough!" Alice yelled. "Open the gate there, Kenny, come around the back of me, and Bruce, take Grandma's cane."

"I'm not giving up my third leg, Alice," Mildred said, white-faced and holding her cane with two hands.

"If we don't corral them properly, Grandma, they'll be everywhere. I'll return it right away," Alice said, still holding the biggest sheep in the bunch, and working to keep her footing through the jostling animals.

Bruce, all of 16 and with a huge head of hair, took Mildred's cane, and, being careful with it, tapped the sheep on the rear as the artist and Kenny stepped to the side. The herd moved toward Alice. "Away from the dog, Kenny, yes, right into Mr. Humphries place – won't he love that," she said, slapping rumps as they went by her in a rush, her hands softened by the lanolin in the wool. "Won't he be surprised."

The last sheep tried to make his getaway, but the artist grabbed him by the neck, and the sheep kicked a little, bleated, huffed and headed in. Now, all the sheep were behind a fence and a proud Pomeranian was in charge, barking and running up and down the fence line as the sheep glared at the tiny animal.

"Good job, Alice!" Mildred clapped her hands, and forgetting she didn't have her cane, almost fell. She grabbed the rail for safety as Bruce headed her way with her fully intact cane.

"Great teamwork," Alice said. She felt her nose. No dampness. Were her bloody noses a thing of the past? That would be great. The boys, Kenny and Bruce, whooped and hollered. The artist headed back to his studio, muttering that madness was afoot in Point Reyes.

Five minutes later Mr. Humphries turned off Route One and drove his Ferrari down his driveway with his trophy wife in the passenger seat. As usual, Buffy was bugging him for more money. He couldn't wait to get home, put her in front of the big screen TV, and have a whiskey. She had turned out to be far more than he'd bargained for. He should have known better. He longed for Cathy, his previous wife of twenty years, whom he'd divorced a little over a year ago. She'd laughed at him when he'd seen her last.

He came down the last stretch of road, being careful with the potholes and the car's very low clearance, and seeing people ahead, slammed on his brakes, and dropped into a pothole. Damn. He rolled forward slowly and pressed the gate release button as people got out of the way. In a second he was surrounded by sheep. One stuck his wooly head into the passenger side of the car and Buffy screamed. Mr. Humphries turned on his wipers and sprayer by mistake, spraying the leather interior. The boys cheered.

"Way to go, Mr. Humphries," they said, while Mrs. Rhinehart, his neighbor, stood by a rail fence holding her cane, and stared at him with determined eyes. She waded through the sheep, marched up to the driver's side, leaned in.

"I told you you shouldn't have bought a house in the country, Mr. Humphries, you stupid man," she said, giving him the eye. "Now look at what you've done."

From the Sheriff's Calls Section in the *Point Reyes Light*,
November 15, 2012

BOLINAS: At 2:04 p.m. deputies gave a man lacking something a ride home.

Thin As a Piece of Paper

"Lacking what, Fred?" Mildred clicked her teeth. They always gave her trouble, especially on cloudy, gray days. "A potato? A gremlin? A car? A fish?"

She was muttering. Even without his hearing aids Fred could hear every word. He was out in the back yard raking leaves. There were so many of them. He opened the kitchen door and peered in. His sweetheart, bless her little heart, was clucking over the paper and shucking peas.

"Fred, we going to your sister's tonight?" Mildred peeled another pea pod. "I'm not up to it."

That's what she always said, Fred mused, she'd never cared for Harriet. Disappointed, he headed back out to the yard. He loved his sister almost as much as he loved baseball. He dug into a pile of leaves.

Hearing no response, Mildred headed outside. He had disappeared. Knowing that a man of Fred's size would not be easy to lose, she walked the postcard sized lot on the Mesa in town. What was good about it was the view; they could see clear across Tomales Bay to the Inverness Ridge, and if it weren't for the oak trees dropping leaves all fall, Fred wouldn't complain at all.

She found him in the shed, hunting for an empty glass jar.

"It's a spider as big as tomorrow, and it was right here. Stand back. Stand back!" He held a hammer over his shoulder while keeping an eye on his workbench.

"Let the cat get it," Mildred said. "Make Max earn his keep."

"This spider's way bigger than Max. It's just a disgusting thing."

Mildred could see he'd been at it awhile. Deep hammer marks were sunk all over the pine bench and sweat stood out on his forehead. All this excitement wasn't good for his heart.

"Darling, sweetheart. Forget about the spider."

He glared at her.

She'd noticed the pile of leaves on her way to the shed. "I'll help you rake."

Fred was moving cans of nails around on his bench. "I'll get him…what's that you said? Help? You said help?" He sounded and felt like a bitter old man, and he had good reason. Ever since she'd come home from the hospital with a weakened ankle, she hadn't done anything much except buy pre-made dinners and bake cookies. It had been his own fault; he'd catered to her too damn much. "Really?"

"Got a spare rake?"

"I have a spare shovel." He looked at her small frame. A shovelful of leaves would knock her over. "Or you can hold the bag."

She smiled, grabbed a fistful of bags, and followed him outside. It was an early December day and the wind was rising. She loved rain. She stood beside him and held the bag open.

He came up with the first shovelful, then the second, and the third made the bag collapse and the fourth made the bag too heavy and she yelled at him.

Fred had been a happy man when she'd started to help him, but with most things and Mildred, there was no future in it. Soon it would be his fault there were so many leaves, and she'd ask him why he hadn't cut the goddamn trees down years ago.

Frustrated, he rested his shovel against a tree.

"Sweetheart, forget it." He took the bag from her. She was as light and thin as a piece of paper. She sat down on one of the recliners, which didn't collapse under her. That surprised Fred no end.

"Feeling better?" He brought her a glass of orange juice.

The drink seemed to enliven her. She sat up with a start, adjusted the flower pinned to her dress. "Forget about the leaves, Fred, let Mario do it."

"Mario?" Fred asked. "Who's Mario?"

"The guy at the market. Don't you pay attention? You've met him a hundred times."

"What does Mario have to do with the price of cheese?" He wanted to sit beside her but did not want to collapse on the cold, wet ground.

"Fred, it's the same guy as in the paper. It has to be. It's Mario. He's always forgetting to ring up all my groceries. He forgot something at the station too. It makes perfect sense. The deputies drove him home, remember?" She noticed the glazed look in his eyes. "Earth to Fred, is anyone home?"

"What does Mario have to do with the leaves, dear?" he asked, still puzzled. He wished the baseball game was on so he could head inside.

"Mario does yard work too! Don't you ever talk to him? I thought so. If you paid attention you would know. I told you yesterday. You never listen." Mildred wrung her hands. "I'm just a little old lady and you're making fun of me."

"I would never do anything of the sort," Fred said, feeling badly, for he had.

"I bet he forgot his glasses," she said, gathering herself into him, into his bulk where she felt safe. "Or his hearing aids." My goodness; he had gained every pound she'd lost.

"You silly thing. It could be anything." He held her close. He wouldn't squish her tight. She didn't like that much.

"Come inside, old man and I'll make you some cookies." She placed her arm through his.

"And I suppose the man at the station had forgotten his?" Fred asked, joking with her.

"His cookies? He didn't lose anything as easy as his cookies, Fred," she chattered as they went inside. "I think he lost his wife, and feels completely alone."

"Then I'm one lucky man." Smoke was billowing out from the oven. "Even with burnt cookies, dear, I still have you," he said, and rushed to turn the oven off.

POINT REYES STATION: At 5:26 p.m. deputies assisted a citizen from Germany who wished to get a picture of a patrol car.

Well, I Never

"Well, I never." Beatrice wiggled her good leg and put the paper down. She was sitting in a chair at Doris' beauty salon getting her hair dyed.

"Mrs. Darcy, I really don't think it's necessary, your hair is fine just as it is," Doris suggested.

"I told you, Doris, and I told you. I've owned my own beauty salon, and when I say color…" Beatrice, 92, was on a tear. Her favorite soap opera would be back on within the hour and she did not want to be late. "When I say color, you say which one. Clear?"

"Yes, ma'am," Doris said, mixing in more blue. Even with gloves on, she could see the blue climbing up her wrists and staining her skin. Gloves, paintbrush and dye, not a good combo in her book. She was never going to get it off.

"Getting back to the paper," Beatrice urged.

"Doris, don't you think the German guy could just take a photo and leave those poor deputies alone?" Mildred asked and tapped her feet. Hair was growing out of her ears and she didn't like it one bit. She hadn't told Doris yet. She hid behind a beauty magazine.

"Deputies are a proud bunch." Doris finished the dye job on Beatrice's head and flipped on a beehive dryer.

"Deputies have too much to do around here to pose for pictures." Mildred snapped her purse shut as Doris floated a smock over her too thin frame. "Honestly, good waste of taxpayers' money, having deputies stand around like that."

"Maybe the German guy was cute." Beatrice waved at Officer Kettleman, who had just walked in the door.

"What was that you said, Mrs. Darcy?" Linda took off her equipment belt and settled into a chair.

"Beatrice is always putting her nose in other people's business." Mildred couldn't hear too well on account of all the water swooshing around her ears. She moaned while Doris' fingers massaged her neck.

"He was great looking," Linda said. "From Dusseldorf. Over in Germany, all of their trucks are Mercedes."

"Nice." Beatrice peered out from under the hair dryer. "Did you take them inside the station too, Officer, and show them the most wanted list?"

"Most Wanted posters are in the post office, Beatrice," Mildred declared. "Everyone knows that." She clucked her tongue and dropped her head into a magazine.

Beatrice, under the hair dryer, scowled.

"Sit up please, Mrs. Rhinehart." Doris held out her comb.

"Cut all of Mildred's hair off, Doris." Beatrice stood up and feeling unsteady, grabbed her chair.

"Mrs. Darcy, Mrs. Rhinehart, sit down, please," Linda ordered. "Or someone is going to get hurt." She turned to Doris. "Just a little off the back, please."

The two old ladies sat down in a huff.

"Was he cute, officer?" Beatrice teased.

"Can't hear you," Linda answered, getting her hair washed.

"The German guy. The German guy who asked for a photo of the patrol car," Beatrice asked.

Linda paused, hearing something over her radio. "Thanks, Doris." She shook her short brown hair. "He looked like a movie star."

"Who? The German guy? Then where is he staying?" Mildred asked.

"Oooh," Beatrice said, "I haven't seen movie stars since Prince Charles and Camilla came to the Western."

"The Royal Family are not movie stars, you nincompoop," Mildred barked.

"They're movie stars in my book," Beatrice declared. "Star power. Don't you think I have star power?" She twirled in front of the mirrors and admired her new, very blue hair.

"You bet." Linda kept an eye on Beatrice's turns. "Be careful, you're 92."

"So?" Beatrice spat. "Lucky me."

"Take him for a ride in the patrol car," Linda joked, twirling her keys.

"The German guy? Really?" Beatrice asked. "Today? Like right now?"

"But you haven't driven in twenty years, you old bat." Mildred admired her new sparkly shoes. Fred had given her a fifty dollar bill as a birthday present, and she'd dumped her old Oxfords in the charity box near the library. "I'll drive, Beatrice." She put her hand out for the keys.

Linda pocketed hers.

"Hey, you promised."

"I was kidding," Linda said.

"You two want to go for a ride in the patrol car – in the back for disturbing the peace?" Doris asked, slipping her combs into solution. "I'm sure Officer Kettleman would be happy to oblige."

"Gotta go," Mildred and Beatrice said in unison and headed out the door.

"You know, Doris." Linda dug into her wallet for a hundred dollar bill. She had reason to celebrate. The adoption papers had come through. "The German guy – he was handsome as hell. Keep the change. He's staying at the Olema, if you're interested."

"You bet," Doris said, and picked up the phone.

My Kind of People

In Woodacre, at 7:43 a.m., a resident reported seeing two men climbing a fence on a vacant property, across the street, and was not sure if they were "workers or bad guys."

At the station Linda put down her bear claw. She knew workers generally didn't climb over fences to get access, they used gates. But what if they were locked? And what if they really were burglars? She stood up, yawned, gazed at a photo of what would soon be her baby, and put on her equipment belt. She would tell Walter where she was going, but he was whispering to his ficus plant and she didn't want to disturb him.

Across the valley in Forest Knolls, Mrs. Willis frowned. At 10:35 a.m. she had reported that her neighbor's dog had come over to her house. She had returned the dog but the animal had mysteriously shown up again. Instead of calling the sheriff, she picked up a stick and went outside.

She ran into Alice and her friend Beth Ann who were playing their iPhone loudly and trying out dance moves in the trees. The dog ran between them but Mrs. Willis wouldn't come near. She let him go and the girls snickered. Disappointed, Mrs. Willis called Alice's mother, but she wasn't home, and Mrs. Willis reached her grandmother Mildred instead.

Mildred wasn't interested in listening to that old biddy and hung up. She had just read in the paper that at 6:48 a.m. someone reported that a 92 year old woman had walked into a table at home and fallen face down. She called Fred and made him drive them over to check on Beatrice.

They found her giggling by the telephone in her 1920s' kitchen with the deep farm sink. She was a day away from her 93rd birthday and too smart to walk into tables, she said. She was all hyped up. She had called the sheriffs to complain about trespassers because - she adjusted her horn-rim glasses that her grandson Justin had given her for her 80th birthday - and busted out with the news. "At 12:47 p.m., someone from the Coast Guard station came by my little cottage and told me that the trespassers I had complained about were actually visiting from Germany, and were taking a nature hike." She took a breath. "I invited them in, gave them all cups of tea and was practicing my rusty German – all I could remember was where is the toilet – but they were kind and everyone was laughing and having a good time. They left just a moment ago."

Back in Woodacre, Mrs. Willis wasn't satisfied. The little dog was still nosing around her gazanias and the girls had left, their chatter and music leaving a void in the air. There were times like these when she longed to have at least someone in the house. Harold had been gone twenty years. She stared at his photo, his favorite one, the one with his pipe and the ill-fitting sweater she'd made for him, sitting in the wing chair by the fire, and her heart tugged, him sitting there, just there, until she heard a crash.

There was a flash of lights and then it went dark. She retrieved a mag flashlight from the drawer by the front door – where Harold had insisted she always keep a flashlight handy – and hurried outside. At 8:29 p.m., in Woodacre, a UPS driver had driven off the road near Madrone Avenue and was about to topple into the creek.

Mrs. Willis, no fool her, pulled out her cell phone, tapped 911, and went over to look. The driver looked scared, hanging by the wheel, and Mrs. Willis fumed. Where were the cops when she needed them? She tapped her feet in her black ballet flats as lights finally came up the road and she stepped out of the way.

Officer Linda Kettleman had just called Cheda's for a tow. He was not far behind, she said to the driver and recognized Mrs. Willis. She gave her a polite hello.

There had been all these sheep in the road, Linda wanted to tell Mrs. Willis, but by the look on her face, changed her mind. There had been nothing but calls all day. She'd just returned from Bolinas where Frederick Thomas

III had complained bitterly that deputies had towed his RV. Luckily, they had found it a block away. Frederick had been drunk, and getting the call about the UPS truck, she had just bundled him up in his RV, given him the keys, and sped up the road.

In Woodacre, Linda listened to the chatter over her radio while Gary, from Cheda's, pulled the UPS truck and driver out of the creek. The driver, Matt Harman, was so grateful he wanted to hug everyone. He was pleased it was dark so no one could see his tears. Mrs. Willis went back inside to sit next to Harold's photo; the girls, Alice and Beth Ann, put on an old James Bond movie – their favorite, *Goldfinger* – and placed popcorn in the microwave.

Back home again in Point Reyes Station, Fred collapsed into his recliner and flipped on World Series reruns. He loved watching Busty Posey hit home runs.

Mildred took up the paper and turned to page three, Sheriff's Calls, and sipped her Earl Grey tea with milk and sugar, just the way she liked it. In Bolinas, at 6:40 p.m., a resident complained that her neighbor's boyfriend had whistled loudly when the two were talking; a driver ran into a cow in the dark; a resident reported that an unfamiliar truck was parked nearby; citizens helped remove a boxy Asian car from a ditch; a citizen reported a solicitor with a limp, and a man, struggling in a relationship, decided to move out.

"My kind of people," Mildred said firmly, folding up the paper and sticking it in a drawer stuffed full of newspapers. "They're keeping the world safe for democracy, Fred," she said, deeply satisfied.

"What's that, Mildred?" He felt her hand on his shoulder. "It's time for bed, sweetheart. Ready, honey?" She leaned over and gave him a smooch.

He rose, flabbergasted, for she had kissed him full on the mouth. He couldn't remember the last time she'd done so. He followed her swishing skirt up the stairs, eager as a young man. Tonight, he was going to get lucky at last.

FINI

About the Author

Susanna Solomon is a grandmother, a wife, a mother and an animal lover. Apart from doing readings of her written work throughout northern California, she also runs her own electrical engineering business. Susanna grew up in Cambridge, Massachusetts and misses the east terribly in the fall, but loves the open spaces of her adopted coast so much that she finds herself remaining there with much contentment. For more about Susanna visit www.susannasolomon.com.

Acknowledgments

This publication would not have been possible without the help and encouragement of the following people: Patricia V. Davis who suggested I write a few more short stories, James N. Frey for his enthusiastic tearing out of his hair during numerous workshops, hollering, "conflict, more conflict," Melba Patillo Beals, my first teacher, Cyndi Cady and the rest of the Tuesday Night Writers, Charselle Hooper from the West End Wednesdays literary readings and members of the Marin and Redwood branches of the California Writers Club. Thank you, all.

Special thanks goes to Patricia Morin, a great friend, Amanda McTigue for the wise counsel, Tess Elliott, editor of the *Point Reyes Light* who first published my stories, J. Macon King, Kelly Preston, Deborah Grabien for the fine editing and Deke Castleman. Thanks also to Inga Silva and Cara Black who were early believers. And finally to Stu, who unknowingly gave me some of my best lines and who is still trying to learn the waltz. (It's one, two, three, Stu — not one, two, three, four.)

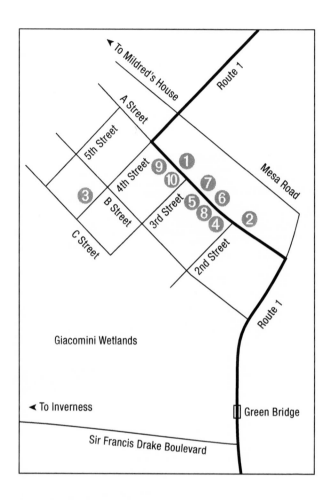

1. Palace Market
2. Station House Café
3. Public Safety Building
4. The Western
5. Cheda's Garage
6. Toby's Feed Barn
7. Toby's Coffee Barn
8. Doris' Saloon
9. Bovine Bakery
10. Fred's Bench